D0467110

This book is a gift of the
Friends of the Orinda Library

Join us at
friendsoftheorindalibrary.org

ALL THAT'S MISSING

Sarah Sullivan

CANDLEWICK PRESS

Copyright © 2013 by Sarah Sullivan

First edition 2013

Library of Congress Catalog Card Number 2013931468
ISBN 978-0-7636-6102-1

13 14 15 16 17 18 BVG 10 9 8 7 6 5 4 3 2 1

Printed in Berryville, VA, U.S.A.

This book was typeset in Dante.

Candlewick Press
99 Dover Street
Somerville, Massachusetts 02144

visit us at www.candlewick.com

For Jane Resh Thomas

Part I
MARSHBORO

CHAPTER 1
Dodging Mrs. Gretzky

Arlo was sitting in math class, thinking about the note Mrs. Gretzky had pressed into his hand five days ago, the one Arlo had opened at home and read through three times just to make sure it was as bad as he thought, the one he was going to have to forge his grandfather's signature on before he could return it to school. Arlo was thinking so hard that he failed to notice Darcy Meadows poking him in the back with a tightly folded piece of notebook paper.

"Here, dummy," she whispered.

"Thanks," Arlo whispered back.

He recognized Sam's handwriting right away. Sam was Arlo's best friend. Some might say his *only* friend. That was because of all the important things they shared in common.

1. They both loved anchovy pizza.
2. They both preferred running to soccer.

3. They both hated fractions.
4. They were both afraid of Nick Halvorson, though neither one of them liked to admit that.

Sam lived with his great-aunt Betty in a frame house in the old section of Marshboro, while Arlo lived with his grandfather a few blocks away.

When Mrs. Gretzky turned to write on the board, Arlo opened up the note and started reading.

Want to go for a run?

Arlo looked over and mouthed, *Yes.*

Sam gave him a nod. "Usual place?" he asked.

Arlo nodded.

At least once a week he and Sam met on the Boulevard near the College to run the two-mile path along the river. So far, it had rained every day this week. Until this afternoon.

"Don't let me interrupt your conversation, Arlo," Mrs. Gretzky said.

Arlo whipped around to face the front of the classroom.

Mrs. Gretzky was staring at him. "Since you don't feel the need to pay attention," she said, "perhaps you'd like an extra challenge."

Lucy Ashcroft giggled from the front row.

"Well?" Mrs. Gretzky tapped her foot.

"Sorry," Arlo said.

"I'm glad to hear that," Mrs. Gretzky said. "Why don't you stop by my desk on your way out? I'll have something extra for you."

"Yes, ma'am." Arlo's shoulders sagged at the thought of what was in store for him. *More homework.* Just what he didn't need.

Sixth grade was different from Arlo's other years at school. It was all because of Poppo—and the weird stuff that was happening in Poppo's brain. Time traveling, Arlo called it, because it was as if Poppo were swept into a time machine and transported to the past. He'd become confused about things and forget how to find his way home. Poppo's memory spells never lasted longer than a few minutes. But while they were going on, they were scary.

This past July, they'd been on their way home from the grocery store when Poppo came to a halt in the middle of an intersection.

"It's this way, isn't it?" he asked.

"No, Poppo, left, toward school," Arlo said. "Then right at the post office."

"Sure," Poppo said. "What was I thinking?"

Arlo hadn't liked the look on his grandfather's face, as if he were lost or, worse yet, frightened.

In the old days, *before this past summer,* Poppo and Arlo used to spend weekends at the fishing camp in Greenbrier County. On Saturday mornings, they would take the canoe out and dangle fishing lines in deep pools where brown trout darted around sandstone boulders. They hiked up Spice Mountain and listened to owls calling in the night.

But this past summer, Poppo never opened the camp at all. First, it rained every weekend from Memorial Day until the end of June. And when the sun finally came out, Poppo kept putting off the trip.

"Maybe next week," he said.

But next week came and went and the week after that, and still Poppo said the same thing.

"Maybe next week, Arlo. I don't feel up to it yet."

In the evenings, Poppo's mind wandered. And Poppo wandered, too. Sometimes. Not often. Not yet, anyway.

"Will I be seeing your grandfather tomorrow afternoon?" Mrs. Gretzky asked when Arlo stopped at her desk.

Arlo's heart skipped as he struggled to keep the panic from showing on his face. "Poppo can't make it," he said.

Mrs. Gretzky frowned. "I thought he understood we needed to meet," she said.

The lie formed in Arlo's head before he knew what he was saying. "The doctor says Poppo isn't supposed to go out of the house till he finishes his medicine." Arlo marveled at how quickly the phony excuse slid out of his mouth. "The doctor says that what Poppo has could be contagious."

Mrs. Gretzky's eyebrows arched to an impossible height, which seemed to Arlo to match how far he had stretched the truth.

"Nothing serious, I hope," she said, putting down her pencil to offer a concerned look.

"Just the flu or something," Arlo said. "He should be OK in a day or two."

For a moment, they stared at each other. Arlo's heart hammered as he wondered if she could possibly believe him.

Arlo counted the seconds ticking past. *One thousand one, two thousand two.*

Finally, Mrs. Gretzky raised her hand and drew a line through one of the notes on her calendar, the one that said, *Meeting with Mr. Sabatini—4 p.m.*

"All right, then, Arlo," she said. "I guess we'll have to make the best of the situation, won't we?"

Arlo forced a tentative smile while his brain beamed the word *VICTORY* in capital letters. His secret was safe.

At least for the moment.

"Tell your grandfather we need to discuss your math grades as soon as possible." Mrs. Gretzky raised her head until they were gazing eye to eye. "You'll do that, won't you?"

"Sure," Arlo said, struggling to control the twitch in his shoulder that came when he told a bald-faced lie.

Mrs. Gretzky kept talking. "Tell him it's important we figure out a way to help you improve your skills." She reached into her desk drawer and pulled out a piece of paper with a list of names, phone numbers, and addresses printed on it. "I was going to give him this list of tutors," she said. "Why don't you go ahead and do that for me? Tell him to call anyone on the list. They're all good. And tell him he'd better do it soon. Their schedules fill up quickly."

Hire a private tutor? Was she kidding? Poppo couldn't afford swim lessons, let alone private math tutors.

"I'm studying a lot harder now," Arlo said, reluctant to accept the list, since there was no way he was going to deliver it.

Mrs. Gretzky gave him a patient smile. "I'm sure you are." She stretched her arm out stiffly until Arlo had no choice but to accept the list. "Everyone needs help from time to time," she said. "It's nothing to be ashamed of. Just give your grandfather this list and tell him what I said. All right?"

Never in a million years, Arlo said silently to himself, but to Mrs. Gretzky he said, "Yes, I will." Then he stuffed the list in the pocket of his backpack.

"Good. I'm glad we had this talk." Mrs. Gretzky closed her eyes and nodded. "Remind your grandfather to call me," she added. "All right?"

"Sure." Arlo nodded his agreement. He hoped his face wasn't as red as it felt. He was a terrible liar. But one conversation with Poppo, and Mrs. Gretzky was bound to know that something was wrong. That is, unless she happened to catch Poppo on a good day. And the good days didn't happen very often anymore. Mrs. Gretzky could ask Poppo a perfectly reasonable question, and Poppo was likely to respond with some crazy comment about watching Walter Cronkite on the news last night. Shoot. Walter Cronkite had been dead for years. Eons, almost.

Or worse yet, Poppo might ask Mrs. Gretzky why she was calling him. *I don't know any boy named Arlo,* Poppo might say. *Do I?*

"Aren't you giving me extra homework?" Arlo asked.

Mrs. Gretzky shook her head. "I'd rather you spend more time on the homework you already have," she said. "And pay attention in class."

Arlo had to hand it to her. She had a way of hitting you right where it hurt. *Bam.* Knocking the breath right out of him.

"Sorry," Arlo said, for what felt like the twentieth time.

"It's all right," Mrs. Gretzky said. "Just do better next time."

CHAPTER 2
Worse Things Than Bullies

Arlo dragged his feet walking home. He hated lying to teachers. He wasn't the sort of kid who did that. But he didn't have a choice—not when it came to covering up the truth about Poppo. It was better that nobody found out what life was like at home.

It had been just last month when Arlo had come home to find Poppo staring at an old photograph in a wooden frame.

"Do we know this girl?" he'd asked.

"That's my mom," he'd said.

Poppo squinted at the face in the photograph.

"She's your daughter," Arlo said. "Her name was Amy. Remember?"

"Was?" Poppo said. "Did something happen to her?"

Arlo's throat swelled, blocking off his breath. "She died," he said.

And Poppo kept on staring at the picture.

Sometimes Arlo felt like one of those mud-and-stick dams

he and Sam liked to build in the creek. They mounded sand and dirt together with twigs and stones and waited for the water to break through. The current welled into tiny pools that pressed against the dam. They broke away a twig here or a pebble there. But the dam usually held. *Usually.*

Poppo's mixed-up brain was breaking away twigs and pebbles in Arlo's life. So far, his dam had held. But how long before Mrs. Gretzky or someone else at school found out? How long before Arlo's dam sprang a leak and the water came gushing through?

As Arlo rounded the corner toward his house, his thoughts turned to running. He headed for his room and changed into gym shorts and a T-shirt. Talking to Mrs. Gretzky had slowed him down. He needed to hurry. Sam would be waiting. After a run, everything would feel all right again. Running evened out the world. It took Arlo's mind off his troubles and let him focus on a quiet place inside, where everything was just as it should be.

Before going outside, he left a note on the kitchen table for Poppo.

Gone for a run with Sam.

Then he hightailed it to the corner, turned onto Jefferson Street, and kept a steady pace as he headed toward the river. Out of the corner of his eye, he spotted movement in the alley behind the West Side Grill. *Three boys.* Arlo groaned inwardly when he recognized them. Nick Halvorson with Mike Ackley and Danny Hyde. Waiting for Arlo. *Obviously.* Ever since Mr. Fanucci had accused Halvorson of shoplifting, when it was really Poppo who had tucked the package of pepperoni rolls inside his pocket, Halvorson and his two goons had made it their personal mission to terrorize Arlo.

"Hey, Jones. Looking for your grandpa?" Halvorson had a way of curling his lip as if it were part of the punch he was going to deliver as soon as Arlo dared to walk in front of him.

"You're as crazy as he is." Ackley pushed up the sleeve of his right arm. "Pathetic," he said.

"Yeah," Hyde added.

"I'll bet your parents didn't really die in that accident." Ackley slid closer. "I'll bet they dumped you at your grandpa's house because they couldn't stand to look at you."

Why didn't Halvorson get it over with? Go ahead and hit him if that's what he had in mind.

Bam. It was Ackley's fist that came out of nowhere. Arlo felt the blow to his left shoulder. He fell back.

"What's the matter with you?" Ackley feinted from one foot to another. "Afraid to fight back?"

"He's chicken. That's what." Hyde's voice was squeaky for a boy his size.

Arlo lifted his head and met Halvorson's eyes, bracing himself for another punch.

"*Bwak, bwak, bwak.*" Ackley made flapping motions with his arms. "Oh, *pwetty pwease,* boys. Don't hurt me."

Both boys looked toward Halvorson, who gave Hyde a nod. Then Hyde slipped behind Arlo and dropped to his knees. While Arlo was trying to figure out what was going on, Ackley shoved him hard. Arlo tried to step back, but Hyde was in the way. Arlo fell backward, landing on his elbow. Pain shot up the back of his arm, while rainwater from the sidewalk soaked into his shorts.

Arlo shot Halvorson a look. *Happy now?*

Halvorson shrugged. He rolled a toothpick from one side of his mouth to the other. "Nice job," he said to Ackley and Hyde.

By that time, Hyde was back on his feet. He and Ackley gave each other a high five.

"Go on," Hyde sneered at Arlo. "Run home to your smelly grandpa."

"Yeah," Ackley added. "Don't he ever change his underwear? Man, he stinks."

As Arlo pulled himself up, he tested his right arm to see if it would still bend. He raised his chin at Halvorson before turning toward the park. Neither one of them spoke. He heard Ackley and Hyde laughing behind his back as he walked away.

"What took you?" Sam yelled when Arlo finally made it to the corner of Chesapeake and Elm. "I thought we were going for a run."

Arlo came to a stop a few feet from the bench where Sam was sitting. He felt Sam staring at his wet shorts.

"Man. What happened to you?"

Arlo's cheeks burned.

"Halvorson?" Sam asked.

"Yeah," Arlo said. "Along with his two friends."

"Geez." Sam shook his head.

"I know," Arlo said.

"How bad was it with Gretzky?"

"I got off easy," Arlo said, pulling his leg back to stretch the muscles in preparation for their run. "No extra work."

"Lucky," Sam said, bending over to tighten his shoelaces. "Too bad you had to run into Halvorson and those two morons."

"I know. Could be worse, I guess."

"Yeah. I guess," Sam said. "You and I should do something about them."

Arlo laughed. *Yeah? Like what?* he thought. The last thing he needed was to get in trouble for starting a fight. "Maybe someday," he said.

Sam smiled. "It would be nice, wouldn't it?"

"Sure," Arlo said. "Really nice." He nodded toward the lower path that ran parallel to the sidewalk along the boulevard. "You sure you want to run down there today? It looks pretty muddy."

"It'll be all right," Sam said. "And besides, we won't have to worry about Halvorson down there. You can't even see the path from up here on the boulevard."

"Good point," Arlo said. He followed Sam down the twenty-six steps that led from the street level to the path.

Sam always liked to run in front. Arlo kept a steady pace behind. He skirted the deep puddles and tried to avoid patches of mud. After the first half mile, Sam's rhythm changed. The mud was deeper here, and it slowed them down. Sloppy goop sucked at the soles of Arlo's shoes, releasing them with a loud *pop* that sent mud spatters up the back of his legs.

They came to a point where the riverbank had slipped and the path was covered with a slough of mud, dirt, and rocks. An orange cone blocked the path in front of them.

"Come on!" Sam yelled, climbing on top of the squishy mound.

Before Arlo had time to argue, the mud pile shifted. There was an odd groaning sound as the whole hillside started to slip.

"Hold on!" Arlo yelled.

Sam dropped to his knees and scrambled to find a way off the mound. But the earth was moving faster now, and after a few steps, Sam lost his footing and toppled onto his side.

Arlo stumbled where the ground had slipped but managed to stay on his feet. He watched helplessly as the mudslide carried Sam toward the river. There was a small bump and then a sickening splash.

"Sam!" Arlo climbed onto a boulder that jutted out over the water. He spotted Sam lying on his back with his legs half in and half out of the water. "Hang on," Arlo yelled. "I'm coming."

Arlo's first thought was *Rats!* The riverbank was inhabited by cat-size rodents that nested in the giant culverts that drained the city storm sewers into the river. Arlo lowered himself to the sand, squinting into the tall weeds. He set his foot down gingerly, keeping an eye peeled for movement. Then, mustering his courage, he sprinted over to Sam.

"I fell," Sam said as Arlo offered him a hand.

"Yeah, I noticed," Arlo said. "Are you all right?"

"I think so." Sam wiggled his arms. He sat up and tried moving his legs. "Everything seems to be working," he said.

"Good."

When Sam stood up, he wobbled.

"What's wrong?" Arlo asked.

"Nothing," Sam said. "I twisted my ankle a little, but it's OK."

Nearby, something rustled in the grass. Arlo glanced sideways long enough to catch two beady eyes staring back at him.

"Uh, Sam?"

"Yeah?"

"Don't look now, but there's something over there."

"Yeah?"

The rustling drew closer.

"Oh, geez." Sam moaned.

"I know. Don't move. OK?"

"Don't worry," Sam said.

Keeping the rat in his peripheral vision, Arlo bent his knees and stretched his left arm backward to pat the ground until he located a rock. He closed his hand around it. The rock was bigger than he'd have liked, but it would have to do. He held his breath as blades of grass twitched again. The creature was close enough to offer a glimpse of its teeth.

"Anytime you're ready," Sam whispered.

"OK," Arlo whispered back. "On the count of three. All right?"

"Sure."

One shot. That's all he'd have. Better make it count. Arlo narrowed one eye and heaved the rock as hard as he could, feeling a sharp pain in his shoulder from swinging at an unnatural angle. No matter. How close had he come to the rat? That's what was important.

"Run!" Arlo yelled.

"No kidding!" Sam yelled back.

They sprinted up the riverbank. Sam must not have been hurt too badly, moving as quickly as he was. Arlo was relieved to see that. It wasn't until they were back on the sidewalk at the top of the hill that Arlo dared to look down. There was the rat, sniffing around the top of the boulder.

"Good riddance," Arlo said.

Sam screwed up his face. "I hate rats," he said.

"I'm not exactly crazy about them," Arlo said. "I mean, a rat's a rat. Right?"

Sam narrowed his eyes. "Yeah, but I got bitten by one once. And it looked just like that rat down there."

"How'd you get bitten by a rat?"

"It was in that foster home they put me in," Sam said.

"They had rats?"

"In the basement. The dad got mad at me one day for messing around with his tools, so I was hiding down there, waiting for him to leave. I was afraid he was going to hit me or something. And then all of a sudden, somebody comes crashing down the stairs. And I knew from how loud his shoes were that it had to be him. So I tried to squeeze in the space between these metal shelves and the furnace. Only I got my hand stuck on one of the shelves. And that's when something bit me. I guess it had been hiding on the shelf the whole time. I must have stuck my hand right in its face."

"Yuck," Arlo said.

"I know," Sam said. "It had these beady eyes. And it was like it was telling me to get out of there before it ate my whole arm. So I moved. I mean, I was on those stairs in minus twenty seconds. Then the dad's yelling at me, and pretty soon, my foster mom comes down the stairs and she sees the rat and she starts screaming."

"Then what happened?"

"My hand was bleeding." Sam pointed to a thin line of raised tissue in the webbing between his thumb and forefinger.

"That's where it bit you?"

"Yeah. Its teeth made this creepy crunching sound."

"Gross."

"I know, but at least it got me out of that foster home."

"What do you mean?" Arlo asked.

"They had to take me to the emergency room because they were afraid I'd get rabies or bubonic plague or something. The nurse gave me a shot. I had to have a bunch of shots. Then the social worker came and she said it was time to find another place for me. She started looking for relatives."

"They hadn't done that before?"

"Sure, they had. But nobody ever found any because I didn't have addresses or phone numbers, and my grandparents were dead. And what did I know? I was only four when my mom died. But this time, there was this other lady. She was real nice and she got obsessed with finding somebody for me. She kept looking till she found my great-aunt."

"So the rat did you a favor," Arlo said.

"Maybe," Sam said. "But there's got to be a better way. Right?"

Arlo shivered.

"You cold?" Sam asked.

"A little," Arlo said. "How about you?"

"I don't know. I was mainly worried about getting bitten. But, yeah, now that you mention it, I'm kind of freezing."

"It's only another block to my house," Arlo said. "You can come in if you want."

"Your grandpa won't mind?"

"Nah. It's OK. He's probably not even home yet."

"Where does he go?" Sam asked. "I thought he sold the doughnut shop."

"He did," Arlo said. "He just likes to take long walks sometimes."

Sam nodded. "OK," he said. "As long as I'm home before six, Aunt Betty won't mind if I go to your place, I guess."

CHAPTER 3
Family Album

"You still have that game we used to play?" Sam asked as they walked in the door.

"You mean Jenga? Sure. It's in the cabinet in the living room."

Arlo led Sam to the low cabinet built into the wall beside the fireplace. Inside was a jumble of tattered magazines, board games, decks of cards, broken video games, old files and letters, and the plastic pumpkin Arlo had used for trick-or-treating when he was in second grade.

"What happened to all your stuff?" Sam asked.

"Poppo must have been looking for something." Arlo's face burned. The cabinet looked like a toddler had been playing in there.

"Not exactly organized, is he?" Sam reached for a tall book with a leather binding. "What's this?" he asked.

"Family pictures," Arlo said, watching as Sam paged through the album.

"That you?" he asked.

"Yeah."

"You had red hair?"

Arlo shrugged. "Only when I was a baby. It turned light brown after that."

Sam turned the page. "Who's that?"

"My grandmother," Arlo said.

Sam pulled the album closer. "She looks mean," he said. "No offense."

"That's OK." Arlo studied the woman in the photograph. It was true she looked like she was angry at someone. "I don't really know her," Arlo said. "She lives in another state."

"So that's why you never talk about her, I guess. Huh?"

Arlo sighed. "She and Poppo don't get along very well."

"How come?"

Arlo's jaw tightened. "Every time I try to ask about that side of the family, Poppo changes the subject." He pointed to the lady in the photograph. "Especially if I ask about her."

"What's her name?" Sam asked.

"Ida Jones."

"So she's your dad's mother?"

"Yeah."

"Something bad must have happened between them." Sam pulled the book closer and stared at the photograph. "What do you think it was?"

"No idea," Arlo said.

"Must be something you're not supposed to know about, then."

"Maybe." Arlo didn't like to admit that he'd had the same thought.

"Hey. Here's what we were looking for!" Sam held up the Jenga box. "Still want to play?"

"Sure." Arlo took one last look at his grandmother before closing the album and sliding it inside the cupboard.

After a few rounds of Jenga, they heard Poppo singing as he climbed the steps to the front porch. It was a song about the moon and pizza. Arlo watched Sam's eyes wander toward the window.

"Geez. When did it turn so dark outside? What time is it, anyway?"

"Almost six," Arlo said.

"I gotta go." Sam jumped up and headed for the door, pausing in the front hallway to listen. "Your granddad sure likes to sing, doesn't he?"

"He sure does," Arlo agreed.

Sam nodded his head in rhythm with the song. "He's pretty good."

"Thanks," Arlo said. "That song's one of his favorites."

Sam opened the door just as Poppo reached the top step.

"Hi there," Poppo said.

"Hi, Mr. Sabatini," Sam said. Then he turned to Arlo. "See you tomorrow. OK?"

"Sure," Arlo said. "See you."

CHAPTER 4
Poppo Goes Walkabout

When Arlo was little, Poppo used to read to him every night. *The Elephant's Child* was Arlo's favorite. Poppo made the words twist and turn like the bends in the Greenbrier River. Arlo recited the words along with his grandfather, the lines about the "great grey-green, greasy Limpopo River."

When Arlo grew older, Poppo told another story.

A dark night. Snow. Ice. The river. A mother and father in an old car careening out of control on a rickety bridge.

He'd told the story again, just a few weeks ago, on the night before school started. Arlo sat on one side of the kitchen table and Poppo sat on the other, keeping a watchful eye on the pot where crushed tomatoes, roasted peppers, garlic, and sweet basil simmered into a thick sauce.

"How old was I?" Arlo asked, though he already knew the answer.

"You were two," Poppo said.

"I don't remember them."

"'Course not. You were too young," Poppo said. "But you'll have part of them when you need them."

"What do you mean?" Arlo asked.

"Angels and spirits," Poppo said, lifting his head to catch Arlo's eyes. "Help comes from the other side."

"You mean, like, ghosts?" Arlo asked.

"Same thing," Poppo said. "They'll help you find your way."

Poppo's mind wandered so much these days. Sometimes he said crazy things. Arlo tried not to think about it too much. Thinking only made things worse.

Hours after Sam had left, Arlo hunkered under the covers in his room. Faces from the album flickered through his mind. For some reason, the house felt much colder than usual. Maybe it was because Arlo was thinking about that night, about icy water and a frozen bridge. Or maybe it was because he'd become chilled running in wet clothes that afternoon. Arlo pulled the quilt up over his ears and fell asleep dreaming about Halvorson and Ackley. In his dream, it was freezing outside—so cold that Arlo lost track of what he was doing. Then somehow, he wasn't in the dream anymore. He was in his bed and he had the covers pulled up over his nose. But it was still frigid.

And it was about that time Arlo realized the temperature was real.

Must be a window open somewhere. Strange. Arlo hadn't opened the window in his room in ages. Poppo must have done it. Poppo had been doing the strangest stuff lately.

Opening windows when it was cold enough to snow out-side. Geez.

After soaking up as much warmth as he could from the covers, Arlo burst out of bed and darted across the floor-boards. His window was closed, so the air must be coming from someplace else. He hurried into the hallway and stood at the top of the stairs. No wonder. The front door was stand-ing wide open.

What the heck?

Poppo.

What had he done now?

Arlo checked Poppo's bedroom. Sheets and a blanket lay heaped on the floor. Otherwise, the room was *empty*. Great. Now what was he supposed to do?

Arlo checked every room in the house. Bathroom. Hallway. Kitchen. Extra bedroom and bath upstairs. Even the basement, which was like an iceberg, and the attic, which wasn't much warmer.

Poppo was gone. Vamoosed. Vanished. Meanwhile, it was getting colder by the minute outside. Arlo checked the clock in the kitchen. Four seventeen.

He needed to find Poppo. *Fast.* Before the police found him. What would they do with an old man wandering around lost and confused in the middle of the night? Arlo pulled on sweatpants and his parka and headed outside.

The sidewalks were filled with puddles from yesterday's rain. The soles of Arlo's shoes oozed water after half a block. It was way too cold for September. And why did it have to be so dark outside? Arlo shivered on his way up South Park

Drive, then crossed over to Maple, and climbed the hill to the ball field behind the high school. That was Poppo's favorite spot, especially when he was time traveling. He used to hang out there with his little brother, Frankie, way back in the fifties when they were in school.

Arlo held his breath as he came closer. A few more steps and he'd have a view of the backstop and . . .

Sure enough, there was an old man huddled on the bench beside the backstop. Arlo ran over to him.

Poppo looked up from the can of sausages he was emptying into his mouth.

"Hey, Frankie. Cold out tonight, isn't it?"

"No, Poppo. I'm Arlo. Not Frankie."

"Huh?" Poppo frowned.

"I'm your grandson. Remember?"

"What happened to Frankie?"

"He died a long time ago, Poppo. Meningitis. You told me all about it."

"Nah. Not Frankie. They done something with him. Why'd they want to go and do something to my little brother?"

"Who did?"

Poppo shrugged. "Those people," he said, blinking at Arlo. He set the can of sausages on the bench. Then he frowned. "I'm confused, aren't I?" he said.

"Maybe a little," Arlo said.

Poppo slid a bandanna out of his left pocket and dabbed at his eyes. "Sorry," he said.

"That's OK," Arlo said.

Poppo pulled his collar higher around his neck.

"Cold?" Arlo asked.

Poppo nodded, shivering.

"You should have worn your coat." Arlo frowned at the sliver of limp lettuce fluttering off the side of the sausage can. He twisted his neck to check the Dumpster in the parking lot. Poppo wouldn't do *that*, would he? The cover was clamped shut on the Dumpster, thank goodness. *So the food had come from . . . where?*

"Something wrong?" Poppo asked.

"No. It's just . . ." Arlo glanced across the grass toward the trash can beside the bleachers. His heart dropped at the sight of wadded-up papers and empty food wrappers littering the ground. He gave the can a sly nudge with his elbow, inching it to the edge of the bench. Then when Poppo turned his head, Arlo gave the can an extra tap, sending it toppling into the mud. *There. At least that was taken care of. Poppo couldn't eat any more of the food he'd salvaged out of the trash.*

"We should go now." Arlo helped his grandfather up from the bench. "Come on. Let's go home and warm you up."

They walked down the sidewalk, across Rotary Street, past Fanucci's Market, toward home. The wind was cold. Poppo's lumbering gait slowed them down. It took three times longer to walk home than it had taken Arlo to walk to the ball field by himself.

As Arlo guided his grandfather toward the porch steps, Poppo lifted his head to the light in Arlo's window.

"My grandson lives up there," he said. "He must be wondering where I am."

Arlo's heart swelled. For a moment, he couldn't speak. "You're still shivering," he said. "Let's get you in the house."

Later that night in bed, Arlo thought about Poppo and Ida Jones and his mom and dad and the whole mystery about why the people on the Jones side of the family hated the people on the Sabatini side.

The thing about families, Arlo thought, was that there was always some question nobody wanted to answer for you, and it was like a stray thread pulling loose in a sweater. You could tug at it all you wanted, but in the end, all you'd have was a pile of twisted yarn.

Ida Jones was a stray thread in Arlo's life. Every time he tried to figure her out, another question popped up. Like today, for instance—the way she looked in that photograph, with her eyes glaring at somebody behind the camera. Why hadn't he noticed that before? Now that Arlo had seen Ida Jones through Sam's eyes, he had another family question. Who the heck was she mad at? And why?

CHAPTER 5
Slocum Jones

By the next afternoon, Poppo was fine. He was having one of his good days, which was kind of unbelievable considering how confused he had been the day before. But that was the way things went with Poppo's wonky brain. One day he was fine, and then for the next ten days, he might wander around in a complete fog.

Arlo pulled the album out of the cabinet and carried it to the kitchen, where Poppo was drinking a cup of coffee. Now was his chance. He should ask Poppo to tell him about the people in the pictures while his mind was clear.

"What you got there?" Poppo asked.

Arlo held up the album.

"Where'd you find that?"

"In the living-room cabinet." Arlo set the album on the table. "Sam and I were looking for a game and Sam found this."

Poppo nodded.

"Mind if I ask you something?"

"Fire away." Poppo pulled out a chair for Arlo to sit down.

Arlo sat. He spread the album open on the table and turned to the page with a photo of his grandmother sitting on a granite bench beside a stern-looking man. Behind them was a large white house, and beyond that, a wide river stretched to the horizon.

"Is this the house where my dad grew up?"

"That's it," Poppo said. "Right there on the river in Edgewater."

"Edge — what?"

"Edgewater," Poppo said. "The town where your grandmother lives."

"How come we never go there?" Arlo asked.

Poppo twisted in his chair. "Too far," he said after a long pause. Then, glancing sideways, he stood and emptied his cup at the sink.

"How far is it?" Arlo asked.

"Three hundred and fifty miles," Poppo said, keeping his back turned toward Arlo. "Probably more. The roads aren't so good, either. Some of them, anyway. Least they weren't the last time we went there."

Arlo waited while Poppo stood at the counter staring out the window at the empty backyard.

"You met her once, you know," Poppo said as he poured himself a fresh cup of coffee.

"I don't remember her," Arlo said.

"'Course you don't," Poppo said. "You were barely two."

"At the . . ."

"That's right. After the memorial service. In Edgewater." Poppo scooped two spoonfuls of sugar into his coffee and stirred it slowly before coming back to sit at the table with Arlo.

"Do you ever talk to her?" Arlo asked.

Poppo raised his eyes. He looked straight at Arlo. "Once in a while," he said, and then added, "she calls to check up on you."

Arlo studied his grandfather's face. He tried to read what was going on behind Poppo's eyes, but it was impossible. "How come I don't talk to her?" he asked.

Poppo stirred his coffee some more. He looked over at the calendar on the door of the pantry, then toward the window over the sink. "Seems like she always calls when you're not around," he said.

Was he telling the truth? Poppo wouldn't lie about something like that, would he? So why was he avoiding eye contact? "What's she like?" Arlo asked.

"I don't know." Poppo waved his hand in the air as if he were searching for an answer. "Always seemed kind of quiet to me. Maybe that was on account of Slocum being so loud."

"Slocum?" Arlo asked.

"Your grandfather Jones," Poppo said. "He was your dad's father. That's him there, on the bench beside your grandmother." Poppo pointed to the stern-looking man in the photograph.

"Was he like you?" Arlo asked.

Poppo made a grunting sound. "Sure hope not," he said.

Arlo frowned. "What do you mean?"

Poppo took a long sip of coffee. He swished it around in his mouth before swallowing. "I guess you could say two people couldn't be less alike than Slocum Jones and Al Sabatini."

Arlo thought about that for a minute. "Did my grandfather Jones do something wrong?" he asked.

"Depends on who you ask," Poppo said, taking another slug of coffee. "I don't mean he went to jail or anything like that, but . . ."

Arlo waited. "But, what?" he said.

Poppo grunted again. "Slocum liked making rules, for one thing," he said. "And he loved telling other folks how to live their lives."

Arlo didn't like the way Poppo's neck was turning red. Something about Slocum Jones obviously bothered him a lot.

"What about my grandmother?" Arlo asked, hoping that would calm Poppo down. "Does she like making rules?"

Poppo looked out the window. "I doubt she ever got the chance as long as Slocum was alive. 'Course, you understand I only saw the two of them a couple of times. She and your mother didn't get along very well."

Finally, they were getting to the important stuff. "Why not?" Arlo asked.

Poppo's eyes turned misty. He cleared his throat. It took him a long time to answer, and when he did, he wasn't looking at Arlo. He was staring at the blank wall and his voice was flat. "There were hard feelings all around on account of the way your daddy and her ran off and got married," he said.

Arlo waited before responding. "Ran off?" he said, keeping his eyes on Poppo's face. "You never told me that."

Poppo frowned. "Nothing to talk about, really."

Clearly there was a *lot* to talk about and Poppo didn't want to discuss any of it. What did that even mean—*running off to get married?*

"I don't understand," Arlo said.

Poppo sighed. "I know you don't. That's why . . ."

"Why *what?*" Arlo asked.

"Maybe when you're older," Poppo said. He got up and dumped his coffee again. Only this time he didn't pour a fresh cup. He stayed at the kitchen counter with his back to Arlo, as if he didn't want Arlo to see his face.

"How come I never see her?" Arlo asked, feeling suddenly desperate to get as much information as he could, knowing that Poppo's patience with his questions was running thin.

Poppo's shoulders collapsed. "Are we playing twenty questions?" he asked.

"No," Arlo said in a small voice. "I'm just curious."

Poppo sighed. "No harm in that, I suppose." He turned around finally and came over to stand behind Arlo's chair. "You'll see her someday," he said. "I promise. But right now you're busy with school, aren't you?"

"I guess so." A mixture of anger and disappointment swirled in Arlo's chest. Poppo was keeping something from him. Something big. Maybe a lot of things.

The air was thick between them. Poppo lifted his hunting jacket off the hook by the back door.

"I think I'll go out for a while," he said. "Leave me a note if you go to Sam's house. All right?"

"Sure, Poppo," Arlo said. "I didn't mean to make you mad."

Poppo sighed again, deeper this time. "It's all right, Arlo. You didn't make me mad. None of this was ever your fault. Remember that. All right?"

None of *what*? Arlo stared at his grandfather's back. He had no idea what Poppo was talking about. But he didn't want to upset him, either. So he answered the best way he could.

"Sure, Poppo," he said. "I'll remember."

"Good."

After he was gone, Arlo studied the photograph once more. He flipped through the rest of the album, stopping at the page with the picture of his parents standing under an apple tree. His father had his arm draped across his mother's shoulders. Her face was turned to his, and they were smiling at each other. They looked so happy. If only Arlo could have known them, *really known* them, before they died. He studied his father's eyebrow, the place where the hair thinned until there almost wasn't a line. Arlo reached up and touched the same spot on his own eyebrow, where it narrowed the same way. He wanted to feel some connection. *Father. Son. Family.* But all that came was a single word. *Gone.*

CHAPTER 6
Busted

Poppo's good days never lasted. By the following Thursday, he was as confused as ever. Arlo sat at the kitchen table, struggling with math problems and waiting for Poppo to come home. By six thirty, he had eaten a bowl of cereal for dinner. Still Poppo wasn't home. Seven fifteen came and went and still there was no sign of Poppo. Cold air seeped through the gap underneath the kitchen door. Then it started to rain, a light sprinkling that barely counted as rain, *at first,* but who knew what might happen later? Poppo was out there alone in the streets, and Arlo needed to find him. He pulled on his parka and headed outside.

He was halfway down the steps when a dark sedan pulled in front of the house. Out stepped a man and woman in uniform. As they moved up the sidewalk, Arlo felt the cornflakes he'd eaten for dinner form a rock in his stomach.

"Your name Arlo Jones?" the man asked, hitching up his pants as he placed his foot on the bottom step.

"Yes, sir?"

"Anybody here with you?" the lady asked.

Arlo gulped. For a moment, he considered lying. But then they would probably ask to go inside, and how would Arlo explain why no one was at home? "I live with my grandpa," he said finally.

The lady glanced sideways at the man.

"Your grandpa named Albert Sabatini?" the man asked.

"Yes." Arlo's shoulders stiffened. "Is he all right?"

"Don't worry," the lady said. "Your grandpa's at the hospital now. The paramedics took him to Marshboro General."

"Hospital?" Arlo's heart ricocheted in his chest.

"Mr. Fanucci was taking out the garbage," the man explained. "You know Fanucci's?"

Arlo nodded.

"Fanucci found your grandpa climbing out of the Dumpster. Or trying to. Seems he didn't quite make it before he passed out."

"Passed out?"

"He was unconscious when they found him," the man said.

Poppo was in a Dumpster? Arlo thought about the garbage strewn around the trash can at the ball field last week and the can of Vienna sausages.

The lady police officer squatted down till she was eye level with Arlo. "We thought you'd like to see him," she said.

Arlo started toward their car.

"Don't you need to call somebody first?" the man asked.

Arlo looked at him.

"You know, an uncle or aunt? Somebody like that."

"You should have somebody with you," the lady added.

The name Ida Jones skipped across Arlo's mind. But even if he thought she could help him, he had no idea what her phone number was or how to reach her.

The man stared at Arlo. "Mr. Fanucci said your grandfather kept calling for some guy named Frankie," he said. "How about calling him?"

"It might be worth a try," the lady police officer suggested.

Arlo looked down at his feet. "Frankie's dead," he said. "He was Poppo's little brother."

"Oh." The man exchanged glances with the woman. "That's too bad, kid."

Then nobody said anything for a minute, until finally, the man cleared his throat and the lady asked another question.

"So, there's nobody?" she asked.

"Just Poppo," Arlo said.

"You're shivering," the lady said. "We'd better get you in the car."

The man parked the police car in the lot for the emergency room. Arlo followed him inside with the lady officer bringing up the rear. They walked through a set of double doors to a window where a woman in a nurse's uniform was typing on a computer.

"They brought this kid's grandpa in an hour ago," the man told the nurse.

"Name?" the nurse asked without looking up.

"Sabatini," the man said.

The nurse stopped typing. She raised her head and looked

at Arlo. Was it Arlo's imagination or did she let out a small groan? Then she looked at the man. "They moved him to ICU," she said.

And Arlo felt the lady officer put a hand on his shoulder.

Both officers stayed with Arlo in the waiting room until a nurse came.

"Would you like to see your grandfather now?" the nurse asked.

"Yes, please," Arlo said.

"I can take him in," the nurse said to the two officers.

The man gave Arlo a small salute. "Take care of yourself, kid," he said as he stood to leave.

"Hope your grandpa's OK," the lady officer said.

"Thanks," Arlo said.

His heart jumped around in his chest as he followed the nurse through the double doors. According to the clock, it was ten minutes past eight.

The lights were dim in intensive care. Curtains on metal rods were all that separated one bed from another. Arlo was almost afraid to see how bad Poppo looked. But when the nurse pulled back the curtain, Poppo looked pretty much the same as Arlo remembered him except for the bandage over his right eye. His hair was scraggly and he hadn't shaved for a few days, but Arlo had gotten used to those changes already. Poppo hadn't looked like his usual self since way back in the spring.

"He's not awake," the nurse said, "but you can talk to him if you like."

There was a tube coming out of Poppo's nose and a needle taped to the back of his hand. The needle was attached to a long plastic tube that connected to a bag of fluid on a metal pole.

"Can he hear me?" Arlo whispered.

"It's possible," the nurse said. "You should try. Sometimes it helps."

"Helps with what?" Arlo asked.

The nurse's eyes widened for a moment, as though she were afraid she'd said something she shouldn't. "The doctor will explain all of that to you later," she said. Then she pulled the curtain shut before adding, "I'll be just outside if you need me."

Arlo pulled a chair closer to Poppo's bed. "Hey, Poppo," he said. "It's me. Arlo."

Poppo lay there with his eyes closed and his chest moving up and down. But he didn't say anything. He didn't groan or blink or even move his hands. Arlo wasn't sure how long he talked. Five minutes? Fifteen? He was all mixed up about time. All too soon, the nurse reappeared.

"I'm afraid you'll have to go out to the lounge now," she said. "The phlebotomist is coming to take a blood sample. And then they're taking your grandfather downstairs for some tests."

The nurse guided Arlo through the ICU and outside to a bright room with sofas and chairs and a television mounted on the wall. It took a few moments for Arlo's eyes to adjust to the light.

"The doctor and social worker will be here to talk to you in a minute," the nurse said. "Would you like a pillow?"

"Social worker?" Arlo's heart jumped.

"You're here by yourself, aren't you?"

"I'm with my grandfather," Arlo said.

The nurse gave him a tight smile. "Let me get that pillow for you," she said.

She disappeared down the hallway for a few minutes. When she came back, there was a man with her.

"Sunil," she said as she led the man toward the sofa where Arlo was sitting. "Over here. This is Arlo."

The man smiled. "Nice to meet you, Arlo," he said.

"Mr. Verma is the social worker," the nurse said. "I'll leave you with him."

Every hair on Arlo's neck stood on end. First the police. Then the hospital. Now a social worker. Forget the mud-and-stick dam. He was drowning.

"How are you doing?" Mr. Verma asked.

"I'm fine," Arlo said.

"That's good. I'm sorry about your grandfather. How's he doing?"

"He's asleep right now," Arlo said.

Mr. Verma nodded. "The nurses will take good care of him. You don't need to worry. And Miss Hasslebarger will be along in a minute."

"Is she the doctor?"

"No, Arlo. She's with Child Protective Services."

"I don't need protection," Arlo said.

Mr. Verma laughed. "Of course you don't. She's with DHHS."

Arlo swallowed. "What's that?"

"Department of Health and Human Services," Mr. Verma said. "They have procedures to deal with situations like yours."

Procedures and *situations* were the kind of words Mrs. Gretzky used when she talked about Arlo's failing grades in math and what they needed to do about them.

Mr. Verma took Arlo downstairs and bought him two packages of peanut-butter crackers and a bottle of orange juice from the machines. Then he brought him back up to the lounge.

"I'm sorry we can't make you more comfortable," he said.

"I'm fine," Arlo said. *"Really."*

Actually, he would feel even better if Mr. Verma would leave him alone. But the social worker stayed and watched television until a red-haired man wearing green scrubs appeared about a half hour later.

CHAPTER 7
The Man in the Green Suit

"Nice to meet you, Arlo." The man wearing green scrubs extended a hand for Arlo to shake. "I'm Dr. Kessel, the resident taking care of your grandfather. Do you mind if we talk?"

"Sure," Arlo said. "I mean, no, I don't mind."

"Excellent."

Arlo's stomach rolled as Dr. Kessel leaned back against the sofa and flipped through a file.

"It says here neither one of your parents is living." Dr. Kessel lifted his glasses and stared at Arlo. "Is that true?"

Arlo nodded. "It's just Poppo and me," he said.

"I'm sorry." Dr. Kessel looked as if he'd been counting on Arlo to correct an error, as if he were hoping Arlo would tell him, *Oh, no, my mom's right down the hall.*

"That's rough," Dr. Kessel said. "How do you manage?"

Arlo shrugged. "We do all right."

Dr. Kessel took his time polishing the lenses of his glasses with the bottom of his scrub shirt. "How long have you been taking care of your grandfather?" he asked.

"I don't really take care of him," Arlo said. "Poppo takes care of me."

"Mmm-hmmm." Dr. Kessel held his glasses up to the light, and Arlo saw that he had dozens of tiny wrinkles around his eyes. He had this odd habit of twisting his watchband. Over and back. Over and back. As if he were nervous about something.

"I was thinking you could help me," he said.

They were in big trouble if Dr. Kessel thought that Arlo knew how to fix Poppo's brain.

"Patient history is important. In most cases, families are the best source of information. It would help a lot if I knew how long your grandfather has been . . ."

Silently Arlo filled in the words. *Confused? Time traveling?*

Dr. Kessel twisted his watchband. "I mean, you know they found him trying to get out of a Dumpster, right?"

"Poppo's fine. What happened tonight . . . he doesn't usually do stuff like that."

Dr. Kessel scooted to the edge of his chair, balancing his clipboard on his knees. "I'm sure he doesn't. The thing is . . . your grandfather may not be able to stay by himself in the house anymore. You understand, don't you?"

Of *course* Poppo could stay by himself. "He's only alone while I'm at school," Arlo said. "And he stays inside mostly. He watches TV and stuff. He never does stuff like he did tonight."

"I believe you, Arlo. Really. I do." Dr. Kessel looked straight into Arlo's eyes. "But something else has happened now. It looks like your grandfather has had a stroke. Do you know what that means?"

Arlo shook his head.

Dr. Kessel stretched his neck as if his shirt collar had grown too tight. "It means that blood spilled in his brain," he said.

Arlo sucked in his breath. "You mean, like a heart attack?"

"Not exactly."

"Is he going to be OK?"

Dr. Kessel looked at Arlo a long time before answering. "I hope so," he said. "We're doing everything we can. And your grandfather appears to be a fighter. That always helps."

Arlo's heart thumped. He thought about blood spilling out of vessels in his brain. He thought about waves of blood pumping through Poppo's head.

"Right now, things are stable," the doctor said. "That's a good sign."

"So he'll be all right?" Arlo asked.

Again the doctor hesitated before answering. "I have to tell you, Arlo, it's unlikely that he'll be well enough to be the primary caretaker for a person your age." Dr. Kessel flipped through the pages on his clipboard. "You're how old?"

"Twelve," Arlo said. After a pause, he added, "In a few weeks."

"I see." Dr. Kessel kept nodding, which made Arlo's stomach churn. "You don't need to worry. The social worker will make sure you're taken care of while we see how things go with your grandfather."

"But I don't need help."

The doctor smiled as he stood up. He clicked his pen shut and slipped it into his shirt pocket. "We'll talk again tomorrow," he said. "Meanwhile, you just take it easy and let the social worker help you. OK?"

"But . . ."

"Good. We'll take good care of your grandfather. Don't worry."

Dr. Kessel was gone before Arlo could finish his sentence.

On his way to the bathroom, Arlo heard two nurses talking.

"Poor kid. Doesn't know what he's in for with Ethel Hasslebarger, does he?" the first nurse said.

"Her heart's in the right place. It's just the follow-through that she's weak on," the second nurse said.

"Hard to believe they called her out of retirement," the first nurse added. "She doesn't really know what she's doing now that they've changed the procedures."

"They needed someone to cover emergency calls at night," the second nurse said. "Can't be too choosy for that shift, I suppose."

"I heard they contacted the shelter," the first nurse said.

The second nurse lowered her voice. "He doesn't have any family except the grandfather, so what else were they supposed to do?"

Arlo thought about making a run for it, but it was pitch-black outside and cold to boot, and the only place he could go was his house — which was the first place they'd look for him. He plumped the pillow the nurse had given him and stretched out on the sofa. It was the sticky plastic kind of sofa material that made terrible noises when you shifted around on it. Sleep was out of the question, but it might be worth trying to rest. Arlo used the remote control to surf from channel to channel, finally settling on an old pirate movie.

Next thing he knew, a large woman wearing lopsided glasses appeared in the doorway. She wrinkled up her nose, squinting around the room until her eyes finally lighted on Arlo. Then she came striding over to him, her worn raincoat dripping puddles on the linoleum.

"Are you Arlo?" she asked.

Arlo nodded, squeezing down a sigh.

The woman stretched out a stiff arm, showering Arlo's pants with rainwater. "My name is Ethel Hasslebarger," she said. "I'm a social worker, and I'm here to help you."

CHAPTER 8
Ethel Hasslebarger, MSW (Retired)

Ethel Hasslebarger had floppy white hair and a pink face and she was about six and a half feet tall.

"Would you mind if we talk a few minutes?" she asked.

"OK," Arlo said. His stomach gurgled.

"Goodness. What's that? Do you need something to eat?"

When she leaned closer, Arlo detected a strong odor of mothballs.

"No, thanks," he said. "Mr. Verma bought me food downstairs."

"That was nice of him. Well, then. Let's get started, shall we? There's an office around the corner we can use. It belongs to the social worker on the day shift."

"OK." Arlo's knees wobbled as he followed her around the corner.

"Have a seat," she said.

Arlo sat. He waited while Miss Hasslebarger fished for

a file in her large bag. She opened it and spread the papers across the desk.

"Ah. Here we go." She moved a blank form to the top and pulled out a pen. "Have you talked to the doctor?" she asked.

"Yes, ma'am."

"So, you know your grandfather's had a stroke?"

"Dr. Kessel told me they *think* that's what it is."

"Well, of course, there are tests to confirm that. He hasn't woken up yet, which means he's going to be with us for a while. My job is to help you find a place to stay."

"I have a home," Arlo said. "Thank you, though," he added after a beat. There was no point in making her mad.

Miss Hasslebarger's smile grew stiff. "There's the question of where you spend the night," she said.

"I'm fine here."

Miss Hasslebarger sighed. "I'm sure you'd like to stay and be near your grandfather, but we can't very well leave you alone in a hospital like this, now, can we?"

Arlo stared at a water stain on the table. If only he could figure out a plan to make her go away.

"No one seems to have a name for your next of kin," she said.

"That would be my grandfather." Arlo forced a smile.

"Of course, dear. We have his name already. I was wondering about other family members."

"Family?" Arlo repeated blankly.

"You know. Uncles? Aunts? Cousins?" Miss Hasslebarger leaned forward over the desk.

Arlo shook his head.

"Does that mean you don't know who they are?"

"No, ma'am. It means, I don't have any."

"No one?"

"Not really. Not around here, anyway."

Arlo watched her draw quick straight lines across the blanks on the form.

"Except a grandmother."

Her hand stopped in midair. She shifted forward, causing the chair to make a loud squeal.

"Her name is Ida Jones," he said.

"So she's on your father's side of the family, then?"

"That's right."

"And do you know where she lives?"

"Edgewater," Arlo said, relieved to have at least one solid piece of information Miss Hasslebarger could write on her form.

"Edge — what?"

"Water."

"Where is that?"

"Virginia."

"OK. Good. Now we're getting somewhere, aren't we?"

Arlo nodded.

"You have her address?"

"No, ma'am."

"A phone number?"

"Not that I know of."

"That you know of?"

"It's just that we haven't called her for a long time."

"A long time?" Miss Hasslebarger kept her eyes on the form, but Arlo could see her eyebrows arching.

"How long?" she asked.

"Pretty long, I guess."

"I see." She put down her pen. "There's a little more to this story, isn't there?"

Arlo shrugged.

"OK, Arlo. You don't have to share family secrets with me. Like I said, I'm here to help you. But, tell me this . . . if you can. There isn't any reason you're afraid of your grandmother Jones, is there?"

"Oh, no, ma'am. I haven't even seen her since . . ."

Miss Hasslebarger locked eyes with him. "Since?" she repeated.

Arlo tried to speak, but his throat closed up on him. "Couldn't I just stay here in the hospital?"

Miss Hasslebarger jotted a few more notes on the form and then closed the file. "For an hour or two, yes. Of course. But I can't very well leave you in the waiting room for days on end."

"But Poppo's going to be all right."

"We hope so, yes. But until then . . ."

"I can stay here. I mean, during the day. At night, I'll go home."

Miss Hasslebarger sighed. It was a long outpouring, as though she were trying to convey how much she regretted what she needed to say. "That's just it, Arlo. With a stroke, there's no way of knowing how long recovery will take." She looked at him a moment. "How old is your grandfather?"

"Seventy-nine."

"And you are?"

"Eleven."

"Exactly." Miss Hasslebarger moved her head up and down sadly. "There's a good chance you'll have to make some changes."

"What kind of changes?"

"Mr. Sabatini is a bit old to be your primary caretaker."

Arlo's stomach tightened. Why did everybody keep saying that? "He goes to all my ball games and he makes sure I do my homework and takes me fishing." *OK. So, they hadn't been fishing in over a year, but still. . . .*

The more Arlo talked, the more pained the expression on Miss Hasslebarger's face became.

"He probably won't be able to drive for a long time, maybe never, and . . ."

"That's OK," Arlo said. "I walk to school. And we buy lots of our food at Fanucci's. It's this little market right down the street. . . ."

"Yes. Fanucci's. I read about it in the police report."

A clammy feeling seeped into Arlo's stomach, as if he had stepped into a dark tunnel and was breathing damp, mold-encrusted air.

Miss Hasslebarger leaned across the desk, and Arlo got another whiff of mothballs, which caused his stomach to churn even harder than it had before.

"Of course, we can *try* to locate your grandmother," she said. "But meanwhile, you need a safe place to stay, so I'll take you to the shelter for tonight and . . ."

Arlo's heart stopped. "But couldn't we wait . . . ?"

Miss Hasslebarger adjusted her glasses. "They're very nice there," she said. "And I'll pick you up first thing in the morning and bring you back here."

If only Arlo had an aunt or cousin someplace who might take care of him, the way Sam's aunt Betty had shown up from Detroit to save him.

Miss Hasslebarger snapped the file shut. Arlo jumped as if someone had fired off a gun. "Wait a second," he said.

She frowned. "My car's right out front," she said as she stuffed the file in her bag and motioned for Arlo to stand up. "It's late. We'd better be going."

CHAPTER 9
A Home Is Not a Home

Calling the Preston Children's Shelter a home was *wrong*. It was a gray building near the airport and looked more like a prison than a home. There were barely any windows, and it was perched on a hilltop all by itself, totally isolated from civilization, as if someone wanted to make sure that the kids living there couldn't possibly escape.

Miss Hasslebarger parked in the visitor's space by the front door. "You'll have to share a room tonight," she said. "They're full at the moment. But it will be nice to have company, don't you think?"

Arlo didn't say anything. It was already quarter of eleven, so it wasn't likely he'd make friends. Not in a place like this. And besides, he wasn't planning to stay, either.

Miss Hasslebarger turned him over to a person named D.W. Whitehair. He was a tall, scrawny man, bald on top with long gray fringes of hair that straggled to his collarbone. He had bushy eyebrows, like antennae, that flopped up and down every time he opened his mouth. As if that weren't disturbing enough, his left eye blinked involuntarily in a kind of nervous twitch. It looked like he was winking at you. Only he wasn't winking. D.W. Whitehair didn't seem like the sort of person who winked. He might frown or scowl or even shake his head, but that was about as friendly as Arlo figured he would get. With his stooped shoulders and lanky arms, he looked a lot like a praying mantis.

"You'll be safe here, Arlo," Miss Hasslebarger said. "Don't worry."

Was she kidding? Arlo was terrified.

Mr. Whitehair jerked his head toward a room on the right. "Come on in the office, kid. Watch out for Rupert there." He gestured toward an ancient-looking terrier who had crusty bald patches where his skin was all scabby and red.

"Nice dog," Arlo said. He leaned down to pat Rupert on the head, and the dog snapped at him.

"Careful of your fingers. Rupert's a little cranky. Hasn't felt well lately. Skin condition, you know."

Arlo nodded. He slid past the dog into Mr. Whitehair's office.

"Sorry you have to bunk with Purvis," Mr. Whitehair said. He handed Arlo a towel and a washcloth and a toothbrush and a tiny tube of toothpaste. "The thing is, we're a little short on space right now. But it's only for tonight. If you have any trouble, you just tap on my door. All right?"

"Yes, sir."

"Good. That's settled, then. Oh. There is one more thing. I'm sort of a sound sleeper, so you may have to knock a few times."

"I'll try to remember that."

Mr. Whitehair led Arlo down the hall. They passed a thin boy with dark hair who was carrying a toothbrush toward the bathroom. He looked like he could use an extra couple of meals.

"Hi," the boy said.

"Hi," Arlo said.

"This is Burton," Mr. Whitehair said. "Burton, meet Arlo. He's going to be staying with us tonight while his grandfather's in the hospital."

"I thought we didn't have any rooms left," the boy said.

Mr. Whitehair cleared his throat. "Well, technically speaking, that's true. But there's an extra bed in O'Dell's room."

The boy's eyes widened to the size of walnuts. "Not Purvis," he said.

"Just for tonight," the man said. Then he raised an eyebrow. "Up kind of late, aren't you?" he asked the boy.

Burton shivered. "Forgot to brush my teeth," he said.

Arlo's stomach pumped acid into his throat. Why exactly was it that Miss Hasslebarger thought Arlo was safer here than in his own home? He followed Mr. Whitehair to the first room on the right. Mr. Whitehair knocked and then opened the door.

"Glad you weren't asleep yet," he said to the refrigerator-shaped boy playing video games on his bed. "This is Arlo. He going to be with us for tonight."

Purvis narrowed his eyes. "You're not thinking of putting him in here, are you?"

Mr. Whitehair cleared his throat. "I'm sure you'll make the best of it."

Purvis got a nasty grin on his face.

"Right, then," Mr. Whitehair said after a pause. "I'll leave you two to get acquainted." He paused at the door. "I know you'll do your best to stay out of Arlo's way, won't you, Purvis?"

"Yeah, right. 'Course I will," Purvis said. He crossed his arms over his chest.

Arlo didn't say a word. He waited until Mr. Whitehair had gone, feeling all hope of survival vanish with him.

"I told Whitehair not to put anybody in here," Purvis said. "I get a single room. Always. That's the rule. So what do they do? Stick some dork in here. Like I'm not going to notice."

Arlo shrugged. "Sorry," he said.

Purvis rolled onto his side and glared at Arlo. "Make that, *Sorry, sir, Mr. O'Dell, sir.* Got it?"

Arlo nodded. He stepped gingerly across the rug and took a seat on the empty bed, keeping his eyes trained on Purvis the whole time. On closer inspection, he noticed a line of red hatch marks where Purvis had had stitches over his left eyebrow. He thought about stories he'd heard about kids getting put in children's shelters, about things that happened to them in their own homes.

"I'll be leaving in the morning," Arlo said. "If you want, I could sleep in the hall."

"Nah. Whitehair don't let nobody sleep outside their rooms."

Purvis stood and walked to the drawers built into the wall. Arlo couldn't help noticing his limp. He was taking something out of one of the drawers when he caught Arlo staring at him.

"What are you looking at?" he said.

"Nothing," Arlo said.

Purvis lunged toward Arlo's bed, taking a swing with his right arm. Arlo rolled out of his way and fell off the bed. Purvis started laughing.

"You're a real wimp, aren't you, Fido?"

"Arlo."

"Yeah. Right. Whatever. What a loser."

All he had to do was survive the night. Arlo kept repeating that to himself. But it didn't help. If he'd had any doubts, he was certain now. *He wasn't staying. Period.* But where was he supposed to go? The shelter was at least three miles from town. And the only road was a narrow two-lane with thick woods on either side, so there was no way to walk on it without being spotted. And there was a fence bordering the woods, so you couldn't duck into them and hide.

Arlo walked down the hall to the bathroom to think. When he came back out, Purvis had locked the door to his room. In a way it was a relief. Now Arlo had an excuse. He was standing there in the dark trying to figure out what to do next when he heard footsteps coming down the hall. It was the boy he'd seen earlier, the one named Burton.

"Hi," Arlo said.

"Hi," Burton said. "I was coming to make sure you were all right."

"Thanks," Arlo said.

"They're not supposed to put anyone in a room with Purvis. Everybody knows that."

"He locked me out," Arlo said.

"You're lucky," Burton said. "You should see what he did to the last kid they put in there."

Arlo shivered.

"You can spend the rest of the night in my room, if you like," Burton said. "You'll have to sleep on the floor, but we have extra blankets. My roommate, Max . . . The thing is, he sleeps pretty soundly. He probably won't even know you're there."

Burton was even skinnier than Arlo remembered from seeing him earlier in the hallway. Poor kid had probably been terrorized by Purvis.

"I don't want to get you in trouble," Arlo said.

"It's OK," Burton said. "You can go to the dining room early. Mr. Whitehair won't know the difference."

"Thanks," Arlo said.

Burton gave him a nod.

They made their way quietly down the hall. Luckily, Burton's room was at the opposite end of the building from Purvis's.

Burton pointed to a spare blanket folded up at the foot of his bed. "You can use that, if you want. There's another one on top of the bookcase."

"That's OK. This is fine." Arlo took the blanket and made a bed on the floor. He stretched out and closed his eyes.

Sleep was out of the question, but at least nobody would hassle him here. He lay awake in the dark, planning his escape. When there was a faint orange glow through the window, he got up and started looking for a way out, but there were alarms on all the doors, and the front door was securely latched.

He was checking out the ground floor, where the dining hall was, when he noticed a panel truck backing up to the loading dock. SEAL'S FINE FOODS was painted in red letters on the door of the cab. Arlo watched the truck inch closer. What he needed was some way to get far enough down the road so that he wouldn't be spotted walking, just far enough to make it back to town. He could walk home from there. It was only a short ride . . . *about the distance a truck might travel between deliveries.*

Of course. He would hide in the back of the truck and sneak out when the driver made his next delivery. With any luck, it would be at a place close to town.

Making it down to the kitchen was the easy part. The driver was carrying boxes off the truck and lining them up in the hallway for the cook. Arlo hid behind one of the tables in the dining room.

"Another box of canned peas?" the cook asked. "Geez, what d'you have, a warehouse of this stuff you needed to get rid of?"

"They're on special this month. Whitehair tripled the order."

"Peas and powdered eggs. What am I supposed to do with that?"

"No idea, Mac. Say, you mind if I use your bathroom?"

"Help yourself. It's down the hall on the right. I'll be peeling potatoes if you need me."

"Sure thing."

As soon as the driver disappeared down the hall, Arlo made a dash through the far end of the kitchen to the loading dock and onto the truck. There were still about ten boxes of food. He squeezed into the back corner behind two cartons of tomatoes.

Riding in back of a truck wasn't exactly comfortable. Every time they made a turn, Arlo braced himself in case one of the cartons toppled over on him. The truck slowed to a stop and then accelerated a short distance, picking up speed as it veered to the left. *Must be going onto the interstate,* Arlo figured. Sure enough, it kept a steady speed for a couple of minutes and then slowed again. *Taking the ramp to the boulevard,* Arlo thought. The driver made two turns and then stopped. Arlo crouched behind the box and waited. When the rear door opened, he peered through a space between the boxes.

There was the sign for the Fairfield Inn. Perfect. He was right across the street from the post office. He waited till the driver wheeled a dolly down the ramp.

Now was his chance. Arlo made a dash out of the truck and across the parking lot. The driver spotted him as he headed toward the boulevard.

"Hey! Where'd you come from? Come back here, kid."

Arlo didn't stop. He kept running. The next stop was his house. All he needed was a couple of shirts and some under-wear and—the most important thing—money for a bus ticket.

He had lawn-mowing money stashed in a box in his sock drawer. He'd been saving it for the school trip to Washington in the spring. But school trips were ancient history now. After an hour in a room with Purvis O'Dell, all Arlo could think about was survival.

CHAPTER 10
Hatching a Plan

Arlo wasn't crazy about going into an empty house before daylight. The house didn't look so good these days. Paint (what little paint remained) was peeling off the shutters, and the screen door hung by a single hinge. People might think the place was deserted if they didn't see any lights on. Still, it wasn't like he could afford to sit around and wait for the sun to come up. So he climbed the stairs to his room and slid the drawer open.

His money was supposed to be there. Second drawer. Left side. In the cigar box Mr. Fanucci had given him last winter. But when Arlo reached into the drawer and moved his hand side to side, he felt nothing. He jiggled the drawer and tried again.

Side to side.

Front to back.

Still, nothing.

He couldn't believe it. After mowing lawns and raking leaves and shoveling snow and even helping Mrs. Beakerbinder clean out her garage — he'd worked his rear end off for that money. He yanked the drawer out of the chest and dumped it over his bed.

two pencil stubs
a rock
three Band-Aids
eight gym socks
five pairs of underwear
six rubber bands
and part of a wooden knob that had
    fallen off one of the drawers

Wait. There was something else.

Two wrinkled bills. A ten and a five.

Fifteen dollars. That's all he had? Out of the hundred and fifty dollars Arlo had saved over the past two years, all that remained was a measly fifteen bucks. The rest was gone.

Vamoosed. Vanished.

The worst part was, Arlo knew who had taken his money. There was only one person who could have done it. Heck, nobody else ever came in their house. It was just the two of them. Poppo and Arlo. OK, maybe Sam came over from time to time. But mostly they went to Sam's house, because Aunt Betty liked to know where Sam was all the time. And even if someone had come in their house, why would they rifle through Arlo's underwear drawer? Unless it was some pervert. And Arlo wasn't going to think about that.

No. It had to be Poppo.

Arlo knew Poppo didn't mean to steal. He didn't even realize he was doing it. It was part of the wonkiness of his brain, being confused and time traveling all the time. Like the way he forgot to pay for food at Fanucci's sometimes. Poppo would wander down the aisles all absentminded, and there would be a package of crackers and they would look pretty good to him, so he'd pluck the box off the shelf and open it up and start eating. And pretty soon after that, he'd spot a bag of pepperoni slices and he'd figure those would taste good with the crackers, so he'd take that bag and pop it open and start eating the pepperoni, too. And before you knew it, he'd be at the front door, and out he'd go, never even remembering he was supposed to pay.

Mr. Fanucci was nice. Sometimes he let Poppo go, and sometimes he called Arlo and asked him to bring money to the store.

"Your grandpa's hungry again," Mr. Fanucci would say. And Arlo would know what that meant. He'd take money out of the underwear drawer and hustle down to the market.

With a wave of his arm, Arlo swept the socks and underwear off his bed. He flopped on his back and stared at the ceiling. *Now what?* The minutes were ticking past. No time to waste. Arlo climbed off the bed, then went downstairs and pulled the photo album out of the cabinet. He opened it to the page with the picture of his mother and father standing in front of the apple tree.

Arlo stared at his dad's face, at that slight irregularity in his left eyebrow. Maybe Ida Jones had a spot like that, too. He would find out as soon as he made it to Edgewater. When he saw his grandmother in the flesh for the first time in nine years, he would check to see if they shared that connection.

He looked at the small wood carving that dangled from the binding of the album. Funny how he'd never paid much attention to it before. It was a bird of some kind. An eagle? Hard to tell. Obviously handmade. Maybe his father had carved it. Arlo unhooked the silver chain that connected it to the album. He wrapped his hand around the wood, feeling how it had turned smooth and furry with age. He rubbed his finger across the grain. Maybe it would bring him luck. If he were living in a fairy tale, a genie would appear and offer to grant his wish. And what would that be? *Easy.* A bus ticket to Edgewater. Yeah. That would work. Arlo would close his eyes and tell the genie his wish, and when he opened them again, he would have a ticket in his hand.

Arlo put the album back in the cabinet. He slipped the wood carving into his pocket and climbed the stairs to his room. He packed two shirts, two pairs of underwear, a couple of pairs of socks, and a pair of shorts in his backpack. Then he headed down to Poppo's room.

Everything looked the same. Poppo's blanket was still bunched on the floor. A pair of dirty khakis, a belt, and two shirts lay in a heap under the window. Dust was heavy on the chest of drawers. There was the brass box where Poppo used to keep emergency cash. It had been empty since a few months after Poppo sold the doughnut shop, but it couldn't hurt to check. Who knows? Arlo might get lucky.

He lifted the lid and pushed the yellowed newspaper clippings aside. There was no money. But there was a piece of jewelry. Arlo held up the gold wedding band with the inscription that read, *To Amy, love forever, W.* His mother's wedding ring. Arlo hated the idea that sprang into his head, but he couldn't help it. He was desperate. And gold was worth money. Enough to buy a bus ticket, probably. And if his mother were around to ask, Arlo figured she would want him to do whatever it took to survive. Besides, a gold ring wasn't doing anybody any good sitting in a box.

All he needed to do was figure out where to sell it. You heard about people selling jewelry all the time. Hadn't Poppo sold his watch when he needed money to fix the roof? He'd taken it to Casey Rader's grandmother. The Raders ran a shop beside the dry cleaner. RADER & SON — WE BUY ESTATE JEWELRY.

Mrs. Rader was a nice lady. She and the lady from the dry cleaners had coffee every morning before the store opened. Arlo could see them through the window on his way to school. Mrs. Rader liked Poppo a lot. And she seemed to understand that Poppo wasn't doing so well these days.

"Afternoon, Albert," she would say in an extra-loud voice when they saw her at the post office. "You doing all right today?"

Mrs. Rader was the type of person who liked helping others. She would buy that ring in a minute. She'd know Arlo wouldn't sell it unless he had to. All he needed to do was tell her how sick Poppo was and that they needed money for medicine. And that wasn't a *complete* lie, because Poppo *was* sick at the moment. And they *definitely* needed money.

Arlo tucked the ring in his pocket. Finally, he had a plan.

1. Walk to Rader & Son.
2. Sell ring.
3. Walk to bus station.
4. Buy bus tickct.
5. Go to Edgewater.

Wait a minute. There was one other thing. Why hadn't he thought of it?

6. Call Sam and tell him what was going on.

He couldn't leave without letting Sam know where he was going and that he would be back as soon as he could.

On his way out the door, Arlo tapped the bottom of his pocket where the carving was safely tucked away. *Help me,* he thought, halfway believing in Poppo's angels and spirits, hoping and *not daring to hope* at the same time that whatever was out there — *some part of his father?* — could hear him.

CHAPTER 11
On the Road?

There was a dim glow in the back of the shop where Mrs. Rader and the dry-cleaning lady sat drinking their morning coffee. Arlo knocked, and Mrs. Rader came to the door. He showed her the ring and explained that he needed money for medicine. "Let's have a look," she said, leading him inside and over to the cash register.

It was easier than Arlo had expected. She paid him seventy-five dollars for the ring. She didn't even ask him many questions, other than, "What can I do to help?" and "Are you sure you've had breakfast?"

"Tell Albert I hope he feels better," she said, ushering Arlo to the door. "And tell him I'm going to hold on to this ring for a couple of months." She gave him a wink. "In case he wants it back. You just call us if you need anything. All right?"

Arlo felt terrible lying to her. She was such a sweet lady. It was a shame he couldn't tell her the truth, but he had to keep the water from crashing over his mud-and-stick dam. He had to get to Edgewater.

Arlo tucked the plastic bag with the cash in his pocket and walked out of the store.

There was one more stop he needed to make. He couldn't leave Marshboro without telling Poppo good-bye.

Arlo hid in one of the stalls in the men's room until he figured the coast was clear. He waited for an opening to slip past the nurses' station to Poppo's bed in the ICU.

Someone had combed Poppo's hair, so he looked better. But he was still frail. His skin looked so thin.

Arlo leaned down and whispered in his ear. "Hi, Poppo. It's me. You doing OK?"

Poppo seemed to choke for a second.

Arlo sighed. This was harder than he'd thought. "Listen, Poppo. I have to go away for a little while. I need to find us some help."

Arlo watched Poppo's chest rise and fall. For some reason, he felt sure Poppo could hear him, though there were no outward signs.

"The nurses are taking good care of you. This is where you need to be right now. But if I don't leave, they'll take me away. You understand?"

"Erp."

Arlo couldn't tell if Poppo was trying to speak or if he was just having difficulty swallowing.

"Don't worry," Arlo said. "I'll be careful. There's this lady named Miss Hasslebarger. She thinks I need to be in the children's shelter while you're getting well."

Arlo put his hand around Poppo's hand, the one that didn't have a needle sticking in it. He felt a slight pressure as Poppo's hand moved. One finger inched over the back of Arlo's hand. Or tried to. It didn't quite make it all the way. Still, Arlo was sure that Poppo was telling him it was all right. He understood why he needed to go.

"You can hear me, can't you?" Arlo gave his grandfather a hug. "Get well, OK? That's all you need to do. I'll be back as soon as I can."

A sound came from his grandfather's lips, barely audible, but at least it was *something*. OK, maybe it sounded like he was choking on spit. But still, Arlo could have sworn Poppo was trying to say the word *love*.

He pulled the blanket around Poppo's shoulders. "I'll be back," he whispered. "I promise."

This time Arlo thought he saw Poppo's hand move, as if he were telling him, *Go on. Hurry.*

He kissed his grandfather on the cheek and slipped silently out of the room.

It was just past eight in the morning. Visiting time was beginning, so there were people milling about. No one noticed Arlo, though his heart thumped wildly as he made his way across the lounge, toward the door beside the restrooms, and then quickly down the stairs.

If Miss Hasslebarger caught him, there would be no escape. Arlo needed to make a clean break *now.*

He burst through the door to the parking lot, only to discover a security guard headed straight toward him.

"Morning, son." The guard gave Arlo a nod.

"Morning." Arlo nearly choked on the word, fearing the guard would stop him.

But he didn't. So Arlo kept moving.

He walked all the way through the parking lot and across the street. Then he started running again. The bus station was less than a quarter mile away.

From a block away, the bus station looked like a crazy spaceship, with its Plexiglas awning and steel girders. Inside, the air was hazy with dust that sparkled when the light hit it, like mica in granite. Arlo took a deep breath and walked straight to the ticket counter. The ticket agent was a skinny man with horn-rimmed glasses that magnified his eyes.

"Can I help you?" he asked.

"I need a ticket to Edgewater, please."

The man lifted his glasses, kneading the red spots where the frames rested on his nose. "What state's that in?"

"Virginia," Arlo said.

"Round-trip or one-way?"

"Round-trip, please."

The man looked at him for a minute. Arlo held his breath. Why was he hesitating? Finally, the man punched some buttons on his computer. Arlo relaxed a bit.

"The nearest station is Richmond," he said. "There's a bus at eight fifty. Gets you there at six twelve. You change at Wytheville."

"How much?" Arlo asked.

The man checked his screen. "A hundred and twenty dollars," he said.

Arlo's stomach tightened. "How much for one-way?"

"Eighty-five," the man said.

Arlo pulled out the plastic bag with the money from Mrs. Rader and what was left of his lawn-mowing cash.

The man put up his hand. "Just a minute," he said. "You have to get the adult who's traveling with you to buy the ticket. You know that, right?"

"Right," Arlo said, struggling to maintain his composure.

"You *do* have an adult traveling with you, don't you?" The man leaned over the counter, glancing around the waiting area.

"Sure. Right over there." Arlo jerked his head toward the orange seats where the passengers were waiting for their buses to be called. There were a couple of ladies who looked about the right age to be his mom.

The ticket agent studied Arlo's face. He checked the passengers in the orange seats. Arlo held his breath, waiting for the man to speak.

"Tell her the bus leaves in twenty minutes," he said at last. "She'll need to come up here and purchase the tickets. It's number seventy-three."

"Thanks."

"You'll have to move out of the way now. There are people behind you."

"Sorry." *What a grump.*

Arlo was careful to choose a seat beside one of the

age-appropriate ladies. The seat on his other side was empty, but Arlo held his backpack in his lap. No sense giving somebody a chance to steal it. He watched the minute hand inch closer to departure time. Now what was he supposed to do?

An old lady hobbled across the tile floor toward the orange chairs. She was lugging overstuffed shopping bags in each hand. The bags were so heavy, they made her shoulders sag. She was headed straight for the chair beside Arlo. *No. Please.* He didn't want to talk to anybody. The best strategy was to keep to himself and avoid being noticed. But the lady had her eyes on that seat.

"Excuse me. Is this one taken?"

"No, ma'am."

"Thank goodness. I wasn't sure I could make it all the way to the back row with these bags." She eased herself into the chair. "Hot in here, don't you think?" She fanned herself with a bus schedule. "Maybe it's just me. I don't know. Seems like they ought to open up one of these doors, maybe get a fan going. A little air circulation would help."

"Yes, ma'am," Arlo said.

Passengers were lining up at the gate now.

"You're not traveling alone, are you?"

"No, ma'am. That is, I wasn't supposed to be, but the thing is . . ." *The thing is . . . what?* Arlo wondered. Another lie. *Quickly.* He didn't have time to waste.

"Yes?" she asked.

"The thing is . . . my mom got called back to work. We were on our way out the door and they had some kind of emergency. She dropped me off and told me to go ahead without her. She said she'd catch up as soon as she could."

Whew. The story was more complicated than he'd like, but the lady seemed to believe him, thank goodness. Her breathing scared him. It was raspy and slow, as if she needed to work hard to get air in her lungs. Each time she bent over to rearrange one of her bags, she had to stop afterward and catch her breath. *Bend . . . rest. Bend . . . rest.*

"Where is it you're headed?" she asked.

"My grandmother's," Arlo said.

"Is it a special occasion?"

Arlo thought fast. "It's her birthday," he said.

"Isn't that nice?" She smiled at him. "I'm a grandmother myself. Seeing those grandbabies is what keeps a body going at my age."

"Yes, ma'am." Arlo sneaked a look at the ticket agent to make sure he wasn't watching.

"In fact, that's where I'm headed today," the lady said.

"Excuse me?"

"To see my grandbabies." The lady squinted toward the loading platform. "Can you read the number on that bus? My eyes aren't so good."

Arlo looked in the direction she was pointing. "Seventy-three," he said, trying to keep the panic out of his voice.

Meanwhile, the voice on the intercom called out destinations. "Wytheville, Richmond."

"Mercy, that's me." The lady rolled forward, gathering up her bags and working her way to her feet. She grimaced when the weight came down on her right side. "What time's your bus?" she asked.

Arlo didn't say anything.

"Son?"

Arlo raised his head.

"What's the matter?" she asked.

Arlo had story-spinning adrenaline gushing through his brain so fast, he couldn't think of an answer. All the ideas were garbled together. He needed a story that would get him on that bus. Finally, the idea came—just in the nick of time. Arlo blurted it out.

"My mom left money for me to buy my ticket, but that ticket agent wouldn't sell it to me." He nodded in the direction of the man with the horn-rimmed glasses.

In ten minutes the bus would be pulling out of the station. And probably two minutes after that, a policeman would show up, looking for "some kid named Arlo whose grandfather is in the hospital."

"You have a phone with you?" the lady asked. "Maybe you could give your mom a call."

"My battery died," Arlo lied.

"You could borrow mine."

Oh, geez. Now what? "She said she was going to be in a meeting," Arlo said, digging deeper into his brain for another lie. "They wouldn't let her take any calls."

"Mmm-mmm," the lady said. "You're in a pickle, aren't you?"

"Yes, ma'am." It was amazing. She actually believed

him. He watched her glare at the man behind the ticket counter.

"Can't say I'm surprised you ran into trouble," she said. "That sorry so-and-so needs a lot of friendly added to his diet, if you ask me." She thought for a moment. "You got your money for that ticket?"

"Yes, ma'am." Arlo offered up the plastic bag with his money.

The lady laughed. "Oh, me. I've seen some fancy wallets in my day, but that one takes the cake. Where is it you're headed?"

"Richmond."

"The same as me." The lady frowned. "You need to hurry, son."

"Yes, ma'am, I know."

She looked at him. Then she slid back in her seat and stared up at ceiling for a minute. "I'd like to help," she said.

"You would?"

She rolled forward again. "You seem like a nice young man, and you and your mama are trying to do a good thing for your grandmother."

Arlo nodded. He tapped the wood carving. Maybe it was helping after all.

"You trust me with that fancy wallet of yours long enough to buy your ticket?"

"*Yes, ma'am.*" Arlo handed over the bag.

"It's a shame about your mama not being able to go. I hope she can catch up with you later on."

"I hope so, too," Arlo said. "She promised she would."

The lady looked closely at Arlo's face. Could she tell he was lying? His cheeks turned red sometimes when he was under stress.

"I'll tell you what," she said. "You wait right here and I'll be back in a minute."

"OK."

If a kindly stranger appeared at just the right moment and offered to help you when it looked like everything was lost, that must be a sign you were doing the right thing. After all, what were the odds that somebody like this lady would show up when Arlo needed help? He pulled the wood carving out of his pocket and looked at it. He could almost see the bird blink. In fact, he would have sworn he saw that eye close and then open again. *Slowly.* Like it was winking at him. If it kept bringing him luck, Arlo ought to be sitting in Ida Jones's living room before the sun went down.

Two minutes later, the lady hobbled back across the floor waving a ticket above her head.

"We've got to shake a leg, son," she said. "Come on."

Arlo tossed his backpack over his shoulder. "Want me to carry one of your bags?"

"Bless your heart." The lady handed him the smaller of the two bags. "Be careful you don't hurt yourself. It's a little heavy."

The bag weighed a ton.

"Books for my grandbabies," she said. "They were selling them cheap at the library. Guess I got carried away."

Arlo followed her to the boarding platform. She favored

her right side when she walked, as if her hip didn't work so well, or maybe it was just that she was off balance on account of Arlo carrying one of her bags. The driver waited for them. He pulled the door shut as soon as they stepped on board.

"You go on ahead," the lady said when they got to the top of the steps. "I can't move that quick."

"I'll save you a seat," Arlo said.

The lady smiled. "That's nice." She pointed toward two seats in the middle of the bus. "Why don't you take the one by the window?" she said.

When she sat down, her skirt billowed up, exposing ankles so swollen that they looked like balloons. The skin was purple and splotchy, as if it was stretched too tight. No wonder she walked the way she did.

Arlo stowed her shopping bags under the seat. He had to rearrange the books so they would fit.

"Thank you, son. Don't believe I could've managed that without your help." The lady patted him on the arm. "You stick with me, and I'll get you to your grandmother's in time to help her blow out the candles on her cake."

"Thank you," Arlo said.

"My name's Bernice, by the way." She left space at the end of the sentence for Arlo to fill in his name. But he'd just as soon she not know anything about him, in case the police came looking later on. Wasn't he in enough trouble as it was? No sense making it easier to find him.

Air whooshed through the hoses on the bus as the engine turned over. Gears ground into place. Arlo glanced out the window. The security guard was talking to some lady on the sidewalk. She raised an arm and pointed toward Arlo, but he ducked before the security guard spotted him. Burrowing deeper in his seat, Arlo pulled a magazine out of the pocket on the seat in front of him. He shoved it in front of his face. All the way to the interstate, his heart raced, waiting for someone to stop the bus and order him off.

But nothing happened. Bernice started humming as she watched the buildings buzz by.

"We're on our way now," she said, giving him a nod.

"Yes, ma'am," Arlo said. And, for the first time in two days, the tightness in his shoulders began to ease.

CHAPTER 12
Angels and Spirits

Riding a bus was like being on top of the world. Compact cars looked like bugs. Bernice got out her cross-stitch and threaded a fresh needle. Arlo glanced at the words spelled out in her work. *The truth will make you free.* His toes itched. He wished he could reach inside his shoes.

Meanwhile Bernice stitched away. "I'm making this for one of my grandbabies," she said. "My son and his wife named her after me. I told Tyrone if they named that baby Bernice, they'd better not go calling her by any nicknames. I had an uncle who used to call me Bernie. I hated that. Speaking of names, I don't believe you told me yours, did you?"

Arlo stared at the magazine in his lap with the glossy photo of the former president who used to be in the movies, way back in the old days.

"Ronald," he said in a quiet voice.

"Is that right? I have a son named Ronald. He lives in Michigan. Don't get to see him as often as I'd like."

She was so nice. It was terrible lying to her, but the less she knew, the better it was for both of them. Arlo decided to change the subject before she asked any really difficult questions.

"How many children do you have?"

"Six living. I lost two. Olive when she was a baby and Lonnie when he was twelve."

Arlo's heart skipped. "I'm sorry," he said. He thought about Poppo and Frankie and the way Poppo was always traveling back to the days when Frankie was still alive.

"The Lord works in mysterious ways," Bernice said. "You got to take the bad with the good, like they tell you in church. Life is full of sweet and sad."

"My dad died." Arlo had no idea what made him say that. Usually he didn't talk about his parents in front of strangers.

Bernice put down her needlework. She stared at the seat-back in front of her, though her eyes seemed miles away. "It's hard to see the reason in a thing like that," she said. "A boy needs a father. How old were you when you lost him, if you don't mind my asking?"

"Two," Arlo said. "I don't really remember him." *Or my mom, either,* he wanted to add. But it was too late to say anything about his mother, not after telling Bernice that story he'd concocted about his mom being called back to work.

"You got a lot of grit, Ronald. I can see that. I'll bet your daddy's looking down right now and feeling proud."

If Wake Jones happened to be looking down right now, Arlo was sure he wasn't feeling proud. He hoped his dad

81

could understand why Arlo needed to lie. *I promise,* he whispered in his head. *I'll do better from here on out.* He felt a little spark coming back at him.

"You're welcome to read any of those books in my bag," Bernice told him.

Arlo leaned his head against the window. "Thanks, but I'm a little sleepy," he said.

"Best way to make the trip go faster. Have yourself a nap. The rest will do you good."

Through cracked eyelids, Arlo watched Bernice go back to her cross-stitch. He must have fallen asleep after that, because the next thing he remembered was the driver's voice coming on the intercom to announce the next stop.

"Wytheville," he said. "Transfers here."

Wytheville was higher in the mountains, which meant the weather would turn cold earlier than in Marshboro. In a few weeks, these woods would look like bowls of hard candy, all yellow and red with the green of the pine trees mixed in.

When they pulled into the station, Arlo checked the clock. In a few hours, he would be in Edgewater. As long as his dam held the water back a few more hours, everything would be fine.

After Wytheville, they stopped at Roanoke. Traffic was heavy from there to the Lynchburg station, where one passenger got off and three got on. The fog lifted on the way into Charlottesville. The bus was nearly full by the time they pulled out of that station.

"Next stop Richmond," the driver announced as he levered the doors shut.

Bernice reached into one of her shopping bags and pulled out little triangles of cheese wrapped in foil. She rooted around until she found a box of crackers in the other bag.

"Hungry?" she asked.

"A little," Arlo admitted.

"Here. Have yourself something to drink, too." She handed him a can of orange pop and some crackers and cheese.

Where did she get all this stuff? No wonder those bags were so heavy. Next thing you know, she'd be pulling out her own refrigerator.

"Thank you," Arlo said.

"Won't be long now." Bernice handed him another packet of cheese. "Is your grandma meeting you at the station?"

"Mmpf." A lump of cracker lodged in Arlo's throat.

"Mercy." Bernice pounded Arlo on the back. "You all right?"

"Yes, ma'am. Must have swallowed the wrong way."

"That's OK. Just drink that pop slowly. I'd like to meet your grandma, if she's not in too big a hurry."

Arlo choked again.

"Good heavens, son. Put your arms over your head and count to ten."

Arlo raised his arms. He hawked up a chunk of cheese.

"Must be the excitement of getting to see your grandma," Bernice said.

"Yes, ma'am. I'm sure that's what it is."

Bernice closed the cracker box and stuffed it in her bag. "Does she know what time your bus arrives?"

Arlo started coughing again.

"Son?"

He shook his head.

"You got her number so you can call her, though, don't you?"

Arlo's cheeks burned. He slid lower in his seat and let his face sink into his shirt collar.

"Ronald? I asked you a question. You have your grandma's phone number, don't you?"

"Not exactly," Arlo mumbled.

"You got some other family coming to meet you? Is that it?"

Arlo tried to find some way not to look at Bernice, but it was hard because she was glaring straight at him.

"Ronald? Did you hear me?"

"Yes, ma'am. I heard."

"Now, I know you got some money left in that fancy wallet of yours, but it's surely not enough to pay a taxi. How *exactly* do you plan to get to your grandma's?"

Arlo shrugged.

"Is there something you haven't told me?" A little edge crept into Bernice's voice.

Arlo shrugged again.

"Oh, Lordy. I know what that shoulder shuffle means. I've seen that business plenty of times. It means, *Well, Bernice, maybe this story I been telling you isn't exactly the truth*. Isn't that right, Ronald?"

Arlo looked at the floor. Back home he was Frankie. Here he was Ronald. When could he just be himself?

"You better look at me now. We're into some serious business here."

Arlo's heart beat so hard, his throat ached.

"After I helped you get on this bus so you could see your
grandma, don't you think you owe it to me to tell the truth?"

"Yes, ma'am."

"What about the grandmother part of your story? Is
that true?"

"Mostly."

"Mmm-mmmm." Bernice looked up at the ceiling of the
bus and shook her head. "Mostly, you say. S'pose you tell me
which part of your story *is* true. Maybe that's where we need
to start."

Arlo swallowed. He sat up in his seat and turned halfway
around to face her. "I *am* going to see my grandmother," he
said. "That part's the truth."

"For some reason, I feel a *but* coming on."

Arlo took in a slow breath and let it out again. "The
thing is, she doesn't exactly *know* I'm coming. That part's a
surprise."

"Go on."

"And she doesn't exactly live in Richmond, either."

Bernice pursed her lips. "And just *where exactly does*
she live?"

"Edgewater." Arlo's shoulders felt like hollowed-out pas-
tries, those crème-filled éclairs, only without the filling inside.
"I don't think it's that far," he said.

Bernice had the saddest look on her face. It made Arlo feel
awful.

"We got us a problem here, don't we?" she said.

"Yes, ma'am. I guess we do."

"Lord, have mercy, what are we going to do now? You have any suggestions?"

"I could try getting her number from Information."

"You think I'm gonna leave you standing in a bus station all by yourself?"

"I don't want to be any trouble."

"It's a little late to be worrying about that now." Bernice fanned herself with one of the magazines from the pocket on the seat. "My son Tyrone's picking me up in Richmond. We could give you a ride to Edgewater."

"I don't want to take you out of your way."

"It's a little late to worry about that, too. I'm not leaving till I see you're with family. You understand?"

"Yes, ma'am." Arlo worked hard to breathe. It felt like someone had tied a rope around his chest. "I'm sorry," he said.

Bernice sighed. "I know you are. But let's us deal with the situation we got. Something tells me there's a big part of this story you haven't told me. That's all right. Maybe it's none of my business. Besides, it's too late to do anything about it today, other than getting you where you're supposed to be, safe and sound. If you and I work real hard on this together, we might just manage that. All right?"

"Yes, ma'am."

"But you got to tell me the truth."

Arlo felt another choking fit coming on. He took a deep breath to squelch it down.

"We'll try Information when we get to Richmond. You're going to have to promise to help. All right, son?"

Arlo's stomach churned. The words didn't want to form in his mouth. It was awful to promise something he wasn't going to do.

"Yes, ma'am," he said, swallowing extra hard to keep the cheese and crackers from coming back up.

CHAPTER 13

Bernice and Tyrone Lend a Hand

At the station in Richmond, a tall man wearing khaki pants and a blue shirt waved from the sidewalk. Bernice put down her bags and opened her arms.

"Tyrone!"

The man walked over and gave her a hug.

"What's in the bags, Mama?"

Bernice grinned at him. "You know I don't like to come empty-handed."

The man bent down to lift one of the bags and grunted when he felt how heavy it was.

"What in the world have you got in here? Bricks? You know you don't need to bring us anything. We're just happy to see you."

The man kept a steady eye on Arlo, as if he was trying to figure out why a white boy would be traveling with his mother.

"You didn't tell me you'd be bringing a friend."

"This is Ronald," Bernice said. "We met at the bus station." She gave Arlo a wink. "Didn't we, Ronald?"

Arlo nodded.

"Ronald is going to see his grandma in Edgewater. You think we could give him a ride?"

Tyrone glanced sideways at his mother.

"It's all right," Bernice said. "He just needs a ride to her house. Isn't that right, Ronald?"

"That's right," Arlo said. He looked at Tyrone and smiled.

Tyrone did not smile back. "The car's out front," he said, giving Arlo a look that made it clear he had his doubts about Arlo's story.

"Ronald needs to make a phone call first, though, don't you, son?"

"Yes, ma'am," Arlo said.

"And he needs to borrow your phone."

Tyrone frowned. He put down Bernice's bags and cocked his head toward Arlo.

"My battery ran out," Arlo explained.

Tyrone ran a hand back and forth across his chin, as if he were thinking hard before deciding what to do next. Finally, he reached into his pocket and handed Arlo his phone.

"Thank you," Arlo said.

"It's all right," Tyrone said.

Bernice patted Arlo on the shoulder. "You go on and call Information, now."

"Information?" Tyrone put the bags down again. "You mean, he doesn't have his grandmother's number?"

"Ronald says he left the number at home."

"Sorry," Arlo said to Tyrone. He lifted one shoulder and let it drop.

Tyrone shifted his weight from one foot to the other, leaning closer to Arlo. "Where'd you say you met my mother?"

"At the bus station."

"Mmm-hmm." Tyrone narrowed his eyes. "I reckon you'd better hurry up and make that call. Mama doesn't do so well standing on her feet a long time."

Arlo looked at the keypad.

"Dial 411," Bernice said.

Arlo felt Tyrone watching as he punched in the numbers. An operator came on the line.

"City and state, please?"

"Edgewater, Virginia," Arlo said. That was the easy part.

"What listing?" she asked.

Here goes, Arlo thought. Better not use a real name. Once Bernice and Tyrone dropped him off, Arlo didn't want anyone to be able to trace him. Better think of a phony name. And better do it fast. Before Tyrone grew any more suspicious than he already was. John Smith was too obvious. *Oh, just say whatever name comes to mind,* Arlo thought. *Sam.* There you go. That was a good first name. Sam *what?* *Gretzky.* That was it. Sam Gretzky. It sounded real enough.

"Mrs. Sam Gretzky," Arlo said into the phone. He had to fight to keep from laughing at the idea of Sam being related to Mrs. Gretzky.

"One moment, please."

"She's checking," Arlo reported as Tyrone stood over him, tapping his foot.

"There's an Arthur Gretzky on Beachcrest," the operator said.

"That's it," Arlo said, smiling and nodding for Bernice and Tyrone's benefit.

Bernice nodded back at him. "If you hold on, they'll connect you at no extra charge," she said.

"OK." Arlo held the line. What's the worst that could happen? Someone answers and he talks to them like it's his grandmother at the other end. Tyrone and Bernice wouldn't know the difference, not if Arlo kept the phone pressed tightly against his ear. And he happened to know that when Information made a connection for you, the number they called didn't register on your phone. So Tyrone couldn't hit REDIAL and check up on him.

The phone rang about six times. Bernice was starting to look worried. Finally, a voice came on the line. It was a man's voice on a recording. "This is the Gretzky residence. Our number has changed. If you need to reach us, please call . . ." And he gave a number.

Arlo smiled. This was perfect. More than perfect. He could say anything he wanted, and no one would know the difference.

"Did you get her?" Bernice asked.

Arlo nodded. "Is that you, Gramma? Yes. It's me. Arlo."

"Tell her you're on your way to see her," Bernice whispered.

"I'm coming to see you," Arlo said, smiling at Bernice. "No. Mom couldn't come. They called her from work. . . . Yeah. I know. It *is* too bad. She really wanted to be there for your birthday."

Bernice gave him a sympathetic look, and Arlo nodded sadly in return. It was working. He almost believed his grandmother was on the other end of the line himself.

"They told her it was some kind of emergency meeting," he said. Then he paused. He had to leave room for somebody else to be talking at the other end, right? "That's OK," he said. "I met this nice lady." He smiled at Bernice. "She and her son offered to give me a ride." Even Tyrone looked like he believed Arlo's story now. "See you soon. OK?" *Pause. Pause. Pause.* "What's that? Oh, yeah. I love you too, Gramma. Bye."

Arlo had never given such a performance. He deserved a standing ovation. He deserved an Academy Award. Sweat dripped from his armpits as he handed Tyrone the phone. Getting away with the lie was all the reward he needed. If it helped him find Ida Jones, the lying was worth all the wear and tear on his body.

Deep down inside, Arlo had known for a long time that he and Poppo couldn't go on living the way they had been. Poppo was likely to poison himself eating food that came out of a Dumpster or from who knows where. He might set the house on fire by forgetting a pan on the stove. Some things you tried not to think about, especially if you were a kid and you didn't know how to fix them. You waited and you hoped the problem would be fixed by somebody else. And then when it wasn't fixed—when the problem only grew worse—well, then all you could do was hope you'd be lucky enough to figure out a way to fix it . . . eventually.

And that's where things had stood the day Poppo was taken to the hospital. And Arlo was working on a solution. So far things were going all right. Sure, he'd hit a few snags along the way, but nothing terrible. Not so far. And look what he'd accomplished. Twelve hours ago, he'd been at the children's shelter, and now here he was, only minutes away from seeing his grandmother.

She'd probably been waiting all these years to see her grandson, only she couldn't on account of some stupid argument between Poppo and her about his parents "running off to get married." Whatever *that* meant. There had to be more to the story, didn't there? Whatever bad blood existed between Poppo and his grandmother, she couldn't hold it against Arlo, could she? What kind of a grandmother would do that?

Besides, he was sure there was a reason for his coming here, as if someone (or some*thing*) were guiding him. Maybe that was crazy. Maybe, on some level, he didn't really believe it. But you couldn't ignore the odd things that had happened or how lucky he had been to find Bernice the way he did. It was like one of Poppo's stories, the ones where magical things happened. Arlo tapped the carving in his pocket. Was that a tiny vibration coming back at him? More likely it was his imagination working overtime. No wonder. When you were under this much stress, every part of your body kicked into overdrive. Of course he was sensing things that weren't really there. He hadn't had much sleep either. That was part of the problem. And, when you thought about it, where was the harm in believing in spirits or angels or whatever. As long as it wasn't hurting anybody.

"You coming, Ronald?" Tyrone yelled from the driver's side of the car.

"On my way!" Arlo yelled back. He pulled the door of the sedan open and hopped inside.

"Won't be long now," Bernice said, winking at Arlo in the mirror on the visor over her head.

Arlo hoped she was right.

Tyrone drove past strip malls and car lots. Eventually the concrete turned to grass, and soon after that, there was nothing but cornfields and tobacco crops that stretched in every direction. Small white churches dotted the landscape. Tyrone drove through little towns with feed stores and service stations and not much else. Just outside Edgewater a construction crew worked in the opposite lane. Tyrone's tires made short clipping noises as they bumped over seams of new pavement.

EDGEWATER, VIRGINIA — FOUNDED 1687 — POP. 1,753

"Not a very big place, is it?" Tyrone asked.

"Looks like a pretty little town to me," Bernice said.

"I haven't been here for a long time," Arlo said.

To their right, a brick building stood beside a hardware store. In the town square there was a pedestal with a statue of a man on the top. The man wore a funny hat.

Arlo snapped to attention in the backseat. He'd been cruising along thinking everything was OK, not even considering the fact that he had no idea where to tell Bernice and Tyrone to drop him off. In another sixty seconds, they would be past the town and it would be too late. He needed to find a house quick, someplace that looked like a grandmother might live there.

On the other hand, if he hadn't been to Edgewater in a long time, why should he remember where her house was? He had to go somewhere. What should he do? Sweat pooled in Arlo's armpits.

"You remember how to find your grandmother's house?" Bernice asked.

"I remember that statue," Arlo lied. "Her house wasn't far from there." That lie seemed safe enough. In a town this small, her house couldn't be far away.

"Looks like there's some houses down that street," Tyrone said, nodding toward a shady street lined with tree-filled yards and flower gardens and mailboxes.

It looked perfect.

"That's it," Arlo said. "I mean, it looks familiar. I think her house is down there."

"You mean, I should turn here?" Tyrone asked.

"Yes, please." Arlo held his breath, watching houses drift past. He needed to pick one, but he wanted to make sure nobody was home first. How could he do that from the backseat of the car? All the houses looked nice. Maybe he'd be lucky and pick one that had the door unlocked. Lots of people left houses unlocked in small towns. OK, maybe not *lots*, but some did. A few. All Arlo needed was one. And if there wasn't a car in the driveway and the house didn't have a garage, then it would probably be safe. He could get out of the car and tell Bernice to wait while he went to the door. Then he'd pretend to ring the bell and act like someone was inviting him inside. After a minute or two, he would step back outside and wave and tell them everything was OK. He'd give Tyrone time to back out of the driveway. And after they were gone, he'd go back outside and . . .

And what?

Who knows?

One thing at a time.

That's all he could handle.

"It's that one." Arlo pointed to a low bungalow with twin pine trees growing on either side of the front steps.

"Nice-looking place," Tyrone said.

"Look at those flowers," Bernice said. "Your grandma must be quite a gardener."

"Yes, ma'am, she is." Arlo crossed his fingers behind his back. Who knows? Maybe it was the truth.

Tyrone flipped on the blinker and made the turn.

"She'll be excited to see you, won't she?" Bernice said.

She sure will, Arlo thought. He looked at Bernice. The way she smiled at Tyrone, you could see how proud she was of him. Then she turned and smiled at Arlo in almost the same way. Arlo figured it was because she was happy they were helping him. She was such a nice lady. It was rotten to lie to her. If it weren't for Bernice and Tyrone, Arlo wouldn't even be here. He'd still be sitting in that bus station back home. Or worse yet, at the police station, explaining why he had stolen his mother's wedding ring, or maybe even at the children's shelter. He owed Bernice and Tyrone a lot. And what had he done for them? Lied, that's what. He took a deep breath and slid forward in his seat. "Thank you for helping me," he murmured. Something fluttered in his chest.

"What's that?" Bernice asked. "I can't hear so well over the engine noise."

"I said thank you." The flutter moved into Arlo's throat, pressing to get out.

"We were glad to do it. Weren't we, Tyrone?"

"Anytime," Tyrone said. He glanced in the rearview mirror and gave Arlo a small salute.

Bernice reached into the backseat and patted Arlo on the knee. "You tell your grandmother she's a lucky lady to have such a fine grandson."

Arlo started coughing. The words on Bernice's cross-stitch flashed through his mind.

"You all right?" Tyrone asked.

"Fine," Arlo said.

"Ronald had a little trouble with the cheese and crackers I gave him on the bus," Bernice said. "I expect he's still working on them. Is that it, son?"

"Yes, ma'am," Arlo said. "I think that's what it is. Excitement about seeing my grandmother—like you said."

Maybe someday he would have the chance to help someone the way Bernice and Tyrone had helped him. He hoped so. It would be one way to repay the debt he owed. There wasn't much else he could do. Not at the moment, anyway.

"You run on to the door and let her know you're here. Tyrone and I will wait in the car."

97

Perfect. Arlo opened the door.

"Don't forget your backpack," Bernice called out to him.

"No, ma'am. I have it. Thank you."

"You wave when you're ready for us to come inside. All right?"

Oh, great. How was he going to make them leave?

"Yes, ma'am."

Tyrone smiled through the car window.

Arlo threw his backpack over his shoulder and started toward the house. He stood in the front yard between the twin pine trees and stared at the door. His knees quivered. Who knew what trouble waited on the other side? *Go on,* Arlo told his feet. Might as well get this over with. The first step would be the hardest, the one where he walked onto the porch of a strange house and waited to see if anybody was home. He needed a miracle. He needed a grandmother to drop down out of the sky. Then he'd have to figure out how to get rid of Bernice and Tyrone. Maybe he could just wave and smile and let them see he was OK. He could always hope. He reached up and pressed the doorbell. *Oh, please.*

CHAPTER 14
Augusta Stonestreet

Nothing happened. No one came to the door.

Arlo stood there waiting while Tyrone's engine idled in the driveway.

"Sure you got the right place?" Tyrone yelled.

"I'm sure." Arlo waved back at him. Couldn't they just take the hint and drive away?

"Maybe she left the door unlocked for you," Bernice yelled.

"Maybe," Arlo yelled back. He reached for the doorknob and closed his eyes. On top of lying and stealing, he was about to add breaking and entering to the list of things he hadn't intended to do. The squeal of the rusty hinge was so loud, it sent vibrations through his toes. Any second, a strange person might appear and demand to know what he was doing in the middle of their front hallway. Arlo imagined police sirens blaring and an officer handcuffing his wrists behind his back. Meanwhile, the clock ticked seconds away. *One thousand one, two thousand two.* Arlo held his breath. When the clock chimed the quarter hour, he jumped and nearly knocked a vase off the hall table.

But nothing happened.

No one came.

Thank you, God.

He was safe.

Now all he had to do was get rid of Bernice and Tyrone. But how? Finally, it came to him. He'd pretend his grandmother was in the bathtub. It was so easy. Why hadn't he thought of it before? He would tell them she had been working in the yard the first time he called and that she'd wanted to take a bath before he arrived. Only they'd appeared sooner than she'd expected.

He stepped back onto the front stoop.

"Everything all right?" Bernice asked.

"She's in the bathtub," Arlo said. "Everything's fine."

Bernice started to get out of the car.

No. Didn't she understand? If his grandmother was in the bathtub, that meant Bernice couldn't see her now. Arlo started thinking again.

"She said to tell you thank you for bringing me here. She asked me to get your address so she could write you a note."

Bernice pulled the car door closed again.

She looked over at Tyrone, then stuck her head out the window.

"You sure everything's all right?" she asked.

"Yes, ma'am. I'll get a piece of paper so you can write

down your address. She probably wants to send you some candy or something."

Bernice smiled, which made Arlo's heart slow to a normal pace.

"That's all right," Bernice said. "You tell her it was our pleasure. We're just glad we could help out."

Please leave, please leave, please leave, Arlo thought as he stood there nodding and grinning like an idiot.

"You take care of yourself, Ronald," Bernice said.

"I will," Arlo said. "Thank you again."

Bernice waved. Then she rolled up her window and said something to Tyrone. Arlo held his breath. Finally, the car started backing out of the driveway. Arlo had never heard such a nice sound as the crackling of tires on gravel.

He stepped back inside the house, watching through the window until Tyrone's car disappeared around the curve. Then, holding his breath, Arlo stepped back outside. He paused long enough to wipe his fingerprints off the doorknob with his shirt.

Then he walked down the front steps and headed toward the road. He wasn't sure where he was going next. He would have to figure that out on the way. Like Tyrone said, Edgewater wasn't a big place. How hard could it be to find a lady named Ida Jones?

Arlo was thinking so hard that he didn't see the lady in the yard across the street.

"They're not home," she said in a loud voice.

Arlo turned around in a full circle before he spotted her lifting a bag of mulch from the trunk of her car.

"They take a walk around this time every evening." The lady leaned the mulch bag against her garage and walked toward the curb. "Should be home soon," she said.

Arlo tried to smile, but the corners of his mouth were frozen in place. Fear did funny things to your body. Somehow, miraculously, he wasn't in trouble yet. But he wasn't exactly home free, either.

"You were looking for the McIlvoys, weren't you? That's their house you were in."

Arlo's heart dropped to his stomach. The best thing to do was agree with her. When in doubt, nod your head yes.

"Thought so." The lady moved closer to him. "Say, you're not Doris's nephew Anthony from Harrisonburg, are you?"

Arlo looked at her.

"No. You couldn't be Anthony. Doris told me he's spending this year in California with his daddy."

She looked a little frightening. She had a sawed-off nose and a jutting-out chin, and her eyes were small and beady looking, like that rat back on the riverbank. Thinking about the riverbank reminded Arlo of home. He wondered how Poppo was doing. *Don't think about that,* Arlo told himself. *He's got nurses and a doctor, and he's doing just fine. Well—as fine as he could be . . . considering.*

Arlo adjusted the backpack strap on his shoulder.

"I haven't seen you around here before, have I?" the woman asked. "Are you sure you're supposed to be going into that house without anybody home?"

A headline flashed through Arlo's mind. LOCAL BOY ARRESTED IN VIRGINIA TOWN. Making up lies was exhausting.

Arlo couldn't think fast enough to make up another one. "Please," he said, "could you tell me where to find Ida Jones?"

The lady frowned. "Why are you looking for her?"

Arlo kept his eyes on his feet. "We're sort of . . . related," he said.

"*Sort of?*" The lady squinted her eyes. She examined Arlo's face. Every inch of it. Especially his eyebrow, the one with the thin spot where the hairs nearly disappeared. "You'd be about the right age," she said.

The right age for what? Arlo took a step away from her.

"You're not . . ." The lady tapped a finger against her cheek. "No. Surely not. You couldn't be. . . . Could you?"

"Couldn't be what?" Arlo asked.

"Ida's grandson, of course. What do you think I'm talking about?" The lady leaned closer. "You *are* Arlo, aren't you?"

Arlo focused on a tiny mole on the lady's cheek. That way he didn't have to make eye contact. "Yes, ma'am," he said. "That's who I am."

The lady dabbed sweat off her forehead with a wrinkled tissue. "Heavenly days. Does Ida know you're coming?"

"I guess you'd have to say it's pretty much a surprise," Arlo said.

"A surprise, is it?" The lady stuffed the tissue back in the waistband of her pants. "Isn't that interesting. But what were you doing in the McIlvoys' house?"

Arlo sighed. "I couldn't remember where my grandmother's house was," he said. "I guess I was confused."

"I'll say." The lady rolled her eyes. "Ida's house is nothing like Doris and Phil's."

"Who?"

"The McIlvoys, son." She scratched at a mosquito bite on her neck. "Bugs are coming out. Time to go in. I suppose you might as well come in, too. I'll give Ida a call."

"Are you good friends with her?"

The lady laughed. "Merciful heavens. I've lived in Edgewater all my life. This ain't exactly the Big Apple, in case you hadn't noticed. We all know each other around here. Ida was two years ahead of me in school."

Arlo followed her inside.

Every room was filled with plants. Ferns. African violets. Those leafy plants like the ones Mrs. Gretzky kept in her room, philo-something-or-other—she had those, too. It was a regular forest.

"You look like you could use something to drink," the lady said. "I've got lemonade. Would you like a glass?"

"Sure. Thank you."

"You're welcome. Have a seat there in the living room. I'll be back in a minute."

Arlo sank onto the couch. The cushions were worn and easy to slide into. When the lady came out of the kitchen, she was carrying a tall blue glass. Ice cubes clinked inside it.

"So, you've come to see Ida, have you?"

"Yes, ma'am."

"It's about time somebody took an interest. Where's your grandfather?"

"He wanted to come, but he couldn't get away." Arlo shifted in his seat. Poppo definitely couldn't *get away* right now. That was an undeniable fact.

The lady lifted her chin, throwing a shadow across Arlo's face.

"I thought you lived someplace near Roanoke," she said.

"No. I live in Marshboro," Arlo said.

The lady's jaw jutted out so sharply, it could slice off his nose. "Marshboro's a good six-hour drive from here," she said. "What was your grandfather thinking, sending you off on a journey like that by yourself?"

Arlo's palms were sweaty. If this lady turned him in, he might never see his grandmother. She walked over to the window and flipped the blind so she could see outside.

"You still haven't answered my question. Those people. Who were they?"

He might as well get it over with. He was going to have to tell his grandmother anyway. Telling this lady would be good practice.

"Well?" The lady drummed her fingers on the windowsill.

"I met Bernice at the bus station," Arlo said.

"You're traveling with a person you met in a bus station?"

"Bernice is real nice. She and her son Tyrone gave me a ride."

"Unbelievable." The lines on the lady's forehead hardened. She leaned toward Arlo. "You sure you weren't looking for something in the McIlvoys' house?"

Arlo shook his head. Was she accusing him of stealing? "No, ma'am. Really. I was just trying to figure out where my grandmother lives."

The lady didn't look convinced. Two minutes ago, she'd been Mrs. Santa Claus. Now she was the Wicked Witch of the West. *Please.* He was tired. And hungry. And he needed to see his grandmother. Tears burned at the back of his eyelids.

Finally, she softened her gaze. "I don't mean to be so hard on you," she said. "But I happen to know it's been years since Ida's seen her grandson. And the way things are out there in the world these days, a person can't be too careful. Especially a person of advanced years, like myself."

"No, ma'am. I mean, yes, ma'am, I understand."

She continued staring at him. "I suppose we might as well go ahead and call Ida now?"

"That would be nice. Thank you," Arlo said. He held his breath. She could call the police for all he knew.

She started to say something else, but she must have thought better of it. "Why don't you just rest there on the sofa?" she said. "I'll be back in a minute."

Arlo leaned back and stuffed a pillow under his head. He wouldn't actually sleep. He would only rest his eyes for a second. A few minutes at the most. Who knows what was happening back in Marshboro? Miss Hasslebarger must have called the police by now. They could be looking for him all over Virginia. They could have bulletins posted across the entire United States, for all Arlo knew. Any second now a police cruiser might pull up to the front door. What if Tyrone had called the authorities? Or what if a neighbor had noticed Arlo going in that empty house—a neighbor besides the jutting-out-chin lady, that is. What if someone had reported a strange boy walking into the McIlvoys' residence? If Arlo heard a siren outside, he'd be out of this house in a flash.

He'd be down the sidewalk so fast, no one would know he was gone until he was so far away they'd never find him.

When the jutting-out-chin lady came back through the swinging door, Arlo jumped about three feet.

"Didn't mean to scare you, son. You're acting awful nervous. Did you do something wrong?"

"I'm just anxious to see my grandmother. It's been a long time."

"Hmph. That's the understatement of the year. Ida said she'd be here in five minutes. I'm going to make a pot of coffee. You need anything?"

"No, thank you. I think I'll just wait here on the sofa."

"Suit yourself."

Arlo took a deep breath and tried to relax while the jutting-out-chin lady fixed coffee in the kitchen. Blood pumped through his body so fast, it made his knees jiggle. He stood up and walked around the room, but that didn't help either. There would be no relief until he saw Ida Jones face-to-face. And even then, there were no guarantees. What if she didn't like him? Without realizing it, Arlo squeezed his fist around the wood carving and made a wish. *Please let her like me,* he thought.

CHAPTER 15
The Other Lady

Arlo had no idea how long he'd been asleep. He couldn't believe he'd fallen asleep in the first place. Not in this lady's house. But he was so tired.

There was another lady standing in front of him now. She was turned to her side, so he couldn't see her face, but she wasn't a large woman, and though she looked to be on the thin side, there was something substantial about her. You could tell she wasn't the sort of person you could steamroll over. If somebody tried to push her around, she would put up a fight. That wasn't how he'd expected his grandmother to look. Shoot. What had he expected? Who knows? Photographs weren't much to go on. Especially not if they were fourteen years old, like the ones in the album back home.

"Is that him?" the new lady asked.

"Well, who else would it be?" the jutting-out-chin lady said.

"Arlo was only two the last time I saw him. I don't remember his hair being so dark."

"Hair darkens as they get older," the jutting-out-chin lady said. "That's what happened with Lucius."

"Maybe you're right."

"Of course I'm right." The jutting-out-chin lady lowered her voice. "What do you suppose he's doing here?"

"I have no idea, Augusta. But I'd feel a lot better if Al Sabatini had called before he sent the boy to Edgewater. Unfortunately, that's not Al's style."

"Who's Al Batini?"

"*Sa*-ba-tini. You remember." Arlo's grandmother pronounced each syllable carefully. "Arlo's grandfather. On his mother's side."

"Oh, him. It's a wonder that man's still alive. I remember all those stories you told me about those people."

Those people? Arlo pressed his eyelids tightly closed.

"Careful, Augusta. The boy might hear you."

"I don't think so, Ida. Looks like he's sound asleep to me."

The other lady, *his grandmother*, sniffed. "It was mostly his mother I had a problem with," she said. "The way she tricked Wake . . . Wait a minute. Are his eyes open?"

"No, Ida. That's just the angle you're looking from."

"You don't suppose he's run away, do you?"

"Now, there's a thought." The jutting-out-chin lady leaned closer. "When I first saw that car drive up, I knew there was something fishy about it. Doris and Phil never have company. They stopped going to church years ago. Keep to themselves

109

mostly. So what would a strange car be doing in their driveway?"

"You'd think Al would have called if Arlo was missing."

"Al?"

"Sabatini. Pay attention, Augusta."

"Sorry. You don't need to be so touchy. I still don't understand why he went in their house. When a strange person wanders around an empty house, you know that means trouble."

"You want to check his pockets?"

Arlo lifted an eyelid. The new lady was glaring at the jutting-out-chin lady.

"Sorry, Ida."

"What if he was kidnapped?"

Arlo tried to open his eye a little wider without being noticed. He wanted a peek at the new lady's eyebrows. Unfortunately, both ladies were watching him like a hawk.

"Arlo?"

"*Uh*. Hi."

The jutting-out-chin lady slid to the edge of her chair, craning her neck like a buzzard swooping down on roadkill.

"I'm Ida Jones," his grandmother said.

"Yes, ma'am. I sort of figured that's who you were."

"Your grandmother," she added.

"Yes, I know."

She leaned closer. "Where's your grandfather?"

"Back home," Arlo said.

Ida Jones's eyebrows shot into sharp points. She didn't have the thin spot after all. Her eyebrows were even all the way across, the same way her sweater was perfectly buttoned and the color of the leather in her shoes matched her pants perfectly, though they were both a bit worn and faded and there was what looked like a mustard stain on one of her sleeves.

"If Albert's not with you, then how did you get here?"

"On a bus." Arlo braced himself for her reaction.

She blinked about seven times. It was as if someone had turned a windup crank in her back that was connected directly to her lids.

"Did you say *bus*?"

"Yes, ma'am."

"By yourself?"

"Uh-huh."

"But we don't have a bus station in Edgewater."

"Yes, ma'am, I know that," Arlo said guiltily.

She waited, and Arlo knew she must be expecting an explanation, but he didn't say anything.

"Mmm, mmm, mmm," the jutting-out-chin lady muttered. "I told you we should call the police."

"Hush, Augusta. Arlo and I are talking."

Arlo's grandmother blinked faster now. She had bulgy eyeballs, too. For a second, Arlo was afraid she might blink her eyeballs clear out of their sockets. "If you didn't take the bus . . ." she said.

"But I did take a bus," Arlo said. "I bought a ticket to Richmond and then this nice lady offered me a ride from there."

"I see," said his grandmother, though it was clear she did not see at all.

The jutting-out-chin lady made a throat-clearing noise, which caused his grandmother to scowl. When the jutting-out-chin lady whipped out a cell phone, Arlo's grandmother shook her head. The jutting-out-chin lady put the phone away. And Ida Jones turned back to Arlo.

"Augusta tells me you went in the McIlvoys' house," she said. *Blink, blink, blink, blink,* went her eyelids.

"I didn't know whose house it was," Arlo said.

"Then why did you stop there?"

"It's where Bernice dropped me off."

"Bernice?"

"The lady who gave me a ride."

Arlo's grandmother narrowed her eyes. "And why did she drop you off there?"

Great question. Unfortunately, Arlo didn't have an answer. Luckily, the jutting-out-chin lady barged in and filled up the silence.

"About this Bernice person . . ." she said.

"Augusta, please!" Arlo's grandmother threw up her hands.

"Sorry."

"It's all right. It's just that we'll never get anywhere unless . . ."

"Actually, it was Tyrone who was driving," Arlo said. "Bernice is his mom."

"Slow down, Arlo," Ida Jones said. "You're confusing us."

"Sorry."

112

"That's OK. But, I still don't understand who this Bernice person is. Did your grandfather ask her to help?"

"No, ma'am. I just met her at the bus station. She helped me buy my ticket."

The jutting-out-chin lady picked up her cell phone again, but this time Arlo's grandmother grabbed it before she had time to punch in a number.

"Control yourself," she snapped. Then she turned to Arlo. "Surely your grandfather bought your ticket for you," she said.

"Not exactly," Arlo said.

"He either bought it or he didn't," the jutting-out-chin lady said.

"Augusta, this doesn't concern you." Arlo's grandmother wagged a finger at her.

"I'm only trying to help."

"I know you are, but I think Arlo and I can handle this nicely on our own."

The jutting-out-chin lady made a huffing noise. "If you ask me, you're not making much progress."

The two ladies glared at each other.

"Do you mind if I use the bathroom?" Arlo asked.

"Help yourself," his grandmother said. "It's down the hall on the right."

"Well, don't mind me," the jutting-out-chin lady said. "It's only my house."

Arlo's chest was tight by the time he closed the bathroom door. The smell of pine disinfectant raised the hairs in his nose. Still, he would rather be here than back in that living room. He needed time to think.

All too soon he was on his way back down the hall. He took a deep breath and let it out slowly. *Here we go*, he thought.

"Now, Arlo." His grandmother leaned toward him. "About that bus ticket. Tell Mrs. Stonestreet and me the truth. Albert bought you that ticket, didn't he?"

She wasn't going to like this, but even with the time-out in the bathroom, Arlo couldn't see any way around telling the truth.

"The *truth* is . . . Poppo wasn't feeling well."

The jutting-out-chin lady scooted back to the edge of her chair.

"Go on," his grandmother said.

Blink, blink, blink, blink, went her eyes. Somebody must have wound the crank while he was in the bathroom.

"So you went to the bus station by yourself?"

"That's right."

"But how did you get there?"

Arlo swallowed. "I walked," he said.

A harrumphing sound came from the jutting-out-chin lady. She mouthed a silent message to Ida. *Call 911.*

Ida straightened her sweater. "I believe Arlo and I need a moment alone," she told the Augusta lady.

They exchanged frosty stares again, but this time the jutting-out-chin lady moved toward the dining room. She paused before pushing open the door to the kitchen.

"Do whatever you like," she said. "You generally do anyway." Then she gave the swinging door an extra jab and disappeared.

Arlo's grandmother waited. She watched the kitchen door. "You're not going to make any phone calls, now, are you?" she called in a loud voice.

"Wouldn't dream of it," the Augusta lady yelled back.

"Good," Ida said under her breath. Then she turned to Arlo. "You think you might tell me the whole story now?"

Arlo kept his eyes on his shoelaces, focusing on the knots, on how loosely they were tied, sort of the way the stories he was telling were loosely put together too. His heart pumped harder.

"Look at me."

Arlo tried looking at the lamp shade beside her, so he wouldn't have to make direct eye contact. "That *is* the truth," he said.

"Let's say I believe you," his grandmother said. "You still left out some parts, didn't you?"

Arlo swallowed.

"Tell the truth, Arlo. Did you run away?"

While he was trying to figure out how to answer, there was the squeal of a metal hinge as the kitchen door opened slightly and then closed again.

Ida narrowed her eyes. Giving Arlo a conspiratorial glance, she put a finger to her lips, then crept silently around the far wall of the living room and up to the door. As Arlo watched, she gave the door a quick shove, then stepped back. From the other side, there was an *oof* and then a loud *"Ouch!"*

"Excuse me," Ida said. "I was just coming to get a cup of coffee."

The jutting-out-chin lady rubbed a spot above her ear. "You might have warned me," she said.

"You must have had your head pressed right up against the door," Ida said.

"Don't be ridiculous. I was on my way to see if you needed anything."

"Mmm-hmmm." Arlo's grandmother backed away from the door. "Arlo and I are fine, but you look like you're in pain."

Arlo stifled a laugh.

Meanwhile, his grandmother collected her purse from the dining-room table. "I'm taking Arlo home now," she said.

"Not a good idea," the jutting-out-chin lady said.

Arlo could feel the anger rolling off his grandmother's shoulders.

"You've been so helpful, dear. Now, put your mind at ease. I'll give you a call later."

"Don't say I didn't warn you," the jutting-out-chin lady called through the front door.

"Wouldn't dream of it," Arlo's grandmother said, leading Arlo down the front walk.

"Thank you for the lemonade," Arlo said.

The jutting-out-chin lady closed the door.

"That woman!" Arlo's grandmother leaned across the steering wheel while her friend peered at them through the front window. "Curiosity killed the cat, Arlo. Mark my words."

Arlo nodded, though he wasn't sure what she meant.

"Some people need to learn how not to stick their noses into other people's business."

The car tires kicked up gravel as Ida pressed down on the accelerator.

Watch and learn, Poppo used to say. This seemed like one of those times when watching was a whole lot smarter than talking. Arlo kept his mouth shut.

The car fender narrowly missed a large boulder marking the boundary between the Stonestreet lady's house and the house next door. Arlo fastened his seat belt. He wished his grandmother would fasten hers, too, but when the seat belt alarm failed to ding, he noticed that she had fastened the seat belt against the seat so that the alarm wouldn't sound. There was a loud *clunk* as the right front end of her car hit the bottom of a deep pothole at the intersection with the main highway.

"Now, where did *that* come from?" Arlo's grandmother asked.

Arlo braced himself for impact when they pulled onto the highway. So far his grandmother didn't seem like the greatest driver. They stopped at the first stoplight in front of Safeway and across from a restaurant named Maury's Seafood.

"Now that we're alone," his grandmother said in an *I'm-in-control-and-that's-the-way-it's-going-to-stay* voice, "perhaps you'll tell me the *real* reason you've come."

Part II
EDGEWATER

CHAPTER 16
Edgewater — Pop. 1,753

The car slowed as they approached the intersection with the main street of town. They were passing the statue of the man on top of the granite pedestal. It was harder to see his face, now that the sun had sunk to the horizon. To their right was a road marker bearing the words: EDGEWATER, VIRGINIA — FOUNDED 1687 — POP. 1,753

"Who is that guy?" Arlo asked.

"Ebenezer Crookshank. Our town founder," his grandmother said.

"Why is he wearing that funny hat?"

She tapped a thin, knob-knuckled finger on the steering wheel. "That's the way they dressed in those days," she said. "Didn't you learn that in school?"

"I guess not."

"Ebenezer Crookshank was quite distinguished."

Was that a dirty look she gave him? How was Arlo supposed to know what kind of hats people wore in the old days?

While the car idled at the intersection, Arlo craned his neck to read the brass plaque under the streetlight on the corner. SITE OF TOWN GAOL 1769.

"What's a *gale*?" he asked.

"That's *jail*, son. Old English spelling. Guess they didn't teach you that, either."

"Is that what Ebenezer Crookshank is famous for building?"

His grandmother tightened her grip on the steering wheel. "Of course not," she snapped. "There was a huge house on the river. Unfortunately, it burned."

The light changed and the car rolled forward.

"You probably aren't aware of this," his grandmother continued, "but your forebears were among the first settlers in the Northern Neck."

"Forebears?"

"Ancestors, Arlo. Your great-great-great-great-grandparents. On your grandfather's side, of course. My people are from farther south."

"I don't think I knew that."

"No, I don't imagine you did. In fact, I'll bet there's a wealth of information you're lacking."

You could almost slice a sandwich on the sharp edges in her voice.

They whizzed past the remaining blocks of the tiny business district. Then the road widened into four lanes and they passed a modern high school and a steel-and-glass public library on the right.

"Modern monstrosities, aren't they?" his grandmother said.

Arlo kept his lips sealed. Sometimes the safest answer was no answer at all. Poppo had taught him that, too.

After the library, they passed a line of small houses.

"I don't suppose there's anything more you'd like to tell me about how you got here," she said.

If Arlo told her the truth, she'd probably call the police as soon as they walked through the door.

"Did you hear me?"

"Yes, ma'am, I heard."

"Well?"

"That's pretty much the whole story."

"*Mmm-hmm.* Well, perhaps you'll feel like talking later."

OK, so she wasn't buying it. She wasn't exactly bending over backwards to make *him* feel welcome, either. Everything about her was sharp and poky, like a pile of old bones.

Arlo imagined a white room with a bare lightbulb hanging from the ceiling. Ida Jones stood over him wielding a large stick. *We have ways to make you talk,* she snarled through a curled lip.

"Did you say something?"

"No, ma'am."

She was eyeing him again, giving him the fish eye as if he were some professional thief plotting how to rob her. Arlo stared at the hillside on their right. The houses had been replaced by a tall grassy mound that sloped down to an open field. Edgewater was a good name for this place. Arlo felt like he was hanging onto the edge of something, all right. In fact, he felt like the ground was about to bust loose underneath him.

Meanwhile, the car bumped over a rough seam of pavement. Then the road narrowed as they crossed a tidal creek. Ahead of them, Arlo noticed a wooden building teetering off a thin spit of land where the creek spilled into the river.

"There's the marina where your father used to work." His grandmother dipped her head in the direction of the river. "That was *before* he met your mother, of course — back when he was saving for college."

"I didn't know my dad went to college."

"That makes two things you didn't know. Or is it three?"

Ouch! Bones again. To think that he could have stayed in Marshboro instead of coming here. . . . But no. He had to find this wonderful grandmother who was going to help him — help them both. Yeah. That was a big mistake.

As the highway straightened out, the small houses were replaced by grassy fields and long driveways that led to places you couldn't see.

When the car hit a dip in the pavement, Ida's foot slipped off the accelerator and the car slowed instantly. Someone in the car behind them laid on the horn.

"You can jolly well wait your turn." Ida frowned into the rearview mirror. "Impatient twerp!"

Meanwhile, the car behind them sped up and zoomed past on the left.

"No manners these days. I tell you, Arlo, it's every man for himself. Civilization has gone to the dogs." She scooted forward in her seat. "What were we talking about?"

"My dad?"

"Ah, yes. Well, maybe that's a subject best left for another day." She glanced sideways again, causing the car to drift into the left lane.

"Look out!" Arlo yelled.

"Goodness. You startled me, Arlo. Passengers shouldn't distract the driver. It's dangerous."

No kidding. Arlo didn't breathe normally again until she flipped on her blinker and signaled a right turn onto a gravel driveway. He wouldn't have known it was a driveway if it weren't for the mailbox. You couldn't see the house. It was obscured by trees.

"I don't suppose Albert told you about my apple trees, did he?" She nodded toward a cluster of evenly spaced trees on their left.

"Not that I remember," he said.

"*Hmph.* Figures," she said.

Then, they rode on in silence. The driveway seemed to go on forever.

"Saved all through high school," she was grumbling as they approached a clearing.

"Sorry. Did you say something?" Arlo asked.

He couldn't tell if she was talking to him or mumbling to herself.

"Won that award. Set for life. Until *she* came along."

"Are you talking about my dad?"

She shifted in her seat and made a small throat-clearing sound. Before conversation resumed, one of her front tires hit a rock and the car lurched to the right. She jerked the wheel to pull it back in line.

"How many times have I told those people at Bert's Auto to fix the power steering?" she said, her voice rising to a shrill pitch. "If you ask me, we were better off with *un*-power steering. At least in those days, all you had to do was put a little muscle behind the wheel and the car turned exactly the way you wanted."

It's the driver who's broken, Arlo thought.

As the car continued on its path, Arlo thought about the photograph of his mother and father in front of the tree. It must have been taken here. In front of one of those apple trees. He wondered if it was before or after his father left school. Did his grandmother already hate his mom then, or had that come later?

The driveway dipped and the land flattened out in a broad lawn with a large house perched on the left. The house was three stories tall, with shutters at the windows. Arlo couldn't see much more than that in the darkness until they drew closer and the headlights shone on a large strip of paint that had peeled loose from one of the shutters. On his way through the yard, Arlo tripped over a piece of broken roof tile.

"Careful," his grandmother said.

"Thanks," Arlo said. He followed her past the front steps.

"You were here years ago," she said, stooping to collect bits of a flower blossom that had dropped onto the brick path.

"I don't remember," Arlo said.

"How could you? Two years old, that's what you were." She eyed him sharply. "Why, I hardly remember you myself."

They moved on to the kitchen door, where a small brown dog with ears like a collie jumped against the screen. As his grandmother held the door open, the dog pranced outside. He ran straight to Arlo and jumped against his legs.

"It's all right, Steamboat. Arlo's our guest."

His grandmother took Steamboat's head in both her hands and kissed the space between his ears. She whispered in a louder-than-necessary voice, "Arlo's hiding something from us, Steamboat. Maybe you can make him tell us what it is."

The dog fixed his eyes on Arlo.

Meanwhile, she moved inside the house and, with a wave of her hand, invited Arlo to follow.

CHAPTER 17
Where She Lives

They climbed a short staircase to the kitchen, bypassing a door which—she informed him—led to the basement.

Everything was white—cabinets, ceiling, tile, refrigerator—the one exception being the large island in the center of the room, which looked to be an old wooden cabinet someone had painted a deep shade of blue. A chipped pottery bowl held a dozen red apples, and beside it a ceramic pitcher boasted a bouquet of sunflowers.

Arlo took a seat on one of the tall wooden stools while Ida fit her keys over a small brass hook on a wooden rack above the light switch.

"Wait till I wipe the mud off your paws, Steamboat." Ida retrieved a towel from under the sink while Steamboat waited patiently on the top step. "You mind turning the light on for me?" she said to Arlo.

"Sure." When the light came on, Arlo noticed that the wood on the key rack spelled out the word JONES. His hand went instinctively to the wood carving in his pocket. Had his father made that rack? Or maybe his grandfather Jones had been a wood-carver. Maybe he had passed that skill on to his son. Arlo didn't know anything about Slocum Jones other than the few things Poppo had told him, which really didn't amount to much information — besides the name and what Poppo thought of him.

Ida finished cleaning Steamboat's paws. Then she carried the towel down the steps and hung it to dry over the boot tray.

"I suppose you're hungry," she said. "A boy your age? Hungry all the time, I expect."

Was there something wrong with having an appetite? "I wouldn't mind eating," Arlo said. "I mean, it's not like I'm starving or anything. Mrs. Stonestreet gave me that lemonade."

"Probably didn't scratch the surface, did it? Why, I'll bet you go through at least a gallon of milk a day. I'll warn you: I don't keep a lot of food around the house."

Arlo swallowed. "Anything's fine," he said.

"You like sardines?"

Was she kidding? Did *anyone* actually *like* sardines? "I eat Vienna sausage sometimes," Arlo said. "Do you have any of those?"

His grandmother's eyebrows came together in a scowl. "Potted meat will kill you," she said. "You know that, don't you?"

Arlo shook his head.

"Of course you don't. Living with that grandfather of yours, how could you? I'll bet he feeds you all manner of things. Potted meat's probably just the tip of the iceberg. No doubt that's his idea of a gourmet meal."

Whoa. When Poppo said there were hard feelings, he wasn't kidding, was he?

Arlo watched as she opened the door to the pantry. The shelves were nearly empty, except for dog food. She reached up to a metal rack mounted on the back of the door and plucked off a can of sardines.

"A growing boy needs protein," she said. "Fish oil doesn't hurt, either. Good for the brain. Wouldn't hurt your grandfather to try some."

Elbow jab to midsection. Direct hit. Ten points for Ida Jones. Was brain food what Poppo needed? Was that the problem?

"Maybe one sardine?" Arlo held up a shaky finger. If it would make her stop saying mean things about Poppo, he'd eat anything.

"Let's have crackers, too. Add a little mustard and you've got yourself a meal. Nothing better. I'll bet your mother never fixed you anything like that."

Did "barely two-year-olds" eat sardines? His mother hadn't lived long enough to feed him anything fancier than mashed potatoes, applesauce, and oatmeal.

"She was partial to *pizza*, as I recall," Ida said. "The greasier the better."

"I don't remember what she liked."

Ida coughed. Good. That silenced her. Temporarily at least. Arlo had time to breathe. He watched her wash her hands and then fill the kettle at the sink.

"How's Albert doing these days?" she asked.

Was she trying to be nice?

"He doesn't own the doughnut shop anymore," Arlo said.

"Retired, is he? I guess he's old enough. But what on earth does he do with his time?"

"We go fishing some." *Not lately, of course. But she didn't need to know about that.*

"Wake liked to fish. Still have one of his old rods in the garage. Thought I might give it to you one of these days. *If I ever laid eyes on you again, that is.*" She plunked the kettle on the gas burner, then pivoted around to glare at him. "How many years has it been? Ten?"

"Nine," Arlo said.

"Yes." She pressed her lips together firmly, creating a thin pressure line between her mouth and her nose. "Exactly. Which means you're in what grade now?"

"Sixth."

"I remember when your dad was in sixth grade." She took a china teapot out of the cabinet and filled the mesh cup inside with loose tea from a small silver tin. "Wake was such a good student. Always at the top of his class. Until he met your mother, of course. . . ."

Oh, geez. Would she give it a rest?

When their eyes met, she pressed her mouth closed again. Then she took the sardine can and fit it under the blade of the electric can opener. As she pressed down on the lever, Arlo felt his chest muscles relax. *Thank goodness. More noise. No talking.*

But it didn't last long.

"Always buy the kind packed in water," she said. "Not that

stuff packed in oil." She emptied the sardines onto a white plate with a dainty silver fork. "Oil has cholesterol. You don't want to start clogging up your arteries."

She tossed the can in the trash, waving a finger at Steamboat, who was nosing around. "Not for you, boy. Go sit down, now."

Steamboat went back to the top of the steps and laid his head between his paws. *Poor dog.* Arlo wondered when she fed him.

"You may think you don't need to worry at your age, but it never hurts to start healthy habits early," she said. "You wouldn't want to block circulation in your brain and go soft in the head now, would you?"

Bam! Another direct hit. Was that what was wrong with Poppo? Was he soft in the head because of too much cholesterol?

It was no wonder she and Poppo didn't talk to each other. They were nothing alike. Arlo could see why Poppo never wanted to talk about her. Poppo didn't like to say bad things about people, and it would be tough to describe Ida Jones without saying something negative.

If she was so careful about making sure everybody ate healthy meals, why wasn't his grandfather Jones still alive? Poppo never said what he died of.

"Crackers are in the lazy Susan. You mind getting them for me?"

"No. I mean, sure, I'll be happy to."

"Thank you."

She hadn't even tried to talk to Arlo all these years. It was Poppo who had taken care of him. Meanwhile, here she'd been, living in this big house. OK. Maybe it was falling down now, but still, it was a lot nicer than the house he and Poppo lived in. And besides, what he and Poppo needed right now was help—not criticism.

Arlo sneezed as the fish oil raised the hairs in his nose.

"Gesundheit," she said.

"Thank you."

Steamboat sneaked out from the doorway and positioned himself at Arlo's feet.

"Sure you only want one?" she asked.

"Maybe two?" Arlo said, trying to be polite.

"Take three," she said, and put them on his plate.

Arlo stared at the fish. The smell turned his stomach. He watched her spread mustard over a saltine cracker and carefully mash a sardine down on top of it with a fork. *Ugh.* She held it out to him.

"Would you like to try one of these?"

"No, thank you."

"At least take a cracker," she said.

"OK." Arlo took four crackers off the serving plate. "Thank you," he said.

"I have regular mustard if you don't like the spicy kind," she said.

"That's OK," Arlo said. He felt Steamboat sniffing around his feet.

If she would only turn her head for a second, he could slip his plate under the counter.

"You're not eating," she said.

"What? Oh, yeah. Well, Poppo always says you should take your time eating your food. It's good for digestion."

She stopped chewing. "Albert told you that? Well, maybe I don't give him enough credit."

When the phone rang in another room, Steamboat barked.

"It's OK, boy," Ida said. "I'll get it."

She headed around the corner toward the center of the house. While she was gone, Arlo slipped his plate to the floor. Steamboat lapped up the sardines in three easy bites.

Arlo just managed to get the plate back on the counter before she came back to the kitchen.

"Telemarketers," she said. "I swear. How do they know when you're eating dinner?"

"We get them at home, too," Arlo said. "Poppo takes the phone off the hook sometimes."

"Good for him." She nodded at his empty plate. "So you liked them after all," she said.

"I think it's the crackers that makes the difference," Arlo said, giving Steamboat a grateful pat on the head.

As she carried their dirty dishes to the sink, Steamboat trotted behind her. He stood on his hind legs with his front paws together and an expectant look on his face.

"Now, Steamboat, you know table scraps are bad for you."

Steamboat whimpered. He looked at Arlo and licked his chops.

"He doesn't have anything for you, either," Ida said. She looked from Arlo to Steamboat and then back at the clean dish in Arlo's hand. Her eyes narrowed.

When she turned back to the sink, Arlo could have sworn that Steamboat winked at him.

CHAPTER 18
Lies Versus Truth

"Now that you've had something to eat, I think it's time we got down to business."

They were sitting in the living room after the sardine *feast*. Arlo stared at his reflection in the shine on her coffee table, intrigued by the way it made his cheekbones look wider and flatter than they really were.

"Arlo?"

"Yes, ma'am?"

She leaned forward in her chair. *"What are you doing here?"*

"Oh. Sorry." Arlo gulped some water. "I wanted to see you," he said.

She raised her eyes to the ceiling. "Isn't that amazing? After nine years, you were suddenly seized with an uncontrollable urge to see your long-lost grandmother."

You could have split logs on the points of her eyebrows.

"Come now, Arlo. If you're going to lie, you can do better than that."

The way she glared at him made it hard to think. Arlo blinked. Her habit must be catching. He'd parcel the truth out carefully. See how she reacted. Give her time to digest each bit slowly and get ready for the next installment.

"What happened was, the police came . . ."

"Police?" Her china cup clinked against its saucer.

"It was after they found him in the Dumpster. . . ."

"Found who? What on earth are you talking about?"

Arlo closed his eyes and kept talking. If he could just get through this part, the rest would be easier. "It was in the alley beside Fanucci's Market."

"You don't mean Albert? Slow down, Arlo. You've lost me. Did you say . . . Dumpster?"

"That's right."

"We're talking about your grandfather?"

"Yes, ma'am."

She was blinking faster now.

"And where is he now?"

"In the hospital." Arlo winced. "They were sending me to this place —"

"Who was?"

"The social worker."

"Police. Social workers. What will it be next?"

Ida set her cup and saucer on the table.

"Those Sabatinis of yours, I swear . . ."

Those Sabatinis of yours? Did she mean for him to hear her? Maybe it came from living by herself. Maybe she didn't realize she was talking out loud.

"Didn't we warn Wake? Didn't we tell him?"

She kept mumbling to herself. Arlo tried not to listen. He set up a humming in his head. It didn't block out her voice, but it helped to blur the words so they didn't have as much sting.

"Arlo? Are you listening to me?"

"Sorry?"

"The hospital. Do you know what it's called?"

"Oh, sure. Marshboro General."

"That's better. Do you have a number?"

"No."

"I should have known. That's all right. We'll call Information."

"No. Wait a minute!"

"Now what?" She held the receiver with her hand poised over the keypad.

"It's just . . ."

"Just what?"

"The social worker."

"Yes. Yes. You mentioned her already. Sending you someplace or other." She waved her hand the way a person shoos away a pesky mosquito. "We'll deal with that later."

Arlo panicked. "If you tell them where I am, they'll send someone after me."

Her eyes narrowed. "Did you do something wrong?"

"No. I swear."

One of her eyes twitched, just the tiniest movement at the inside corner of her right eye. "So, that's why you came," she said. "You needed to escape."

Arlo nodded.

"So you ran away?"

He shrugged. *What would you do?* he wanted to ask.

They stared at each other a full five seconds before she spoke again.

"For heaven's sake, don't stare at me like I'm the Wicked Witch of the West. I'm not going to bite."

Arlo jumped. Could she read minds, too? "Sorry," he said.

"And, for heaven's sake, try to sit still." She frowned at Arlo's knee tapping up and down. "You make me so nervous, I can't hear myself think."

Arlo pressed his hand down on his knee. He needed to make her understand. "I have this friend Sam," he said. "His mom's dead, and he lives with his great-aunt. He used to live in a shelter, and then he lived in a foster home. And he got bitten by a rat."

She put up her hand. "You've lost me again, Arlo. And all that stuff's not important right now. First things first. Let's make this phone call, shall we? We can worry about rats later."

Arlo held his breath while she was on the phone, straining to catch a word here and there, words like *stable now* and *keeping a close watch*. The longer the conversation continued, the pinker his grandmother's face became.

"Of course, I didn't realize," she said, glancing at Arlo. "No. No. That won't be necessary. . . . Yes, I'm sure. I was just calling to let you know that Arlo is here with me."

There was a pause.

"Yes. Yes, he's fine. I'm his grandmother."

Another pause.

"No, dear. On the *other* side of the family. Mr. Sabatini and I are not related."

The next question must have been especially difficult, because Ida's cheeks went from pink to crimson.

"Well, I don't know about that. How soon would you need an answer?"

When she met Arlo's gaze, Ida looked away. "Yes, yes. I understand. I'll get back to you as soon as I can."

Then there was another pause and some throat clearing before she spoke again.

"Of course. I understand. Yes. And, you'll let us know if there's any change, won't you? Thank you."

Can I speak to him? Arlo mouthed the question silently so as not to disturb her.

His grandmother shook her head. *Sleeping,* she answered.

After hanging up, she moved to the window and stared blankly at the river.

"Is Poppo all right?"

"He's about the same as when you left him," she said. "Maybe a little stronger and certainly no worse. That's the good news."

Water sloshed against Arlo's dam. That was the *good* news?

"The doctor says he needs to stay right where he is for the time being, but he's not in any *immediate* danger."

"When can I talk to him?"

"I don't know. The doctor didn't say."

"Can you call him back and ask?"

"I wasn't talking to the doctor. I was talking to a nurse."

"Maybe she could tell you. We could call her back."

Ida's mouth twitched again.

"Is there something else?"

His grandmother cleared her throat. "He's still unconscious, Arlo."

Water surged. *Plink*. There went a twig. And then a clump of mud.

"Now, don't be frightened. That's not surprising, considering the stroke. The doctor says we have to wait and see."

Wait and see? That was supposed to make him feel better? "How long?" he asked.

"I beg your pardon?" she said.

"How long do we have to wait?" Arlo asked. He was staring back at her now. Letting her see what that felt like.

She started blinking. "The nurse promised someone would call if there's any change," she said. "If we don't hear from them tonight, we'll call tomorrow."

Oh, why had he ever come here? Why hadn't he stayed in Marshboro where he belonged? What's the worst they could have done to him there? Stick him in a shelter for a few nights? Big deal. At least someone would have taken him to see Poppo. Surely, they would have done that.

She was studying him closely.

Arlo shifted uncomfortably. "What is it?" he asked.

"Nothing," she said.

"You were going to say something, weren't you?"

His grandmother sighed. "If they really think we need to be there, they'll call," she said.

Their eyes met long enough for Arlo to understand what she wasn't saying. . . . Poppo was in danger. And here Arlo was, 350 miles away, staying with a woman who was supposed to care about him but who seemed to have the heart of an armadillo.

CHAPTER 19
Wake Jones's Bedroom

Arlo lay atop the quilt on the squeaky double bed in his father's old room. He wasn't sleepy. In fact, sleep was the last thing on his mind. Sure, he was tired, but his mind was swirling. He couldn't make it stop.

"Just knock on my door if you need anything," his grandmother had said when she *retired for the evening*. That's the way she had said it, as if they were in some grand English manor and the butler was going to bring up a breakfast tray in the morning. It was just a house. OK, it was a big house. It had two staircases, the one behind the door off the kitchen and another grander one between the living room and the dining room. And it had probably been a nice place once . . . a *long* time ago. But there certainly weren't any butlers roaming the halls today. The spare bathroom had a pile of broken tile cluttering the tub, and there were squirrels in the attic. At least that's what Arlo thought they were. They made a lot of noise.

He stared at the ceiling, at a dark-brown spot in the shape of a brontosaurus. In his mind's eye, he gave the brontosaurus an eye and a mouth and then two giant feet. He imagined climbing onto the back of the brontosaurus and riding all the way home to Marshboro.

But then there was a clicking of toenails on wood floors, and Arlo glanced across the room to see Steamboat bounding toward him.

"Are you checking on me?" he asked.

Steamboat trotted over to the bed. When Arlo held out his hand, Steamboat licked his fingers.

"Want to sleep in here, boy?"

Steamboat wagged his tail.

"Come on up, then."

Arlo tapped a spot on the quilt. Steamboat hesitated, glancing over his shoulder toward the hall.

"Ida's asleep, isn't she?" Arlo surprised himself referring to his grandmother by her first name, but that's what Poppo always called her, so it seemed to be what he should call her, too.

Steamboat dipped his head and then raised it again, confirming what Arlo had said.

"Good," Arlo said. "If she's asleep, then it's OK for you to sleep here. Come on." He tapped the quilt again.

Steamboat gave his tail another wag and hopped onto the bed.

Arlo couldn't help wondering if Ida had always been as prickly as she was now. And what about his grandfather? If Slocum had been sterner than Ida—Arlo shivered at the thought—who could blame his father for leaving home?

Arlo tried to imagine his father growing up in this room. Had he and Slocum Jones done things together the way Poppo and Arlo did? Had they gone fishing in the river? Or taken hikes in the woods? Or had his father lain awake the way Arlo had done in the children's shelter, plotting how he might escape?

First thing in the morning, Ida tapped on Arlo's door.

"The shower's broken in your bathroom," she said. "You don't mind sharing, do you?"

Arlo rubbed his eyes. Steamboat was gone already. Probably outside by this time.

"Arlo? Are you awake?"

"Yes, ma'am, I'm awake. And no, I don't mind sharing."

"Good. I generally have half a grapefruit and bran flakes for breakfast. Would you like some?"

Arlo's stomach rolled. "No, thank you," he said.

"You need to eat something."

"Do you have any milk?"

"Afraid not."

Should have known, Arlo thought. "Orange juice?" he asked.

"How about cranberry?" Ida said.

"Sure. That's fine." *Better than sardines, anyway, wasn't it?*

"We'll go to the store this morning. Oh, and Arlo?"

"Yes, ma'am?"

"If you don't mind, just toss my nightgown in the laundry

basket while you're in the bathroom. I forgot to do that. It's hanging on the hook on the back of the door."

"OK."

Arlo wasn't used to women's nightgowns. This one looked sort of flimsy. He plucked it up by the lace collar and dropped it in the wicker basket. The whole room smelled like bath oil. Lavender, he thought. He'd smelled lavender air freshener before. It smelled like this. Ida smelled of it, too. He hoped he wouldn't end up smelling the same way. Luckily, there was a bar of plain white soap under the sink. It looked about a hundred years old, but it was probably OK.

When he came downstairs, Ida was making a list on a pad of paper. "So much to do," she said. "You'll need some things, won't you?"

"Things?"

"You arrived with barely a change of underwear."

Arlo blushed.

"There's no place left in town to buy clothes other than Val-U Mart. Takes half a day just to walk from housewares to the checkout line. And all the money goes out of state. Not like you're helping local businesses. Still, it's the best we can do, I'm afraid.

"We'll take Steamboat with us. He likes to ride in the car."

The cranberry juice was better than Arlo expected, and it turned out that Ida had a few apples from the orchard. They tasted good, too. After breakfast, she drove them to a strip mall on the road toward Washington. Arlo had to admit the stores here didn't have the same feel as the rest of town. Ida circled the lot four times before she found a row of three empty spaces next to each other. She turned the wheel and guided the car into the middle space.

"You wouldn't believe the way people drive around here," she said. "It's like asking for a dented fender the minute you turn off the engine." She pressed the window buttons and lowered all four windows partway. "We won't be long, Steamboat. You wait right here."

Steamboat settled into a spot behind the driver's seat as Ida got out of the car.

Arlo followed her through the parking lot.

"Ready or not," she muttered, taking a deep breath and straightening her spine as she stepped onto the doormat signaling the automatic door opener. Her neck stiffened the minute they were inside.

"Look at all this junk," she said. "Where on earth do we start?"

"Boy's clothes are in the center," Arlo said, pointing to a sign hanging in the middle of the building.

"You go ahead," she said. "I'll catch up."

Arlo found a pair of jeans and four T-shirts. "Two for one," he pointed out.

"Very nice," Ida said. "And what about these?" She held up a pair of khakis with neatly pressed creases. "With a nice plaid shirt?"

"Are we going someplace fancy?"

She handed them to him. "Check the size," she said. "Then we'll find socks."

After paying for their purchases, they headed to the car. Ida stuck her head through the window.

"Steamboat?" She yanked her head back out and frantically yelled his name.

Arlo glanced in the car. Steamboat was gone all right. Ida gave him a panicked look.

"Help me find him," she said.

Steamboat was a small dog, medium-size at best. In a parking lot, with all those SUVs, trucks, and minivans, he would barely stand a chance.

They moved down the rows of cars, calling his name.

"He'll think I've gone to meet Augusta at Frog Creek for tea," she said

"Where's that?" Arlo asked.

"In town. It's Lucius and Delia's bookstore."

"Who are Lucius and Delia?" Arlo asked. Was that a chain like Barnes & Noble?

"Lucius and Delia Stonestreet," Ida said, pronouncing each word carefully. "Lucius is Augusta's son."

"Oh," Arlo said. "Maybe we should go there."

Ida gave him an exasperated look. "Well, of course. That's where we're going, just as soon as we make sure he isn't here." She blinked a few times, looking around the lot again. "We need to divide it up. You take that side over there, and I'll take this one."

"OK."

Ida rolled her eyes at him. "Let's hurry, shall we?"

Arlo walked up and down the rows, calling Steamboat's name. After the first row, he had a bad feeling. Surely

Steamboat would have come by now if he was anywhere close.

"Any luck?" Ida asked.

"No. Sorry," Arlo said.

Ida's shoulders drooped as she moved toward her car. "Come on," she said. "Let's hope he isn't on the highway."

Arlo shivered at the thought of Steamboat in the middle of the two-lane.

If riding with Ida was a dicey business when she wasn't in a hurry, that was nothing compared to riding with her now.

"Oh, dear. I didn't scrape that woman's fender, did I?" she said after a near-miss with a blue sedan.

"Not sure," Arlo mumbled. He was hunkered down in the seat with his arms braced for impact.

"I'm sure she was taking more than her share of the road, don't you think?"

Arlo raised his head long enough to catch a glimpse of a terrified woman pulling onto the shoulder of the road.

"Keep your eyes peeled," Ida snapped. "Steamboat could be anywhere."

Look out, Steamboat. If the dog was out there, Arlo hoped he was nowhere near the road.

CHAPTER 20
Frog Creek Books and Café

Ida parked in a space opposite the statue of Ebenezer Crookshank. She didn't wait to see if Arlo was behind her. She marched straight across the sidewalk and into the brick storefront, passing under the sign shaped like a giant frog.

There was an entire wall of magazines to walk past before turning right into the café, where a tall black man was making cappuccino.

"Morning, Ida," the man said.

"Oh, thank heavens, Matthew. I'm glad you're here."

The man put down the cup. "Maywood tried to call you," he said.

Ida lifted an eyebrow.

"You're looking for Steamboat, aren't you?"

She nodded. "We were at Val-U-Mart," she said.

"We?" The man tilted his head.

"Arlo and I." Ida patted Arlo on the shoulder. "Sorry, Matthew. I'm so rattled. This is my grandson, Arlo Jones."

The man's eyes nearly popped out of his head.

"Arlo, meet Matthew Healy," Ida said.

Arlo shook the man's outstretched hand.

"When did you come to town?" he asked.

"Yesterday," Arlo said.

"Matthew and your father went to school together," Ida said.

Arlo smiled. "Nice to meet you, Mr. Healy."

The man smiled back at him. "Call me Matthew," he said, sliding the fresh cup of cappuccino to the far side of the counter.

"How is it you talked Ida into taking you to the mall?"

Arlo looked at his grandmother.

"Arlo needed a few things," she explained.

"Did your grandfather come with you?"

Arlo shook his head.

"Not this time," Ida said.

She and Matthew exchanged glances over Arlo's head. Then Matthew picked up a dish towel and wiped a drip of milk off the cappuccino machine.

"We tried calling you," he said. "When Steamboat showed up here by himself, we knew something was wrong. And then, when nobody answered at your house, Maywood decided she'd better check up on you. She's headed out to your place now."

"How long ago did they leave?" Ida asked.

"You just missed her." Matthew said.

He moved on to polishing the spout where the steam came

out to froth the milk. Meanwhile, Arlo surveyed the room. There was a large platform suspended above the children's section. It extended clear to the back of the store. On the front side of the platform, just above the bakery case, was a small house. A clubhouse, of sorts. It had windows on two sides, with checked curtains, and a shingled roof and even a WELCOME sign by the door. Stretching beyond the platform were branches. *Real, live tree branches* growing out of a *real tree* in the middle of the store. Above the branches were skylights, where a two-story atrium opened over the children's section. Arlo lost track of Ida's conversation with Matthew. He was too busy staring at the contraption above him.

"Arlo?" Ida said. "Did you hear me?"

"Sorry," Arlo said. He pointed to the tree house.

"Yes. Yes. It's nice, isn't it? That was Maywood's idea. But, right now it's Steamboat we're worried about. Don't dilly-dally. We need to hurry."

"Maywood?"

"Lucius and Delia's daughter. You remember I told you that Lucius is Augusta's son. Delia is his wife. And Maywood is their daughter. Come on. We need to find her." Ida tugged on Arlo's sleeve.

"Bye, Mr. Healy." Arlo raised his arm in a wave.

"Matthew," the man said. "Remember?"

"Sorry."

"That's OK. Come back anytime, all right?"

"Sure. Thanks." Arlo followed Ida to the door. The floorboards made a satisfying creak as they padded over them.

When they were outside, Ida crossed the street and stopped in front of the Watermen's Café. She pointed toward the river.

"See those stone pillars at the end of the street?" she asked.

"Yes." Arlo followed her outstretched arm.

"That's the entrance to the path that leads to Riverside Park. If Maywood went that way, I'll never catch up with her."

Arlo looked at his grandmother. "I'm a good runner," he said.

She looked back at him. "That path goes at least a mile," she said.

Arlo shrugged. "Sam and I run that far all the time."

"You wouldn't mind?" she asked.

"I like to run," Arlo said.

The fine lines eased out of her forehead then. "The path leads straight to the park," she said. "There's no danger of your getting lost. I'll take the car and meet you in the parking lot at the bottom of Cemetery Hill."

Arlo frowned. "Cemetery Hill?"

"You'll see," Ida said. "It's on the far side of Riverside Park."

"OK." Arlo was trying to keep everything straight, but there was a lot to take in. *River path. Cemetery Hill. The park.* And a *girl* named *Maywood.*

"Don't worry. I'll find you." Ida waved him off with the back of her hand. "Just keep your eyes peeled for Steamboat."

Arlo started running. That was one thing he knew how to do. It was a relief to turn onto the river path, even if he didn't really know where he was going. At least he was doing something that made his grandmother happy.

CHAPTER 21
Maywood Stonestreet

The path followed the riverbank, which gradually changed from a gentle slope to a sharp drop-off as Arlo moved away from town. After half a mile, he was running along steep cliffs that loomed above the water. On his left, a tall, wooded hillside rose to a rounded peak.

He'd been running about ten minutes when he spotted Maywood at the end of the path. She was standing inside the entrance to the park. At least there was a girl standing in that spot, and Arlo figured she must be Maywood, because Steamboat was standing right beside her. He sped up so he could catch them before they moved on. The air was humid this close to the river, but at least there was a cool breeze.

After a short burst of speed, he came to a fork in the path. To his left was an iron gate with the words EDGEWATER ACRES across the top. Stone grave markers dotted the lawn behind it. To his right, the path spilled into a grassy park with picnic tables and a swing set, as well as a sandbox for little kids.

The girl eyed Arlo warily as he approached. Meanwhile, Steamboat jumped up and down and then licked Arlo on the hand.

"Who are you?" the girl asked.

"I'm Arlo," he said. "Ida Jones's grandson."

She stared. "What are you doing in Edgewater?"

Arlo felt as if he had been slapped across the cheek. Why shouldn't he be in Edgewater?

"I came to see my grandmother."

The girl lifted her chin. "When did you get here?" she asked.

"Last night." Arlo stooped to rub Steamboat's ears. At least the dog was friendly to him. When he stood back up, the girl was craning her neck to peer behind him.

"Where's Ida?" she asked.

"Looking for you and Steamboat," Arlo said. He blushed. "I mean . . . well, you *are* Maywood, aren't you?"

"*Yes.*" She took a step away from him. "How did you know my name?"

"Matthew told us you were on your way to Ida's house."

The girl folded her arms over her chest. "How do you know Matthew?"

"I don't really. We just met. I mean, Ida introduced me to him. We were at the bookstore. Looking for Steamboat."

At the sound of his name, Steamboat started wagging his tail. He barked and then jumped against Arlo's knee.

"Good boy." Arlo stroked the fine hairs on Steamboat's head. "We've been searching all over for you."

Steamboat's reaction seemed to put Maywood at ease. She dropped her arms and stepped toward Arlo again.

"What happened to Steamboat, anyway?" she asked. "Ida never lets him out of her sight."

"We were at Val-U-Mart," Arlo explained.

Maywood's eyebrows shot up. "Ida took you to the mall?"

"She said I needed some things and that there was nowhere else to buy them."

"She took Steamboat with you?"

"That's right."

Maywood started nodding. "Don't tell me," she said. "You left Steamboat in the car, and he jumped out the window while you were in the store."

"How did you know?"

"Because the first time Ida brought him to the bookstore, he did the same thing. He followed her into the shop."

"Your parents must have loved that."

Maywood tossed her head. "They didn't mind. My dad loves dogs, but my mom says we can't have one because we live in an apartment over the store. They like letting Steamboat come inside."

"I thought dogs couldn't come in restaurants."

Maywood rolled her eyes. "If the inspector shows up, we sneak him out the back door." She bent down and patted Steamboat on the head. "It's not like he's hurting anything.

Mom and Dad love Steamboat. They told Ida to be sure to bring him anytime."

"Does she do that?"

"All the time," Maywood said. "Steamboat's sort of our store mascot. If we didn't already have that frog on the sign, my parents would probably put Steamboat's face there."

Arlo looked down at Steamboat with new respect. "So that's why Ida figured he'd run to the store."

"Naturally," Maywood said.

"Naturally," Arlo repeated.

Steamboat let out a yip.

"We're talking about you, all right." Maywood ruffled his ears. "No wonder you were confused. Poor doggy. That mall's a mess, isn't it?"

Steamboat lifted his head and let out a howl.

"Wow," Arlo said. "I didn't know he could do that."

Maywood patted Steamboat's head again. "Only when he has something to complain about," she said.

"Matthew told us you were walking him home," Arlo said.

"I needed to be sure Ida was all right."

A loud thunk caused Arlo and Maywood to turn their heads in time to see Ida's dark-green sedan bounce its way through a pothole in the parking lot and coast to a jerky stop in a space isolated from the other cars.

"There she is," Arlo said.

Maywood grinned. "Have you ridden in the car with her yet?"

Arlo rolled his eyes. "Three times," he said.

Maywood giggled. "That must have been fun."

Arlo drew in his breath and let it back out slowly. "A thrill a minute," he said.

When Steamboat spotted Ida's car, he took off running. Arlo and Maywood chased after him.

Ida stepped out of her car and threw her arms around Steamboat.

"Thank goodness," she said as she kissed the top of his head. Then she shook a finger at him. "You scared me to death," she scolded.

Steamboat hung his head. He let out a small whimper and ran his tongue over his teeth, as if he were worried about how much trouble he was in.

"You're sorry now, though, aren't you?"

Steamboat wrinkled up his forehead.

"And you won't ever do that again, will you?"

This time Steamboat let his tongue loll out of his mouth, as though he were trying hard to say how sorry he was and that he would never, ever jump out of a car again.

"All right," Ida said. "You're forgiven." She hugged him again. "I suppose it's really my fault for dragging you along to that awful mall."

This time Steamboat wagged his tail so hard he shook the entire back half of his body.

Meanwhile, Arlo noticed two boys passing by on bicycles. They pedaled across the lot and then bumped through the grass in the park, nearly running over a picnic spread out on a blanket.

"Hey!" a man yelled.

But the boys kept moving.

"Oh, great," Maywood muttered.

"You know them?" Arlo asked.

"I go to school with them," Maywood said. *"Unfortunately."*

Arlo watched the two boys pedal through the iron gate into the cemetery and begin climbing the one-lane path up the hill.

"Everyone in Edgewater knows those two," Ida muttered.

"Hafer and Boyle," Maywood explained. "That's who they are."

"You'll want to stay away from them," Ida added. "Trouble with a capital *T.* That's what they are."

Arlo watched Maywood watch the boys. She didn't move until they were out of sight. Then she edged sideways toward Ida.

"Matthew said you were probably working in your garden," Maywood said to Ida. "He figured that's why you didn't answer the phone. But I was afraid something was wrong."

"That's sweet of you, dear. Worrying about an old lady like me."

"Arlo said you went to Val-U-Mart."

"That's right. Arlo needed a few things."

"But you hate the mall," Maywood said.

Ida's face turned pink. "That's true, dear. But there are times when a person has to put personal feelings aside."

Arlo was silently grateful she didn't mention the word *underwear.*

"No wonder Steamboat was confused," Maywood said. "He's never been to the mall before, has he?"

"That was his first trip," Ida said. "And I believe he feels exactly the same way I do about the place." She gave Steamboat an approving nod. "Couldn't get out of there quickly enough, could you, Steamboat?"

As Steamboat wagged his tail, Maywood glanced down the path toward town. "I should be getting back," she said. "My dad will wonder where I am."

"How about if Arlo and I give you a ride?" Ida asked.

Maywood looked sideways at Arlo. He struggled to keep from laughing.

"Yeah," he said. "You should ride with us."

When Ida wasn't looking, Maywood stepped on Arlo's foot. He rolled his eyes at her.

A moment later, something exploded on the hill above them. There was a series of short popping noises, followed by a louder boom.

"What on earth?" Ida looked up at Cemetery Hill.

Steamboat yelped and took off running. First he ran toward the river. When another, louder pop echoed off the rocks near the cliffs, he whipped around and started running toward the cemetery.

"Poor baby," Ida said. "He's terrified." She cupped her hands around her mouth and yelled. "Steamboat! Come back!"

The loud popping noises drowned out her voice.

"Hafer and Boyle," Maywood whispered to Arlo. "They must have firecrackers."

CHAPTER 22
Hafer and Boyle

Ida yelled for Steamboat again. Meanwhile, there was another loud pop that echoed off the rocks.

"He'll never come back as long as he hears that noise," Ida said.

"I'll go after him," Arlo said.

"I'm coming with you," Maywood said.

"You two be careful," Ida said. "Just find Steamboat and bring him down here. And whatever you do, stay away from those boys."

"Don't worry," Maywood said.

Arlo was surprised by how fast she ran. He was running hard, yet she had no trouble keeping up with him. They were both winded by the time they reached the top of the hill. Hafer and Boyle were slumped against the brick building that housed the office for the cemetery. They looked like evil twins in their stained jeans and black T-shirts.

"There he is," Maywood whispered, tilting her head in the direction of a tall evergreen on the right side of the building.

Steamboat peeked from behind the tree as if he believed no one but Maywood and Arlo could spot him.

"Come on," Arlo said. "We need to get him out of there."

"Wait a second." Maywood put a hand on his arm. "Let's see what they're up to first."

The boy with the greasy black hair spoke first. "Hey, Mayflower, who's your boyfriend?" he yelled. Arlo couldn't help noticing the thick mud covering the boy's leather boots.

"Pretend you don't hear him," Maywood whispered. She darted past the office to the tree where Steamboat was hiding.

"Wait up," Arlo yelled.

"Look, Boyle," the other boy yelled. "They want to be alone."

The boy with the muddy boots made loud kissing noises.

"Mind your own business, Hafer," Maywood yelled back.

So much for ignoring them, Arlo thought. He bent down to make sure Steamboat was safe. "Are you OK, boy?"

Steamboat looked up at him with wide eyes. He was panting hard.

"Come on," Maywood said. "Let's get him out of here."

"I'm ready when you are," Arlo said.

And with that, they took off through the trees, weaving a path down the hill to the park.

"Where you going, Mayflower?" Hafer called after them.

"Yeah. Who's your boyfriend, Freak Girl?" the other boy yelled.

161

This time Maywood *did* ignore them. She made sure that Steamboat stayed between them as they made their way through the woods. They didn't stop until they reached the bottom of the hill.

"What's the story with those creeps?" Arlo asked, catching his breath and wiping the sweat off his forehead.

"They're just your basic morons," Maywood said. "Eddie Hafer's dad is the mayor. So Hafer figures he can get away with anything. Chip Boyle's not so bad. He's just dumb. And he does whatever Eddie tells him to do because nobody else will talk to him."

Arlo nodded toward the parking lot, where Ida was waving at them from her car. "We'd better go," he said. "She'll be worried about you-know-who." He pointed toward Steamboat, who promptly lifted his head and howled.

"You can say that again," Arlo said, ruffling Steamboat's ears.

Maywood smiled. "Trouble with a capital *T*," she said.

Then they made their way over to the parking lot. Just before they reached Ida, a black sedan drove past the parked cars and turned up Cemetery Road.

"Wonder who that is," Maywood said.

"Maybe somebody who works in a funeral home," Arlo said. "Look at that car."

"Maybe," Maywood said.

They watched the car take the first switchback curve.

Arlo groaned when he saw the look on Maywood's face. "Don't tell me you want to go back up there," he said.

"Come on," Maywood said. "We need to check this out."

When they reached the top of the hill they tiptoed through the woods, watching the black sedan snake its way up the hillside and pull into a space beside the office. Hafer and Boyle had obviously been waiting for it. They walked over to the driver's side and waited until the window went down and a black-suited arm emerged. An envelope passed from the hand of the man in the car to Hafer's hand.

"What's going on?" Arlo asked.

"Nothing good," Maywood said. "You can bet on that."

Steamboat rubbed his nose against Arlo's leg. When Arlo looked down at him, he whimpered and tilted his nose downhill toward the park.

"Shh. Quiet, Steamboat," Maywood whispered.

Arlo patted Steamboat on the head. "Just hang on, OK?" He glanced again at Hafer and Boyle. They were leaning against the car now with their heads ducked forward, as if some sort of discussion were taking place.

"We've seen enough," Maywood said. "Let's get out of here."

Ida was still waiting when they returned to the parking lot.

"What happened to you?" she asked. "Why did you go back up there?"

Maywood told her what they'd seen.

"I noticed that car," Ida said. "It doesn't belong to anyone around here."

"What do you think they were doing?" Maywood asked.

Ida shook her head. "That Hafer boy's liable to end up in prison at the rate he's going."

Nobody said anything on the way to the bookstore.

"Call me, OK?" Maywood whispered as she got out of the backseat.

Arlo nodded.

On the rest of the ride home, Ida seemed thoughtful. She didn't speak until they had reached the bridge over the creek at the marina. Her voice didn't sound as sharp as it normally did, either, so Arlo was surprised by what she asked.

"I suppose Albert must have had some choice words to say about me over the years," she said, tilting her voice up a notch at the end, making it clear she expected a response.

Arlo thought for a moment. He needed to be careful. The wrong answer might turn her against him for good.

"Poppo said he met you a couple of times and you seemed nice," he said after a pause.

That was the truth after all, though it was leaving out a lot of other things Poppo had said that Ida probably wouldn't want to hear.

She glanced over at him. "Albert told you I was nice?"

Arlo nodded.

"What else did he tell you?"

She had her eyes trained on his face, so Arlo had to control his reactions. His tendency to blush usually gave away when he was stretching the truth. He hoped she wouldn't figure that out.

"Poppo said it was a shame that you and my mom got off on the wrong foot."

Ida tilted her head as if she were trying to map a path from the relationship she remembered to the one Arlo was describing.

"That's one way of putting things, I guess."

At that moment, a large, brownish-white bird swooped low in front of the car, then came to rest on the telephone pole at the side of the road.

"Was that an eagle?" Arlo asked.

Ida smiled, and with that, the tension in the car eased.

"That's an osprey," she said. "I'll bet you've never seen one before, have you? Unusual to see one this late in the fall. That fellow must be reluctant to head south for the winter. Your father was particularly fond of those birds."

"Osprey and eagles, right?" It was a guess, but Arlo felt pretty sure his father had loved eagles too. He patted the wood carving in his pocket. He felt one step closer to finding out if his father had made it.

"How did you know?" Ida's hands tightened on the wheel, bleaching her knuckles white.

"Poppo told me," Arlo lied. He didn't want to lose this chance to find out as much as he could. He kept his hand over the carving. He would show it to her eventually. But not now. The time didn't feel right. He wanted to be able to watch her face when she first saw it. And besides, he couldn't stand it if she took it away from him. He needed to keep it. At least for the time being. He couldn't explain why. He just knew it was important. The way Poppo knew things about angels and spirits. That same old superstitious feeling.

"I'm sure I've never seen one," he said.

"Not surprising," Ida said. "Considering where you live. Osprey like water. So they can fish. They don't usually come as far inland as where you live." She slowed the car to get a closer look at the bird. "You know, we nearly lost them all in the seventies. Pesticides were killing them off. But they're back now. Stronger than ever."

The words *tough old bird* floated through Arlo's mind. It was an expression Poppo used to describe Mrs. Beakerbinder down the street. Or maybe he had used it to describe Ida. Arlo wasn't sure.

"Can we call Poppo when we get home?" Arlo expected her to protest, but his grandmother surprised him.

"That's a good idea," she said. "We should see how he's doing today."

Back at the house, Ida filled Steamboat's water bowl and then made the call. Once again, Arlo asked to speak to Poppo, and again, Ida shook her head.

"He's awake," she said, after she'd hung up the phone. "That's a milestone, Arlo. He's even speaking a bit."

"Then why can't I talk to him?"

A twinge of sadness flashed over her face, then disappeared as her features flattened into her normal expression. "They said he's very weak and not quite up to talking on the phone."

Arlo couldn't help wondering what part of the conversation Ida was holding back from him. "He's going to be all right, though, isn't he?"

She parceled out her words carefully. "The doctor says there's room for hope."

Arlo's chest tightened. *Room for hope* didn't sound hopeful at all.

"Waking up and speaking are good signs, Arlo. One step at a time, OK?"

Her voice was sharp again. All angles and bones. Every time Arlo thought she might be turning less prickly, something happened and the pointy edges came poking back out.

Arlo's eyes burned. But he wouldn't cry in front of her. No matter what.

CHAPTER 23

Reasons to Stay, Reasons to Go

Two days had passed since Steamboat jumped out of the car in the Val-U-Mart parking lot. Aside from trips to the grocery store for food and the post office for stamps, Arlo stayed close to the house with Ida. They talked to the nurse on the morning shift just before noon and to the evening nurse around seven.

Each day Ida spoke to the doctor after he'd completed his morning rounds. Poppo was "holding his own," according to Dr. Simon, who was the neurologist taking care of him.

"They think he's out of danger, but they need to keep a close watch for another couple of days," Ida reported.

"Then what?" Arlo asked.

"Then they decide what to do next."

What did *decide what to do next* mean, exactly? Whatever it meant, it did not sound promising.

At least Miss Hasslebarger wasn't a problem anymore.

"She won't bother you for a while anyway," Ida had told him. "I called Nathan about her."

"Who's Nathan?" Arlo asked.

"My lawyer. He and your grandfather were cousins once removed. He takes care of all my business. And he contacted someone in Marshboro to call off Miss Hasslebarger."

"Thank you," Arlo said.

Ida's face softened. She gave Arlo a sympathetic look, as if to let him know that no matter how she felt about his mother, she hated what Arlo had been through with the social worker.

"What a horrible woman," Ida said.

"You talked to her?"

"Only briefly. That was more than enough. The idea that you might be better off in a shelter . . ."

That comment was followed by a sour expression and more head-shaking. Arlo looked at his grandmother's profile. If you were in a battle and you had to choose sides, you would definitely choose hers.

Sitting at the wooden desk in his father's old room, Arlo reached in the drawer and took out a small pad of paper. He drew a line down the middle of the page. On one side he wrote MARSHBORO, and on the other side he wrote EDGEWATER. Under each heading he listed the names of the people who were important to him. He was surprised to find more names under the Edgewater heading than under Marshboro. Of course, he had never felt closer to anyone than Poppo and Sam. But everything was different now. He stared at his list.

MARSHBORO	EDGEWATER
Poppo	Steamboat
Sam	Maywood (?)
	Ida (?) — no rats in the basement

Arlo added question marks beside Maywood's and Ida's names because he wasn't really sure how they felt about him. Maywood seemed nice, but she was also nosy and had a sharp tongue like Augusta Stonestreet. As for Ida, he wasn't sure what to make of her. She must care about him because she was allowing him to stay in her house. But, she wasn't exactly friendly yet. Or, maybe she was, in those moments when they managed to avoid the subject of his mother.

Who knew what was going to happen? Going home to Marshboro wasn't going to work. But staying in Edgewater didn't feel all that safe, either. Arlo supposed he could get used to Ida's prickly ways if he had to. It wouldn't be the same as living with Poppo. But it would be better than dodging rats in the basement of a foster home, or being terrorized by a bully in a shelter. And if he had to change schools because of a foster home, he'd never see Sam anyway.

Later that morning, Ida managed to get Poppo on the phone.

"He's asking for you," she said.

"I can talk to him now? Really?" Arlo stumbled over the vacuum cleaner in his rush to get to the phone.

"Poppo?"

"Is that my number one grandson?"

"It's me," Arlo said. "You sound good."

"I'm doing fine," Poppo said. "For an old man whose memory is failing."

"I miss you," Arlo said.

"I miss you, too," Poppo said.

Arlo swallowed a huge knot in his throat. "I'm sorry I had to leave," he said.

"Leave?" Poppo said. "Where are you?"

Arlo gulped. Surely Poppo understood where he was. "With Ida," he said. "You know. In Edgewater."

"Ida?" Poppo said. "Who's that?"

A quiver ran down Arlo's spine. He struggled to keep the disappointment out of his voice. "My grandmother in Virginia. Remember?"

"Oh, yeah. I knew that. Didn't I?"

"Sure you did," Arlo said. He glanced over at Ida. She was staring at him.

"OK, buddy," Poppo said. All of a sudden, he sounded like he was in a hurry. "You take care. All right?"

"Sure, Poppo." Arlo felt his shoulders drop as the image of a back-to-normal Poppo dissolved in his mind. "You take care, too," he said.

Arlo handed the receiver back to Ida. There was no escaping her eagle-eye gaze.

"I told Augusta I'd meet her at Frog Creek this afternoon," she said. "I happen to know that Maywood's out of school early because of teachers' meetings. Perhaps you'd like to come with me."

Might as well, Arlo figured. What else was he going to do?

171

CHAPTER 24
Tree House

The tables were all filled when Arlo followed Ida into the café that afternoon. Augusta Stonestreet was seated at the table in the window.

"Augusta's early, as usual," Ida remarked as they stood in line to give Matthew their orders.

Arlo studied the menu board. Would he rather have a turkey-and-cheese pita pocket or macaroni and cheese? They were next in line when a voice trickled down from the tree house above them.

"Want to come up?" Maywood gave Arlo a mysterious smile.

"Go ahead," Ida said. "You can give Matthew your order and eat up there."

Matthew nodded his agreement. "What'll it be, Sky-walker?"

Arlo frowned. *"Skywalker?"* he asked.

"Maybe he hasn't seen *Star Wars,*" Maywood said.

Arlo felt the color rise in his face. *Luke Skywalker. Of course.* "I'll have a turkey-and-cheese pita pocket," he said, trying to appear unruffled in front of Maywood.

Matthew nodded. "I'll give you a yell when it's ready," he said.

It was a quick trip up the ladder. Maywood was seated in one of six beanbag chairs. Arlo explored the small clubhouse before joining her. It was lined with low bookcases that were filled with used books.

"Nice place," Arlo said.

"Thanks," she said. "I designed it. I drew pictures, and then Matthew and my dad built it."

"Pretty impressive," Arlo said.

Maywood lifted her chin. "I'm going to be an architect someday," she said. "Like Julia Morgan."

"Julia who?" Arlo asked.

Maywood sighed. She got up from her beanbag and went inside the clubhouse long enough to retrieve a large art book.

"Here she is," Maywood said, opening to a spread with a photograph of a small woman wearing wire-rimmed glasses on one page and a photo of an ornate building on the opposite page. "She was the first woman to earn a degree in architecture from a famous school in Paris," Maywood said. "And she designed Hearst Castle."

"Hearst what?" Arlo asked.

Maywood lifted her eyes to the ceiling in disbelief. "*San Simeon,*" she said. "Surely you've heard of that?"

Arlo stared at her blankly.

"It's this estate in California built by a guy who owned a

bunch of newspapers back in the nineteen hundreds." She got up again and walked to the clubhouse, emerging a moment later with another large book. "Look, I'll show you." Maywood flipped through the book until she found a photo of a huge white building.

"Nice," Arlo said.

"Nice?" Maywood scowled. "Are you kidding? It's amazing. Look. This is my favorite." She paged through until she came to a series of rustic-style buildings surrounded by tall trees.

"Where's that?" Arlo asked.

"Asilomar," Maywood said. "It used to be a YWCA camp. Look at the dining hall. Wouldn't you like to eat there?"

"Not bad," Arlo said

"It's *beautiful*," Maywood said. "Someday I'm going to design buildings just like these."

Arlo looked around the tree house again. "This is beautiful, too," he said. He could tell from the way Maywood looked at him that he had said the right thing, though that wasn't the reason he'd said it. It wasn't to please Maywood. It was because the tree house really *was* beautiful. Arlo wouldn't mind spending a lot of time here.

Imagining spending time in the tree house made him think of Sam and the apartment over Aunt Betty's garage. That was where they used to go when they needed to stay out of Aunt Betty's way. The two rooms over her garage were filled to the brim with a hodgepodge of used furniture, boxes of broken appliances, and storage bins filled with old kitchen utensils and faded curtains. Arlo liked the privacy and the feeling that it was their own kingdom. No one bothered them up there. They could talk about anything they liked.

Maywood closed the book and laid it carefully against the railing.

"So, your apartment's up there?" Arlo asked, pointing toward the doors on the second floor.

"That's right," Maywood said. "It's the one with the blue door." She pointed to the other side of the atrium. "The one with the yellow door belongs to my grandmother."

Arlo gave her a puzzled look. "But I was in your grandmother's house," he said.

"That's my *other* grandmother," Maywood said. "Gramma Stonestreet. I'm talking about Mama Reel."

"Mama who?"

"It's short for Aurelia. She's my mom's mom. She's taking care of me while my parents are in Washington for my mom's meeting. Mom's an art professor in Richmond."

Arlo nodded. He wondered what it would be like to have an art professor for a mother. Not that he had anything to compare it to. Having a mother was more than he could imagine. He leaned back and watched the clouds drift past the glass in the skylights. "Must be interesting to watch storms from here," he said.

Maywood leaned back too. "Sometimes we bring sleeping bags down at night," she said. "You can see the stars."

Arlo tried to imagine what it would feel like to sleep in a pretend tree house inside a bookstore in the dark. He was imagining a warm summer night and a sky filled with stars when Maywood's voice broke through his dream.

"Is it true you ran away from home?" she asked.

Arlo sat up with a start. "Who told you that?"

Maywood gave him a guilty smile. "Gramma Stonestreet. She says you came on a bus to Richmond and someone gave you a ride from there."

Arlo rolled his eyes. He leaned back and stared at the clouds again. One of them reminded him of Ebenezer Crookshank. Arlo could see his funny hat. "That's true," he said. "Only, I didn't run away."

"I don't understand."

Arlo sighed. Might as well get this over with. She was going to find out eventually, and it was better that she know the truth rather than some garbled version she heard from Augusta Stonestreet.

"Poppo had a stroke," Arlo said in as matter-of-fact a tone as he could muster. "I ran away because he was in the hospital and a social worker wanted to put me in a shelter."

Silence.

The beanbag made a loud scrunching sound as Maywood rolled around on it. "That's terrible," she said at last. "I didn't know."

Arlo nodded. "That's why I had to run away." He kept his eyes on the Ebenezer Crookshank cloud. Gradually, wind currents dispersed the vapors, making it look as though Mr. Crookshank were tipping his hat. *Good day to you, too,* Arlo thought.

When Maywood spoke again, her voice was small. "Your grandfather's going to be all right, isn't he?"

Arlo pressed his lips together tightly, trying to control the fear that came when he repeated the doctor's words. "They say there's room for hope."

Maywood didn't say anything.

The silence was uncomfortable between them until Matthew's voice boomed up from below. "Gobbler and cheese in a pocket," he yelled.

Arlo climbed down the ladder and collected his sandwich and a bottle of water. Then he climbed back up.

"What are you going to do?" Maywood asked.

Arlo put down his sandwich. Then he smiled. "First, I'm going to eat my lunch," he said. She smiled back at him with relief.

"You should move in with Ida," she said.

Arlo laughed. "Yeah. She'd love that, wouldn't she?"

"No, really." Maywood sighed. "Ida's not as cranky as she seems." She scooted closer to Arlo. "And maybe you can stop her."

Arlo swallowed a bite of sandwich. "Stop her from what?" he asked.

"Selling her house and moving to Richmond, that's what," Maywood said.

Arlo looked up. "What are you talking about?"

Maywood's tone was firm, letting him know she was sure of the truth of what she was saying.

"I'm not supposed to know this, but Ida's selling her house and moving into a condo."

"Who told you that?"

Maywood rolled her eyes. "Gramma Stonestreet knows everything Ida does. I heard her tell my dad."

Arlo thought about how all the glasses in Ida's kitchen were arranged according to size and about the way the towels in the bathroom were sorted by color. If a person was moving, they'd be emptying out drawers and giving things away, wouldn't they? Ida's house was way too neat for that to be going on.

On the other hand, Arlo thought, if a person was selling her house, she'd need to keep it neat and clean to make people want to buy it. Ida's house sparkled. It was like something out of a television commercial.

A chair leg scraped the floor beneath them, and Ida's voice drifted up.

"You haven't lost them again, have you, Augusta?"

"I distinctly remember putting them in my purse this morning before I left the house," Mrs. Stonestreet responded.

Maywood stood up. "Here we go again," she said.

Arlo frowned at her. "What are you talking about?"

"Gramma Stonestreet. She's left her key in the house and locked herself out. She does it all the time. I'm going to have to walk her home and help her break in."

"You're kidding?" Arlo said.

Maywood raised an eyebrow. "Watch what happens," she said.

Sure enough, a second later, Augusta Stonestreet stood at the bottom of the ladder and yelled up through the platform.

"May-wood!"

"Yes, Gramma?"

"I've left my key at home, dear. Do you think you could . . . ?"

"Sure, Gramma. I'll be right down." Maywood gave Arlo a *see-what-I-mean?* look. Then she started down the ladder. "See you tomorrow," she said, struggling to hold down a grin.

Arlo leaned over the edge. "Wait a minute," he said. She paused and looked up at him. "You pick locks?" he asked.

She laughed. "I found a book that explained how to do it," she said. "Gramma Stonestreet says I have a real flair. Of course, I've had a lot of practice."

Arlo watched, openmouthed, as Maywood descended. She was the most interesting girl he had ever met.

"See you tomorrow?" he called down from the tree house.

She looked up at him and waved. "Sure," she said. "Meet you back here after school."

As he watched her leave, Arlo caught Ida staring at him. She had an odd expression on her face and somehow Arlo understood that she was pleased with him, though he wasn't sure why.

CHAPTER 25
Linen and Good China

That evening at dinner, Arlo sat beside Ida at the counter in the kitchen.

"I never thought I'd be entertaining company here," Ida said. "Slocum would never have approved."

"Why not?" Arlo asked.

"Slocum liked linen napkins and good china for one thing," she said. "He believed in *formality*."

The way she pronounced the word—*formality*—sounded to Arlo like some sort of dreaded disease. What was wrong with eating in the kitchen? Ida's kitchen was the brightest room in her house. Everything sparkled—the stove and refrigerator and sink. Even the paint on the island was a cheerful shade of blue.

"If I lived here, I'd eat in the kitchen every day," he said.

That seemed to please her. "I like it, too," she whispered. From the guilty look on her face, you would have thought Slocum was in the next room.

Steamboat barked at their feet.

"Well, of course, you love the kitchen, don't you, boy?" Ida said. "That's where we keep all the food."

Arlo waited until they had moved on to dessert before bringing up his conversation with Maywood.

"Mind if I ask you something?" he said.

"Go ahead," Ida said.

Arlo cleared his throat.

"Is something wrong?" she asked.

"No, ma'am. It's not that." Arlo wiped a drip of ice cream off his chin. "It's something Maywood told me this afternoon."

She gave him a puzzled look.

"Maywood says you're moving to Richmond." Arlo kept his eyes on his dessert dish, waiting for her to take that in.

"I suppose you were bound to hear eventually, weren't you?" she said.

He raised his head. "You mean, it's true?"

She gave him a sad smile. "A person needs to make plans, Arlo. I'm an old lady living alone." She folded her napkin and placed it next to her plate.

"Maywood says you bought a condo in a retirement community."

She rolled her eyes. "It's like taking out an ad in the newspaper, isn't it?" she said. "All I need to do is share one tiny detail of my private life with Augusta and a few days later, everyone in Edgewater knows about it."

Her body seemed less substantial now, as if her bones

were shrinking. Her shoulders seemed to cave in on them-selves too.

"It's true that I signed a contract to buy a condominium near Richmond," she said. "But they told me I don't have to go through with it unless I sell this house first."

Arlo felt his stomach roll. "You aren't selling the house, are you?"

"I haven't yet." Her voice was shaky now.

"There isn't even a sign in the yard," Arlo said.

"That's right. And I don't want one either. Once you put a sign in your yard, all manner of strangers think they have a perfect right to come cruising down your driveway, checking things out on their own. I couldn't stand that. And I didn't want everyone in town knowing about it. Too late now, it sounds like."

She ran a finger along the grout in the tile on the island, scraping up a tiny grain of pepper, then wiping it on her nap-kin. "A month ago, selling seemed the only reasonable alter-native. Things have been a little tight around here. I haven't been able to take care of things the way I'd like. There was someone interested in the house. I let a Realtor talk me into looking at places in Richmond." She blotted her cheek with her napkin. "Honestly, Arlo, I'm not even sure how I let her talk me into signing that contract."

"Which contract?" Arlo asked.

"The one on the condo."

"But the person who was interested—they didn't buy your house?"

Ida sniffed. "I haven't let him look at it yet."

Arlo's heart settled back to its normal rhythm. "Is it someone from around here?"

"That's just the thing," Ida said with a puzzled look on her face. "The man doesn't even live in this state. The Realtor says he has a niece who teaches in some town close by. And he thought Edgewater might be a good place to settle down." She picked up Arlo's plate and scraped what was left onto her own. "I still don't understand it. Why, you know as well as I do, you can't even see this place from the road. So, why on earth would he be interested in it?"

Arlo could tell that her mind was racing from the way she wasn't paying attention to what she was doing. She opened the refrigerator and started to put their dirty plates in it, until she glanced down and realized her mistake. Then she bent down and scraped the combined leftovers from their two dinner plates into Steamboat's dish.

"The whole thing gave me a funny feeling," she said. "That's why I canceled the appointment to show the house."

Something made Arlo slip the wood carving out of his pocket. Why now? He wasn't sure. It just felt like the right time. He set it down in front of her. Ida leaned in close, squinting at it. There was a long pause followed by a tiny gasp.

"What on earth?" *Blink. Blink. Blink.* There she went again. "Where did you find this?" she asked.

He told her about the photo album and how the carving had been attached to its binding.

A tear spilled onto Ida's cheek. It took her a few moments to compose herself before she could speak. "Your father made that, you know. It was when he was at camp." She traced the knife marks in the wood with the knobby tip of her finger. "He carried it for luck."

Arlo smiled. "I sort of figured he'd made it," he said.

Ida stared at the carving a long time. "I suppose it's only right you should have it," she said finally.

Arlo's heart speeded up.

"Promise you'll take good care of it?"

He nodded.

"Yes, I believe you will." She placed the carving in his hand.

The wood was warm when Arlo slipped it in his pocket.

That night, he curled up in bed with the book Maywood had given him. *Ghost Stories of the Tidewater Country.* She said it was one of her favorites. Usually Arlo loved ghost stories. He liked the way they set his mind churning, conjuring up all sorts of weird things. But in a strange house, all alone late at night, it was creepy. Still, what else was there to do with Ida asleep and the house closed up? Arlo turned to the page Maywood had marked and started reading. Half of his mind was mulling over the idea of living here in Edgewater. What would he do if Ida asked him to stay? The question made his head spin. He tried to focus on the words of the story.

The fog was thick and blue over the swamp that evening. . . .

But his eyelids drooped, and then somehow the book was on the floor. And Arlo was dreaming. He dreamed of a monster made out of swamp mud, a monster who came to life and chased him through a murky bog. Every time Arlo thought he was getting away, another monster rose up out of the muck and made a grab for him. The monsters all had giant toothless mouths that yawned wider as they lunged toward him.

Arlo woke soaked with sweat. The book of ghost stories was sprawled open on the rug. He carried it to the dresser by the window and pressed it closed. It was bad enough to have Miss Hasslebarger chasing him. He didn't need mud monsters, too. What he needed was a home, with someone to take care of him. Why was that so much to ask?

CHAPTER 26
Matthew Healy

"You're looking a little pale there, Skywalker," Matthew said the next morning when Arlo and Ida walked into the café. "Maybe you need some fortification."

"Matthew's asking if you're hungry," Ida said.

"How about a Frog Creek Special?" Matthew said.

"What's that?" Arlo asked.

"Scrambled-egg sandwich with cheese on homemade bread. Plus a glass of fresh-squeezed orange juice," Matthew told him.

"Sounds good," Arlo said. "I'll try it."

"Good deal," Matthew said.

"And I'll have my usual," Ida said.

"One Frog Creek Special and one Darjeeling with a hazelnut scone." Matthew took two eggs out of the small refrigerator.

Meanwhile, a sharp voice scratched the air behind them.

"Are you two going to stand there lollygagging all day, or are you going to come sit with me?"

Arlo recognized the voice without turning around — Augusta Stonestreet, jutting-out chin and all, glared at them from the front table. Her *usual* spot.

"Coming, dear." Ida gathered her change and walked to the table. Steamboat followed and settled on the floor between them.

Meanwhile, Arlo watched Matthew crack eggs onto a hot griddle. Soon the smell of hot butter, eggs, and melted cheese wafted through the air.

"Know how long you're staying yet?" Matthew asked as he scraped the edges of the egg and blended it with the melting cheese.

"Not really," Arlo said. "It sort of depends."

"Waiting to see what happens with your grandfather, I suppose," Matthew said.

"That's right."

Matthew flipped the egg onto a slice of toasted bread and handed Arlo his orange juice. Arlo took the plate and started eating.

"This is good," he said through a mouthful of food.

Matthew gave him a small salute. "Glad you like it," he said. "How's your grandfather doing, anyway?"

Arlo shrugged.

"That good, huh? Sorry to hear it."

"They say he's not any worse."

"Well, that's something, I guess. Good thing you have Ida."

"Yeah." Arlo didn't mean for his voice to crack. Every time

someone said something that made him think about staying in Edgewater, it was like a valve quit pumping in his heart, just for a second, but enough to put a catch in his voice. Is *that* what he wanted? To stay here? In a place he'd never known?

"Were you good friends with my dad?"

Matthew paused as he lifted the metal basket out of the coffee machine. "Wake and I played on the same basketball team. . . ."

"My dad played basketball?"

"Among other things. You didn't know that?"

"No."

"That's a shame." Matthew dumped the used grounds in the trash and then measured out a fresh scoop of coffee. "Wake was a good man." He poured the fresh coffee grounds into the paper filter, then snapped the lid on the coffee canister. "I could tell you some stories."

"I'd like that." Arlo's heart pressed against the back of his throat. While the water heater on the coffee machine roared, he thought about the questions he might ask.

"You know," Matthew said, lining up clean coffee mugs on the counter, "I've been telling Lucius that I could use an assistant on deliveries. Maybe you could help me out."

"Really?"

"It would give us time to talk." Matthew wiped his hands on a dish towel.

"You could tell me about my dad," Arlo said.

"As long as you don't have other plans," Matthew said.

"I don't have any plans."

Matthew gave him a nod. "Good," he said. "What do you say I talk to Ida?"

"OK."

"Maybe we could start tomorrow." Matthew looked over at him, raising an eyebrow.

"I'd like that," Arlo said. He carried his plate and glass around the counter to the small sink.

"Looks like you know your way around a galley," Matthew said. "Had some experience, have you?"

"I do a lot of cooking at home." Cooking was a glorified way to talk about the meals Arlo fixed, but it was true that he'd been in charge of the kitchen back in Marshboro lately.

"In that case, would you mind wiping off that table for me?"

"Sure."

"Better wash your hands first. Ms. Nosy-Bones is watching us."

Arlo followed Matthew's gaze to the front table, where Augusta Stonestreet was eyeing them intently.

"Bathroom's in back of the children's section."

"Thanks." Arlo smiled as he walked under the tree house. When he came back after washing his hands, Matthew tossed a dish towel to him.

"You and Ida haven't spent much time together, have you?" Matthew asked.

"Poppo and I live pretty far away," Arlo said, wiping down the table. "He always promised we'd come here someday."

"Just never got around to it, I suppose."

"I guess that's right," Arlo said.

Matthew filled the cream pitcher with fresh half-and-half. "You know, it's a good thing you came when you did," he said.

"Why's that?"

"I don't guess Ida's told you about selling her house."

The dish towel slipped in Arlo's hand, but he grabbed hold just before it hit the ground.

"Nice save."

"Thanks." Arlo carried the dish towel to the sink behind the counter, then rinsed it out and hung it over the side to dry. "Maywood mentioned something about it," he said.

"Is that right?" Matthew kept his eyes on the reflection of Ida and Augusta in the mirror over the sink. "Did you ask Ida if it was true?"

Arlo nodded. "She told me she's found a place in Richmond, but she doesn't have to buy it unless she sells her house. She says she had to make plans since she didn't have any family close by."

"'Course if she had some family around here, it might be a different story," Matthew said.

Arlo felt Matthew staring at him. His stomach rolled.

"You know, Ida's been going around telling folks she doesn't want to end up one of those strange old ladies who wanders around a big house not knowing what day of the week it is."

"Ida wouldn't be like that," Arlo said.

"I don't think so, either, but I heard there's this fellow named Garringer in Richmond who's itching to get a look inside the place."

Arlo met Matthew's gaze in the mirror over the sink. In the background he could see Ida and Augusta having a heated discussion at their table. "She told me there was a man who wanted to see it," he said.

"Is she going to show it to him?" Matthew lifted the fresh pot of coffee off the burner and started filling a thermos for the serving table.

"I don't think she wants to," Arlo said, reaching for a dish towel to hand to Matthew when some of the coffee spilled on the table. "Not now, anyway."

They looked at each other.

"It would be a mistake for her to sell that place. And you can tell her I said so."

Arlo took the now-damp dish towel from Matthew and hung it over the rack by the sink. There was no doubt that Ida ought to stay in Edgewater. He didn't need convincing about that.

"Seeing you has already done her a world of good," Matthew said. "You ought to stay as long as you can. Might help her decide to stay."

Arlo didn't like to take credit for things he hadn't done, but Matthew was right about one thing. Selling the house would be a mistake. And besides, he'd barely had a chance to see where his dad had come from. It wouldn't be fair to lose that before he'd even had time to explore.

In the car on the way home, Ida nodded at Steamboat, who was nuzzled under Arlo's arm.

"Looks like you've made a friend," she said.

"I like dogs," Arlo said.

"Do you have one at home?"

Arlo paused longer than he meant to before answering. "Poppo says we can't. He says we don't have a big enough yard."

Ida pressed her lips together so that the white pressure line appeared again. "A boy needs a dog," she said. Then she was silent for a long time.

Arlo thought about what Bernice had said during the bus trip to Richmond. *A boy needs a father.* It seemed like a boy needed a lot of things Arlo didn't have. Things like parents and a home and family. Not to mention a dog.

His mud-and-twig dam was beginning to feel squishy again. What it needed was a little *fortification,* to use one of Matthew's words, something to make sure it stayed strong enough to withstand a full-blown wave.

CHAPTER 27
Betwixt and Between

Just before bed, they called the hospital. This time Ida handed Arlo the receiver.

"He'd rather talk to you," she said.

"Poppo's on the phone?"

"The doctor said it might be good for him to talk to you."

Arlo took the receiver. "Hey, Poppo."

"Where are you?" Poppo asked.

He sounded kind of wild, which caused Arlo's heart to race. "I'm still here with Ida," he said.

"With who?"

"Ida Jones. My dad's mother. Remember? The one who lives in Virginia?"

"I don't know. . . ." Poppo sounded really confused.

"You doing OK?" Arlo asked.

"Doing great. I had cherry pie," Poppo said.

"Your favorite, right?"

"One of them. You coming to see me?"

Arlo's chest tightened. "Can't right now," he said.

"'Course you can't. You're in school, aren't you? Come over later. OK?"

"Sure. I'll get Ida to bring me." Arlo tried to keep his voice easy and relaxed, so Poppo would think they were having a normal conversation, like the ones they used to have at home . . . a year ago. *Or maybe longer.*

"Who?" Poppo asked.

"Never mind. I'll see you soon. OK?"

"OK, buddy. You take care, now."

"I will, Poppo. You take care, too."

Arlo handed the receiver back to Ida and watched as she hung up the phone.

"I talked to the doctor this afternoon," she said.

Her voice did not sound promising.

"He's getting better, right?"

"Yes," Ida said. "And no."

Arlo sighed.

"Dr. Simon said Albert was very lucky. There doesn't seem to be any serious permanent damage from the stroke."

"So, he's OK."

"But there are issues with his memory. . . ." She studied Arlo for a moment. "I believe you already knew that, didn't you?"

Arlo shifted on the stiff cushion. The upholstery poked the back of his knees. Whose idea was it to put spikes in fabrics?

That's what those wiry fibers felt like, short little nails poking holes in Arlo's skin.

"He gets confused sometimes," Arlo admitted.

"Funny you hadn't mentioned that." His grandmother's eyebrows were tiny pinpoints again.

Arlo maintained a poker face, the way Poppo had taught him during their card-playing evenings at camp.

"I was going to tell you," he said.

"When?"

Her sharp old-lady's voice sliced at him again. Arlo stared so hard at the peppermints in the candy dish, the stripes blurred into pinkish swirls.

"I thought he was getting better," Arlo said.

"But he wasn't," she said.

"Some days he seemed fine."

"And other days he had trouble again?"

"Yes."

"Does anybody else know?" She cocked an eyebrow at him.

"You mean, besides the doctors and nurses and Miss Hasslebarger?" Arlo asked.

"That's right. What about the people at school?"

Arlo shook his head. "But we were doing fine before. . . ."

"You aren't doing fine now, are you?"

It was a statement rather than a question. Arlo's chest was so tight he could hardly breathe.

"You wouldn't be here unless there was a serious problem," she said. "Albert needs *professional* help. You can't take care of him on your own."

195

"But I can learn how. . . ."

This time her sigh was so deep, it seemed to cast a pall over the room. "No, you can't, Arlo. You're twelve years old, for Pete's sake."

"Eleven," Arlo corrected her.

Ida's face turned crimson. "All right. Eleven. That's even worse. Adults are supposed to take care of children. Not the other way around."

Later that night, Arlo lay awake in the dark listening to the thrum of mourning doves huddled under the eaves. Was it ungrateful to feel relief at the thought of not keeping Poppo's secret any longer? There had been times when Arlo had worried all through the school day if Poppo might set the house on fire. It had nearly happened once, when Arlo had come home from school to find tomato soup melded to a dry saucepan on a hot burner. If he had stayed to play soccer that day, the house might have burned to the ground.

Arlo thought about Poppo propped up in his hospital bed. He thought about the nurses pouring Poppo fresh cups of water and adjusting the pillow under his head. He wondered if Poppo missed him, or if it was only Frankie that Poppo wanted to see. In a way, Arlo hoped Poppo wasn't thinking about him. If it was only Frankie that Poppo missed, then Arlo wouldn't feel so guilty about leaving him.

If you added up all the moments over the past three months when Poppo had actually recognized Arlo as his grandson, they didn't amount to much time, really. Funny how Arlo hadn't considered that before. Now that he was here with Ida, he saw the past differently. He saw the present differently, too. It was strange how you could talk yourself into believing things were better than they really were. Arlo supposed that was a good thing, too. It was how a person got himself through the tough times. If you realized how bad things were when you were in the middle of them, you might never make it to the other side.

CHAPTER 28
Matthew Tells Stories

The next afternoon, Arlo helped Matthew with the bakery deliveries. Matthew drove his van, and Arlo helped carry boxes inside.

"Tell me what you already know about your dad," Matthew said after they had made their last delivery and were on their way home to Edgewater.

"Not much," Arlo said. He slipped the wood carving out of his pocket and held it up for Matthew to see. "I know he made this."

Matthew glanced over at the object in Arlo's hand. "The eagle," he said. "I'd forgotten about that. Did you show it to Ida?"

"Yes."

"She recognize it?"

"Uh-huh."

"What'd she say?"

Arlo's stomach churned. "She said he made it at camp."

"That's part of the story."

"Will you tell me the rest?"

Matthew didn't say anything for the longest time. His eyes were glued to the empty road in front of them as if there was something out there that Arlo couldn't see. "You ever heard anything about your other grandfather?" Matthew asked finally.

"You mean my dad's father?"

"That's right."

"Not much," Arlo said. "Ida mentioned him a couple of times."

"What did she say about him?"

"She said he liked to eat in the dining room."

Matthew snorted. "Sorry," he said, regaining his composure. "That sounds like Slocum, all right. What else?"

"She said he liked linen napkins."

"I'll bet he did."

"Did you know him?" Arlo asked.

Matthew squinted at the sun, working the muscles in his jaw like he was trying to figure out how to say something unpleasant. "Everyone around here knew Slocum," he said. "He was a man of strong opinions, I guess you'd say."

"Did you like him?"

Matthew coughed. "Slocum wasn't the kind of person you warm up to. Besides, things were different in those days."

"Different how?"

"Between black and white people." Matthew took a long, slow breath. "You know what I'm talking about?"

"Yeah." Arlo tucked the wood carving back in his pocket.

"No offense, Arlo, but there're a lot of folks around here who wouldn't have crossed the street to help Slocum if he collapsed on the sidewalk."

Arlo paused a moment to take that in. "My dad wasn't like that, was he?"

"No. Nothing like that. You have your grandmother to thank for it, too. Partly, anyway."

"She's not like that, either, right?"

"That's right. Ida had sense enough to send your dad away to camp as soon as he was old enough. Wanted to get him away from your grandfather. Wake carved that bird the last summer he went to camp. Showed it to me the day he came back. Said it was a reminder that there was another world out there and all he had to do was make it through high school and he'd get away from your grandfather."

"Did you go to camp, too?"

Matthew laughed. "Camp wasn't exactly an option for me, Arlo. Least not the kind of camp your daddy went to. I had my share of church camp, though. And believe me, I wouldn't have traded places with Wake for anything."

CHAPTER 29
Mama Reel

On Saturday, Maywood was tossing pennies into the fountain outside the post office when Arlo and Ida caught up with her on their way home from mailing a get-well card to Poppo.

"Mama Reel wants to know if you can come for lunch," Maywood said.

Arlo looked at his grandmother.

"It was nice of Aurelia to invite you," she said. "We already talked about it this morning. I told her you'd love to come."

Arlo didn't really appreciate people planning his life without consulting him, but he guessed he didn't mind having lunch with Maywood's other grandmother. Maywood talked about Mama Reel constantly. In a way, he was anxious to meet her.

Ida kept on talking. "I scheduled a meeting with my lawyer," she said. "Nathan and I have some business to tend to, so this works out perfectly."

"What do you need to see Mr. Tretheway about?" Maywood asked.

"Well, Miss Nosy, I suppose that's for me to know, isn't it?" Ida gave Maywood a sharp look.

Arlo stifled a laugh. He kept his eyes focused on the pennies at the bottom of the fountain. Maybe Ida was getting advice about how Arlo could move in with her. Or maybe she was trying to figure out how to get out of buying that condo in Richmond.

"I'll pick you up after my meeting," Ida was saying. "Run on, now, and have a good time." She made a shooing motion with her hand.

On their way through the bookstore, they passed a tall man with curly brown hair who was sorting index cards behind the counter.

"You must be Arlo," he said, stretching out a hand.

"That's my dad," Maywood said.

"Lucius Stonestreet," the man said. "I think you've met my mother."

Arlo appreciated the way Lucius offered an apologetic smile when he mentioned Augusta Stonestreet, as if he recognized, as well as everybody else, what a character she was.

"Nice to meet you," Arlo said, reaching across the counter to shake hands.

"Where's Mom?" Maywood asked.

"She had a meeting with a couple of grad students," Lucius said. "She'll be home this evening. Mama Reel's up there waiting for you."

"We're on our way," Maywood said.

Arlo followed her to a staircase at the back of the store. They climbed the stairs to a small balcony where there were two desks positioned opposite each other and a copy machine.

"This way," Maywood said, leading him through a narrow door that opened onto the atrium. To their left was the yellow door. Maywood opened it up and stepped inside.

Arlo found himself in a small kitchen with sliding glass doors that opened onto a roof garden. Beyond the kitchen was a large open room with brick walls on either side and windows across the front. The walls were covered with oil paintings in bold colors.

"She'll be outside," Maywood said. She slid open the glass door and stepped onto a wooden deck, dodging giant pots of ferns on the way. Mama Reel stood in front of an easel, squinting at the turret on the building across the street. She was a tiny woman with closely cropped gray hair and dark skin.

"So, you're Arlo," she said.

"Yes, ma'am."

"I'm Aurelia Pridemore. Maywood's grandmother. I'd offer to shake your hand, but I'm afraid there's paint on it."

"That's OK."

Mama Reel put down her brush. She was barely taller than Arlo, but her presence seemed to fill the space around them. Her voice was strong and gentle, like water lapping at the shore. She wore a long skirt of orange and white with yellow swirls and a loose cotton sweater with a scarf tied around her neck.

"Come over here, so I can have a look at you," she said.

Her eyes were quick and lively. She examined Arlo from head to toe, then uttered a grunt of approval. "You've got a little from both sides of the family, haven't you?"

Poppo always said Arlo looked more like the Sabatinis than the Joneses, but Arlo had never had the chance to judge for himself, not aside from those few photographs in the album.

"It's good you're here . . . *at last.*"

Arlo braced himself for another scolding about not having visited earlier.

"Ida's waited a long time," she said.

"Yes, ma'am. I know."

"A child can't make up for the mistakes grown-ups make, now, can he?"

Arlo looked up at her.

Mama Reel gave him a nod. "You can't help the bad blood between the Sabatinis and the Joneses," she said. " 'It was pride that changed angels into devils.' "

"Excuse me?"

"She's quoting again," Maywood said.

"That's right, child. And who is the wise person who said that?"

"Socrates?" Maywood guessed.

"No," Mama Reel said.

"Martin Luther King?"

"Two good guesses, but that's not right, either."

"I give up." Maywood plopped into one of the cast-iron chairs around the glass-topped table.

"Saint Augustine," Mama Reel said. "And here's the rest of it: 'It is humility that makes men as angels.'"

Arlo had no idea what she was talking about, but it was a relief not to be blamed for Poppo not bringing him to see Ida sooner. "I wish I knew why they were so mad at each other," he said.

Mama Reel shifted her gaze toward the turret on the old building. "It's not my place to tell you that. You'll need to talk to Ida." She paused, then turned her eyes to him. "I will say this," she began, "once they traveled down that road, it was mighty hard to turn back. Neither one of them was willing to admit they'd been wrong."

It was easy to see how Ida wouldn't admit she was wrong, and Arlo supposed that Poppo could be the same way, especially when it came to forgiving someone who'd been critical of Arlo's mother.

"You must be hungry," Mama Reel said, suddenly changing the subject. "Plates are in the refrigerator. You don't mind if we sit outside and enjoy the breezes, do you?"

"No, ma'am," Arlo said.

"Come on," Maywood said.

Arlo held the door open while Maywood slid the plates off the middle shelf. She handed one to Arlo and carried the other two herself. They came back outside and ducked under the broad umbrella rising from the center of the glass-top table. Maywood pushed aside a large art book to make room for the plates.

"Careful you don't lose my place, child."

"What's this book about?" Maywood turned the cover over so she could read the title. *Masters of African-American Art.*

"Your mother is doing research on a man named Solomon Brokenberry. The museum in Richmond is opening an exhibit in the spring. They asked her to give a talk."

"These pictures look old." Maywood paged through the book.

"Not that old, as museum paintings go. Brokenberry died in 1933. You're related to him way far back. His mother was from around here. She was your great-great-great-great-granddaddy's first cousin."

Arlo looked over Maywood's shoulder. On the right side of the page was a color plate that showed three children standing in front of a large tree.

"That one's a portrait of a family in Normandy. Brokenberry spent most of his life in France. It offered more opportunity for black artists."

An object in the corner of the painting caught Arlo's eye. "Are those berries?" he asked.

"They are." Mama Reel gave Arlo a curious look.

"They're just sort of hidden there in the corner."

"That's right."

Arlo frowned. "Why?" he asked.

"Turn the page." Mama Reel gestured at the book with a knobby finger.

Arlo did as she directed.

"Now look at the next one," she said.

There was the same symbol, tucked in with a jumble of objects behind a chair. Arlo pointed to it.

"That's right. Now try the next one."

Arlo kept turning the pages. The berries were in every one of Brokenberry's paintings.

"Those two stems of red berries were his hallmark," Mama Reel said. She came over and sat beside Arlo. "You have a discerning eye," she said. "That's a gift." She flipped back three pages and pointed to the portrait of a man standing in front of a bookcase filled with leather-bound books. In the man's right hand was a rolled-up map.

"Art scholars believe that that man was Brokenberry's grandfather," Mama Reel said. "No one knows for sure. There's a document in a courthouse somewhere that says his granddaddy was a white man. That much seems certain. We also know that his mama escaped on the Underground Railroad."

"How do they know that?"

Mama Reel smiled. "Family history," she said. My great-granddaddy told me that story, and he heard It from his great-grandmother. There are records from an old plantation proving it was true."

"Will we see the exhibit?" Maywood asked.

"We most certainly will," Mama Reel said. "And maybe Arlo would like to come with us."

"I don't know if I'll still be here," Arlo said.

"Mmmm-hmmmm." Mama Reel looked down over her glasses as she closed the book. "Something tells me you'll be here, all right, but don't ask me how I know."

Arlo felt a twinge. What about Poppo and Sam? A week ago, he wouldn't have considered living with Ida for one minute. But things were changing. She was becoming less prickly, though she still had her moments.

"How are you and Ida getting along, anyway?" Mama Reel asked.

It was as if Arlo's thoughts were being telegraphed directly into her brain.

"Ida's been on her own nearly seven years now," Mama Reel continued. "A person is likely to get set in her ways."

Arlo thought about the underwear hanging on the line in the basement and the cans of sardines in the pantry. "It was a little hard at first," he said, "but we're doing OK now."

Mama Reel covered up a smile with a paint-smeared hand. "Did your grandfather talk about her much when you were growing up?" she asked.

"Not really."

"Didn't figure he would."

"Poppo says Ida and my mom didn't get along."

Mama Reel laughed. "You can say that again."

"Ida says my mom's the reason my dad never finished college." Arlo watched for her reaction.

Mama Reel stared at the open page of the book as if she was trying to avoid making eye contact. Arlo figured she was trying to hide her reaction.

"The truth's not quite that cut-and-dried," she said. "But that's not *my* story to tell."

After lunch, Arlo and Maywood walked up and down the public beach. They gathered bits of driftwood and studied the osprey's nest on top of an old bridge piling.

"Where's the bird?" Arlo asked.

"Gone south for the winter," Maywood said. "They'll be back in the spring."

"*They?*"

"There's a pair of them who have a nest on that piling. They come back every spring."

Arlo told her about the osprey that he and Ida had seen.

"Must have been a straggler," Maywood said. "They're usually gone by the middle of September."

After thanking Mama Reel for lunch, Arlo walked downstairs to the bookstore to meet Ida.

"How was your afternoon?" Ida asked.

"Nice," Arlo said. "Mama Reel sent you this." He offered up the plastic container filled with chicken salad.

"Lovely." Ida closed her eyes. "That will be dinner," she said. "For me, anyway. I have crab cakes for you."

"Where's Steamboat?" Arlo asked.

"Waiting at home."

It wasn't until they had crossed the creek at the marina that Arlo realized calling the house in Edgewater *home* hadn't felt the least bit uncomfortable. He must be getting used to the idea.

CHAPTER 30
What About Steamboat?

Two days later, when Maywood was out of school for Columbus Day, she and Arlo were playing cards in the tree house when they overheard Augusta and Ida quarreling below.

"They're at it again," Maywood said, leaning over the edge. Arlo scooted over beside her, letting his head extend just far enough to catch what they were saying.

"I've given the matter considerable thought," Augusta said, "and I've decided you should plan on taking Steamboat with you."

"No pets allowed, Augusta. I told you that."

Augusta tapped her finger on the glass-top table. "Then we're back to my first piece of advice, Ida. Cancel the contract. Tell them you've changed your mind."

"You know I can't do that. It wouldn't be honorable."

"Phooey. You don't worry about honor when you're dealing with developers."

"I always worry about being honorable in my business dealings," said Ida.

"Developers!" Augusta let out a hoot of disapproval. "A fancy name for *thieves* is more like it. Have you talked to Nathan yet?"

"We met on Saturday," Ida said.

"Did you talk about Arlo?"

"Well, of course we talked about Arlo."

"And?"

"He wanted me to talk to Albert first."

"Who's Albert?"

"Arlo's grandfather."

"Oh, right. That Satarini person."

"*Sabatini*, dear."

"Sorry. Go on."

"I called him yesterday while Arlo and Maywood were having lunch with Aurelia."

"You talked to him?"

"I did."

"Well?"

Ida sighed. "Physically he's in good condition. At least that's what the doctors tell me. But his mind comes and goes."

"Comes and goes?" Augusta asked.

"Mostly goes, I'm afraid. He's not likely to improve."

There was a brief pause before Augusta started speaking again.

"What are you going to do?" she said.

"I don't know. They've asked me . . ."

"Who has?"

"The social worker at the hospital asked . . ."

"Asked you what?"

"Well, you can imagine, can't you? Arlo needs a place to live. He needs someone to take care of him."

"How are you going to do that in a retirement complex?"

"I don't know, Augusta. That's why I made the appointment with Nathan."

"Does Arlo know?"

"About what?"

"Mr. Satarini."

"For heaven's sake, Augusta. The man's name is *Sabatini*! Can't you get that straight?"

"Sorry. You're awfully touchy today."

"Arlo knows some things, but he seems to think that Albert will get better. I'm not sure how much he understands."

Another pause. Longer this time. Then Augusta spoke. "You should never have signed that contract."

"It's too late to talk about that now."

"They tricked you. They never told you about that dog thing."

"What dog thing?"

"That you couldn't take Steamboat with you."

"I wish I could remember if I'd asked them about dogs."

"But surely you did. Tell that horrible Garringer person you're not interested in selling."

"Nathan says I have to show him the house."

"Nonsense. You never even advertised the property."

"Careful, Augusta. Your tea's spilling."

"They're getting up," Maywood whispered. "Scoot back from the edge so they don't see us."

"They're not going anywhere," Arlo said. "Ida's just getting a fresh napkin."

"Shh. She's saying something."

"Mr. Garringer wants to come next week," Ida said. "He's bringing along a contractor to see about tearing down a few walls."

"Heavens. He hasn't even seen the house and he already wants to tear it down?"

"I'd rather not have him come through the place more than once. The real estate agent suggested that this way we could kill two birds with one stone."

"What you need to do is talk to your lawyer."

"Go, Gramma," Maywood mumbled.

"Mr. Garringer says he needs to make sure that the house would suit his needs."

"Suit his needs. Honestly! The nerve of some people. Cancel the contract on the condo and tell the Realtor you have no interest in selling. Tell them you have *ex-ten-uating* circumstances."

"Nathan's working on it."

"You have responsibilities now." Augusta looked up toward the tree house, causing Maywood to yank Arlo away from the edge again.

"I've made a mess of things, haven't I?" Ida said.

"I've seen worse." Augusta poured the last of her tea from

a small china pot. "But I'll admit your situation is not without its challenges."

That night they ate dinner later than usual.

"Can we still call Poppo?" Arlo asked when they were putting the dishes away.

"It's awfully late," Ida said. "Are you sure you want to? You know he gets tired in the evenings."

"Please?" Arlo said.

"All right. Let's finish putting the dishes away, then I'll make the call."

Arlo was careful to line the glasses up so they made neat rows in the cabinet. His grandmother was particular about that. Then he found the dish towel and hung it on the hook under the sink, making sure the cloth did not catch in the door. He walked through the dining room and made the turn toward the middle hall that separated the living room from the dining room. Ida was sitting on the bottom step of the staircase. She handed Arlo the phone.

"Hi, Poppo."

"Hey there, Grandson. How are things in Edgewater?"

"Fine. I made a friend."

"That's good. What's his name?"

"Her name. She's a girl. Her name is Maywood."

"I made a friend, too," Poppo said. "Well, Eldon's not a new friend. We went to high school together."

"Where'd you see him?" Arlo asked.

"Right here in the hospital. He had a hip replaced. We have physical therapy at the same time."

"That's nice," Arlo said.

"Yup. Eldon's been telling me about this apartment complex for folks like us. He's moving there when they let him out of here. Says I might like it, too."

Poppo in an apartment? What about the house?

After an extended silence, Poppo spoke again.

"Eldon's probably waiting for me in the lounge," he said. "I'd better go. We'll talk again tomorrow. OK?"

"Sure, Poppo. Take care of yourself."

"You, too," Poppo said. Then he hung up the phone.

Arlo lay in bed that night thinking about his phone conversation. If Poppo moved into an apartment, what would happen to their house? He watched clouds pass over the full moon. He wondered about the view outside Poppo's hospital window. The mountains in Marshboro were so close together, a person couldn't find a wide-open vista like the views across the river in Edgewater.

Shoot. You'd have to drive all the way to Canaan Valley for that. Everything was different here. But different didn't necessarily mean bad. That was one of Poppo's sayings. Funny how Poppo had a saying for just about every situation. Before coming to Edgewater, Arlo hadn't realized how useful those sayings were.

CHAPTER 31
Hauntings of the Tidewater

It didn't take Arlo long to figure out that Maywood was obsessed with ghosts. He had been in Edgewater almost two weeks and already he understood that she loved cemeteries, black cats, full moons, dark roads, and haunted houses. She had a bookshelf full of ghost stories in her room, books with titles like *Hauntings of the Tidewater* and *Civil War Ghosts of the Potomac*. They were right below the shelf with books about architecture.

On the Thursday after the Columbus Day holiday, the two of them were spying on customers in the café after school when Maywood whipped out a new book of ghost stories.

"This just came in," she said. "I sneaked it out of the box. The stories are really good. Want to hear one?"

"Sure." Arlo knew better than to say no. When Maywood was excited about something, there was no holding her back.

She read in a slow dramatic voice:

> "When the Meyercrofts bought the stately home on
> Lofton Creek, a neighbor told them she hoped they
> didn't mind sharing it with a ghost. The Meyercrofts
> paid no attention . . . until one still autumn afternoon
> when they heard horse hooves clopping over a dirt
> road. Though their driveway was paved, the sound
> came from right outside the window."

"Ghost horses," Maywood said. "Isn't that great?"

"Not bad," Arlo said.

"Not bad?" She swatted him with the book.

"Sorry." Arlo put down his copy of *Hatchet*. "If you heard
ghost-horse hooves outside your window, you'd run screaming for help," he said.

"No, I wouldn't," Maywood said. "Not if I was in my own
bedroom."

"What if you were alone in the apartment? What if there
wasn't anybody else in the building?"

Maywood put down her book. "As long as the door was
locked, I'd be OK."

Arlo leaned closer to her. "What if there was a storm and
the power went off?" he said.

"As long as it was daytime, I'd be fine," Maywood told him.

Arlo rolled his eyes. "I'm talking about in the middle of
the night."

Maywood rolled her eyes back at him. "I'd still be OK."

"I don't believe it."

"Want to bet?" Maywood stuck out her chin. For a split second, she looked exactly like Augusta Stonestreet.

"How are you going to do that?" Arlo asked.

"I'll take you to a haunted house."

Arlo gave her a look. "Where are you going to find one of those?"

"That's easy," she said. "There's one on Cemetery Hill."

Arlo laughed. "Cemetery Hill," he said. "That figures. How do you know it's haunted?"

"Everybody says it is."

"That doesn't mean anything."

"Wait till you see it," she said.

"If it's really haunted, you'll never go inside." Arlo said.

"Want to bet?"

"Sure. How much?"

But Maywood didn't answer. She was already on her way down the ladder.

"Wait up," Arlo yelled. "You want to go right now?"

Maywood climbed back up the ladder. "You have a problem with that?"

Arlo couldn't help smiling to himself. Would it *matter* if he had a problem with going now? Probably not.

"OK. I'm coming," he said. "But what's the bet?"

"How about that?" She pointed to the book with the story about the ghost horse.

"I thought you were reading it," Arlo said.

"I've already read all but the last story. And you'd loan it back to me, wouldn't you?"

"Sure."

"Not that it matters," Maywood said, as she started back down the ladder. "Because you're going to lose, anyway."

Arlo smiled. "We'll see about that," he said. Then he hurried down the ladder and ran to catch up with her.

They walked toward the river and started down the river path.

"Tide's in," Maywood said as they strolled along the cliff.

Arlo looked over the edge. He still wasn't used to the idea of a tidal river, but sure enough, the water was all the way up to the cliffs now. Last time he'd been here, it had barely touched the shore.

They climbed Cemetery Hill to the small brick office where Hafer and Boyle had met the man in the black car.

"The older graves are up there." Maywood pointed to a grassy knoll above them.

"What about the house?" Arlo asked.

"It's above the graves," Maywood said. "Come on."

They hiked past a decrepit iron fence that formed a rectangle around a field of ancient stones. Some of the inscriptions were so worn that they were no longer legible. But others had survived.

"I've always wanted to check these out," Maywood said, kneeling before the first stone.

"You mean, you've never been up here before?"

She shook her head. "Shh. I'm reading."

LYDIA MARCUS STONEHAM
BORN DECEMBER 2, 1756
DIED NOVEMBER 21, 1759.

"She wasn't even three," Arlo said.
Maywood moved to the next marker.

ELIJAH STONEHAM
BORN JUNE 17, 1782
DIED DECEMBER 27, 1788.

"Six," Arlo whispered.

"I feel sorry for them," Maywood said.

She glanced around the field, her eyes settling on a spot where yellow flowers twined around the fence. She marched over, plucked one, and carried it to Lydia's grave.

"That's better," she said.

"What about Elijah?"

Maywood looked higher up the slope. At the edge of the woods, she spotted a clump of blue wildflowers. She walked straight to them, picked one, and laid it on Elijah's grave.

"I'll bet nobody ever visits them," she said. "I'll bet they've been up here for more than two hundred years and nobody even knows they're here."

Arlo thought about Frankie. Who remembered Frankie now besides Poppo?

A crow's squawking interrupted his thoughts. When Arlo looked up at it, the bird tilted its head and aimed a shiny black eye at him. Arlo shivered.

"Why is that bird staring at you?" Maywood asked.

"I don't know."

"It's creepy," she said.

"It's OK. He's gone now." Arlo watched the crow spread its wings and soar higher up the hill.

"Good," Maywood said. "We should go, too."

"I thought you liked spooky stuff."

She shivered.

"So remind me why we're going to a haunted house," he said, "if a measly crow scares you."

She ignored him. "You have to go through the woods first," she said. "Come on. I'll show you."

Under the canopy of pine, the air was cool. Arlo slowed his pace, waiting for his eyes to adjust to the darkness. They dodged tree stumps and lumpy hillocks until they were on the other side of the woods, in a clearing where a gloomy house stared down at them. *Leered*, actually. As if it were daring them to step inside.

Maywood lifted her chin. "It's just an old falling-down house," she said. "It can't hurt us."

"Right," Arlo said.

The house was made of weathered gray boards, some of which had rotted away, leaving gaping holes in the walls. None of the windows had glass in them. And the front door was missing.

When a crow squawked again from the top of a giant hemlock, Arlo whipped around.

"It's following us," Maywood whispered.

"No," Arlo said. "It was here before we got here."

"How do you know?"

Arlo nodded. "I saw it in that hemlock."

"But that's worse." Maywood shivered. "That means it knew we were coming here. Maybe it understands what we're saying."

The wind stirred up dust from the bare dirt around the foundation. Arlo's nose twitched. He peered through the open doorway.

"We can't go in." Maywood squared her shoulders. "The whole thing could collapse any second."

"You mean we came all the way up here just to stand outside and look?"

Arlo tapped on the bottom step. It felt solid enough. Though Maywood put a hand out to stop him, Arlo couldn't ignore the irresistible pull to go inside.

Even afterward, he didn't fully understand what had happened. It was as if some force had lifted his foot and planted it on the step. That was followed by a splintering crunch as the wood gave way. Pain shot across the top of Arlo's foot.

As the pain subsided, he experienced the strangest sensation. It was as if a damp cloud moved over him. Or maybe *into* him, seeping through his pores. He felt cold all over. He was chilled everywhere, except for the space around the carved bird in his pocket, and that burned like fire.

"What happened?" Maywood asked. "Why did you do that?"

"I'm not . . . sure," Arlo said. He surveyed the damage. His foot was caught in a web of splintered wood that used to be the bottom step. Gingerly he worked it free.

"You're bleeding," she said.

"Nothing serious," Arlo said. "Just a scratch." The truth was, his foot was throbbing.

Meanwhile, wind whooshed up from the cellar, stirring up mildew and a foul odor that raised the hairs inside Arlo's nose.

"Phew. It smells like something dead in there," Maywood said.

It was a supremely unpleasant odor. They both coughed. Above them, the crow squawked like crazy.

"Let's get out of here!" Maywood yelled.

"What about the bet?"

"You win. OK?" Maywood started running toward the woods.

Arlo did his best to keep up with her, though the pain slowed him down. When they stopped, she examined the angry-looking scrape on his foot. A trickle of dried blood made it look worse than it was.

"Does it hurt?" she asked.

"Not much," Arlo said. "Maybe a little."

They kept running all the way past the brick office and down to the picnic tables at the bottom of the hill.

Arlo couldn't stop thinking about how unnatural the air around the house had felt—heavy and damp, as if there were something dead in it, something twisted and wrong. He could believe the house was haunted, the way those horrible smells seeped out of the ground around it and the way the air was thicker near the front door. Evil spirits seemed a distinct possibility.

They found an empty table and stretched out on their

backs. It was late afternoon — that slow time when light turns into a golden haze on the leaves.

"Mama Reel says the last Stonehams who lived in that house were bad people," Maywood said. "They owned slaves and treated them horribly. She says it has evil in it."

"Now you tell me," Arlo said, sneezing out dust.

Maywood reached in a pocket and handed him a rumpled tissue.

When Arlo sat up to blow his nose, he noticed Hafer and Boyle pedaling their bicycles up the hill.

He jabbed Maywood with his elbow.

She sat up quickly. "Yeah, and look who else is coming." She tilted her head in the direction of the black sedan making the turn up Cemetery Hill.

They waited until the car was out of sight.

"Come on," Maywood said. "Let's get out of here."

Arlo was silently grateful she did not want to follow them up the hill. The incident at the haunted house must have really upset her. It was kind of a relief to know there was something that scared her. Still, how strange that she loved reading about ghosts so much, but could not handle the real thing.

CHAPTER 32
Mama Reel Tells the Story

Mama Reel was sitting on the patio sipping a glass of iced tea while a citronella candle burned on the table.

"Been wondering if something happened to you," she said. "Bet you went in that old Stoneham place, didn't you?"

Funny how she used the word *bet*.

"How'd you know?" Maywood asked.

Mama Reel gave them a funny smile. "Old ladies know things sometimes," she said, tapping the side of her head.

"We didn't actually go inside. Arlo tried to, but . . ."

"My foot got stuck," Arlo finished for her.

"Is that right?" Mama Reel said. "You ought to know better than to go messing with evil spirits. Let's have a look at it."

"I'm OK," Arlo said.

Mama Reel pointed at an empty chair. "I'll be the judge of that," she said. "Come on over here."

Arlo sat in the chair. He held his foot up as she moved over to examine it.

"Mercy, you've had a tug-of-war with the spirits, haven't you? Whose bright idea was it to go up there, anyway?" She looked straight at Maywood. "As if I didn't know."

"We only stayed a second," Maywood said.

"Mmm-hmmm. Long enough for them to do their work, wasn't it?" She leaned closer and inspected the scratch on Arlo's ankle. "Doesn't look too bad. Still, you're lucky you made it out of there in one piece. Come on in the bathroom so I can clean it for you and put something on it."

"I'll just wait out here," Maywood said.

"Girl can't stand the sight of blood," Mama Reel whispered. She led Arlo to the bathroom. "You need to be careful what you let her talk you into. Maywood's headstrong. She doesn't stop to think."

"I noticed," Arlo said.

Mama Reel chuckled. "Smart boy," she said. "'Course, you had to learn the hard way, didn't you?"

Arlo shrugged. "Could be worse, I guess."

She propped his foot on the side of the tub and sat on the lid of the toilet seat. "Let me warm the water up before we wash it."

"Yes, ma'am."

"You know, having you here's been good for that girl. Maywood doesn't have many friends. There was a girl in her class named Cassie, but her family moved to Baltimore last fall. It's been hard on Maywood ever since."

"Some of the kids aren't very nice to her."

"You're talking about those two boys now, aren't you? Those two don't treat anybody right." Mama Reel spread ointment on Arlo's wound. "Sure wish you could stay. Seems a shame to send you back to Marshboro when you're just getting to know Ida after all these years."

"I'm not sure Ida would like that."

"Shoot, Arlo. You don't know anything, do you?" Mama Reel shook her head at him. "Keeping you here is what she wants more than anything. Maybe she hasn't told you that. May not realize it herself, poor soul. That woman's spent her life trying to smother feelings inside. It's what she had to do to survive life with your granddaddy. No offense, but he wasn't a nice man."

"That's what everybody says."

Mama Reel tossed the used cotton pad in the wastebasket. "Slocum made life hard on a lot of folks, especially your daddy."

"Is it true my dad gave up a scholarship to get married?"

Mama Reel grunted. "You don't pussyfoot around when you start asking questions, do you?"

Arlo shrugged.

Mama Reel focused on wringing out the wet washcloth. "Ida's the one who needs to answer that question."

"I know, but she won't talk about it."

"Don't I know that?" Mama Reel looked him dead in the eye.

"Poppo told me that he and Ida didn't get along on account of my mom and dad running off and getting married. But I didn't even know that until just before I came here. And now, everywhere I go, people keep asking me how come I don't know my grandmother." Arlo held his hand up in a sign of resignation. "It's not my fault. Nobody ever told me the truth."

"I know that, Arlo." She glanced at the ceiling, as if she were asking for help. "You put an old lady on the spot, don't you? If I answer your questions, do you promise not to tell Ida?"

"I promise," Arlo said.

"Then you better listen close, 'cause I'm only going to say this once." She stopped for a moment and took a slow, deliberate breath. "Hope I'm doing the right thing," she said.

"You are," Maywood said from the door behind them.

"Where did you come from?" Mama Reel asked.

"It was getting cold out there," Maywood said. "And I was lonely."

"Lordy, now I've got two mouths to worry about keeping quiet. You promise not to tell?" she asked Maywood.

"Yes, ma'am."

"All right. But we don't have to do this in the bathroom, do we?" Mama Reel stood up and made a shooing motion toward the door. "Go on out in the living room," she said.

Arlo and Maywood sat down first and waited for Mama Reel to pour herself another glass of tea before she joined them. Arlo felt so jumpy, it was hard to sit still.

"There's a few things you need to understand first. All right?"

"Yes, ma'am," Arlo said.

"Number one. Living with Slocum Jones was no picnic. For Ida or your daddy. You got that?"

"Got it," Maywood said.

"Was I talking to you?" Mama Reel asked.

"Sorry," Maywood said.

"That's all right," Mama Reel said. "Only go back to listening and don't talk."

"Yes, ma'am."

"Good."

Mama Reel turned to Arlo. "Number two. Your daddy was the only bright spot in Ida's life. She adored that boy. And it nearly killed her when he died. But that stone-hearted grandfather of yours expected her to go on taking care of him like nothing had ever happened. She did take care of him, too. Till the day he died. Lord only knows why. There wasn't an ounce of give in that man."

"Everybody talks about how unfriendly he was, but nobody ever says what he did."

"We're getting to that. Number three. Your granddaddy Slocum is the one who ran your daddy off. It wasn't your mother."

"How'd he do that?"

"Orneriness. Greed. Stupidity. He was filled up with all those things. Wanted your daddy to be just like him. But Wake was having none of that."

"What do you mean?"

"Mercy. You're not going to settle for less than the whole story, are you?"

Arlo smiled as he shook his head.

"OK. Here's the saga of Slocum Jones and S. W. J. Pressure-Treated Lumber Company."

Maywood chimed in. "I've heard about them. They're the ones who were poisoning the water."

"Did I ask for your help?" Mama Reel said.

Maywood pouted.

"Your granddaddy manufactured lumber for outdoor decks and the like. He started back before people knew about what the chemicals from that stuff did to the environment. Things changed, but that didn't slow him down. He kept on doing things the old way, even after the government told him he needed to change. They fined him. Even shut him down temporarily. But Slocum kept sneaking around the regulations."

"What's that got to do with my mom and dad getting married?"

"I'm getting to that. You see, Slocum wanted your daddy to take over the family business. But Wake wanted no part of that. He and Slocum hadn't gotten along for years. That's why Ida started sending him to camp."

Arlo thought about how Ida had reacted when she saw the wood carving. He took it out of his pocket and held it up for Mama Reel to see. "Does this have anything to do with it?"

"The eagle," she said.

"Can I see it?" Maywood asked.

When Arlo handed her the carving, Maywood held it carefully in her hand.

"That carving has everything to do with it," Mama Reel said. "Chemicals were killing eagles and osprey, not to mention the fish. Your daddy couldn't stand that. When he refused to go into the business, Slocum threw him out of the house. That didn't accomplish much, because your daddy was already going off to college. He'd managed to win a scholarship. But only for the first year. After that, he was on his own."

"Why does Ida say my mother made my dad drop out of school?"

Mama Reel gave Arlo a funny look. "When time came for Wake's second year of college, he had a family to support."

Arlo thought about the photos of himself as a baby with his parents. "You mean, they were already married?"

Mama Reel wrinkled up her face, as though she were trying to figure out how to deliver delicate news. "Sometimes the family's already on its way before the wedding comes along, if you know what I mean."

Arlo felt a hollowness spread inside. He looked from Mama Reel to Maywood, watching as Maywood's eyes grew rounder by the second.

"So, that's why Ida . . ."

Mama Reel interrupted Arlo before he could finish. "Your mama and daddy eloped a few weeks before you were born," she said. "Slocum was furious. Ida was heartbroken. She thought your daddy was too young to start a family." Mama Reel paused for a moment, gazing off toward the patio and then turning back to Arlo. "Ida needed someone to blame, Arlo, so she chose your mother."

"But my mom didn't do anything wrong."

"No, of course she didn't."

"Then, why . . . ?"

Mama Reel reached over and patted Arlo on the knee. "All either one of those people was ever guilty of was loving you too much." She shot a sideways glance at Maywood.

"Mothers can be hard on the girls their sons marry. Especially if they think their sons got married too young or were trapped in some way."

"Trapped?" Arlo asked.

"Never mind," Mama Reel said. "Ida's not the first woman to make life difficult for a daughter-in-law. Unfortunately, in the process, she made an enemy of your grandfather. Can't blame him really. She treated his daughter shabbily. And, before you know it, nobody was talking in your family. Then the accident happened and . . ."

"It was too late," Maywood finished.

"I'm afraid that's right." Mama Reel leaned back in her chair. "Not long after that, the government shut Slocum down for good. Darn near lost everything he had. Somehow he managed to hang on to the house. That and your daddy dying are what broke him finally. He died a couple of years later."

"That explains a lot," Arlo said.

"The truth's kind of difficult to hear sometimes," Mama Reel said.

Arlo thought about Bernice's cross-stitch again. He felt lighter already. All the terrible things he had imagined drifted out of his mind. The message in the cross-stitch was right. The truth could set you free.

CHAPTER 33
Steamboat to the Rescue

Lucius gave Arlo a ride home. Maywood came along for the ride.

"It looked like you and Mama Reel were settling all the problems of the world back there," Lucius said while the truck idled at the light.

"Only the important ones," Maywood said.

Arlo turned around in the front seat and looked at her. She gave him a sly smile.

When they reached the house, Ida was sitting on the granite bench in the front yard.

"What's she doing?" Maywood asked.

"I don't know. She told me she'd be in a meeting with Mr. Tretheway till dinnertime." Arlo scanned the yard. "Do you see Steamboat?"

"No," Lucius said.

He parked the car and the three of them hurried to the bench.

"I've done something stupid," Ida said, shaking her head as she looked from Maywood to Lucius to Arlo. Her cheeks were pink. "I was on my way outside to pick some mint. Just as I came through the door, the wind gusted and blew it shut. Now I'm locked out."

"That's not stupid," Lucius said. "That's just bad luck."

"The worst part is, I have a chicken in one oven and a pie in the other. They'll burn to a crisp if I don't get inside soon." She stared bleakly toward the window.

"I don't suppose you have a spare key hidden someplace?" Lucius asked.

"Not since the neighbors had a break-in," Ida said. "I decided it was better to risk being locked out than to be broken into."

"Any windows unlocked?" Lucius asked.

"No," Ida said. "I used to leave two of them open upstairs, but I quit doing that because —"

"Of the break-in," Maywood finished for her.

"That's right."

"That's too bad." Lucius stroked his beard. "Anybody have any other ideas?"

The wheels were turning in Arlo's head. Ida's lock didn't require a key to unlock it from inside. All you needed to do was push on the doorknob and turn it slightly to the left. If there was someone to bump against it . . .

"I could pick the lock if you have a coat hanger," Maywood offered.

Ida smiled. "I suppose we could borrow one from the neighbors."

"Wait a minute," Arlo said.

Everyone looked at him.

"Where's Steamboat?" he asked.

"Inside," Ida said.

"You don't have any food out here, do you?" Arlo asked.

Ida gave him a curious look. "You might find some apples in the orchard. . . ."

"I was thinking of something more like hamburger," Arlo said.

"Really, Arlo. I know you're a growing boy, but this is hardly the time. And besides, there's a lovely meal waiting for you inside if we can get to it soon enough."

"The food's not for me," Arlo said. Pictures of Steamboat jumping against the door on the day he first arrived were running through his mind.

Lucius tugged at his beard. He looked at Arlo. Then he looked at the door.

"We need something for Steamboat," Arlo said. "To make him jump against the doorknob."

A smile started spreading across Lucius's face. He moved his head slowly up and down. "That might work," he said.

Ida looked puzzled. "There's a freezer in the garage," she said, studying the two of them.

Arlo followed her across the lawn. She stopped in front of an old white Kelvinator freezer that took up half of the right-hand wall. "Nathan sent me some of those Omaha steaks for my birthday," she said. "I'm not much of a meat eater, so I stuck them in here. Would they work?"

Arlo opened the freezer. The first thing he pulled out was a plastic bag with something white inside.

"Not that, Arlo," Ida said.

"What is it?"

"My grandmother's tablecloth."

"You keep it in the freezer?"

"Only when I don't have time to iron it. It's still damp when you thaw it out. Best way to get rid of the wrinkles. Oh, never mind that. Let me have a look."

She lifted a metal basket and reached underneath. "Here you go." She held up a T-bone. "What do you think?"

"Perfect," Arlo said. He carried the steak back to the kitchen door, tapped on the glass, and called for Steamboat. "Come on, boy. Look what I've got."

Steamboat looked up at the glass. His tongue lolled out and he wagged his tail.

"Looks good, doesn't it?" Arlo said.

Steamboat barked. Then he sniffed around the bottom of the door.

"No, Steamboat. Don't sniff. Jump."

Maywood came up behind Arlo. "Come on," she said through the glass. "We need your help, boy."

Steamboat scooted back from the door. He sat down and gave Arlo a puzzled look. He tilted his head, as if he couldn't understand why Arlo didn't hurry up and open the door.

"This will never work," Maywood said.

"Give him a chance to figure it out," Ida said. "Steamboat's smart."

Time was running out. Arlo caught Ida checking her watch.

"Come on, Steamboat," Arlo pleaded.

On the other side of the door, Steamboat lifted his chin.

"Come on," Arlo said.

Steamboat hunkered down.

"That's it," Arlo said.

Then he jumped.

"Good boy!" Ida yelled.

"But he missed," Maywood said flatly.

"One more time, Steamboat. Please," Arlo said.

They gathered around the door. Arlo held his breath while Ida checked her watch.

"Come on, Steamboat," Ida prodded gently.

Steamboat looked straight at her. She gave him a smile and then a nod. "I know you can do it."

And Steamboat jumped again. And this time there was a lovely click as his paw made contact with the doorknob and an even more satisfactory bump and louder click as the lock released.

Arlo pushed the door open and rushed inside. Ida was right behind him. She went straight for the pot holders and pulled the pie out of the oven.

"A little browner than I'd like around the edges," she said, "but an extra scoop of ice cream should take care of that."

Maywood hugged Steamboat around the neck. "Smart dog," she said.

Arlo stroked Steamboat's head. "Thanks, Steamboat," he whispered.

Steamboat's tongue hung from his mouth. He panted as if the excitement of opening the door had worn him out. Then he sat down in front of Arlo and held up his right paw.

"You want to shake hands?" Arlo took Steamboat's paw and gave it a good shake. "You deserve more than a handshake for that."

"There'll be a special treat this evening," Ida said.

"That's some dog," Lucius said.

"He's a genius." Ida rubbed his ears. "Aren't you, Steamboat?"

Steamboat wagged his tail. He trotted from Arlo to Ida to Maywood to Lucius, accepting head rubs. Then he walked back over to Ida and sat up and begged.

"A biscuit for now," she said, plunging her hand into the cardboard box of dog treats. "And something special for dinner."

CHAPTER 34
Secret Plans

Later that evening, as Ida and Arlo sat around the kitchen counter eating ice cream and pie, Ida asked Arlo about his afternoon.

"Aurelia said you were gone a long time. Where did Maywood take you?"

"Nowhere much."

Ida rolled her eyes. "Just like your father, aren't you?"

Arlo looked up from his apple pie. "What do you mean?" he said.

"I used to ask Wake what he and Matthew had been up to, and all he would say was, *Oh, nothing much. The usual.*"

"Oh." Disappointment spread through Arlo's body. He had hoped for something more, a real story about his father like the ones that Matthew told. He took another spoonful of ice cream, allowing it to melt slowly on his tongue.

"We explored the old cemetery," he said finally when she failed to offer any more information about his father.

"Maywood and her ghosts," Ida said. "That girl has an imagination, doesn't she? Don't let her get you into trouble."

"I'll be careful," Arlo said, smiling to himself. *Too late now,* he thought, staring at the Band-Aid on his ankle.

Almost as if she could hear his thoughts, Ida fired a question at him. "She didn't take you in that old house, did she?"

Arlo choked on a piece of apple. "We just looked at it from the outside," he said. "Maywood told me it was too dangerous to go inside."

"The old Stoneham place makes me nervous," Ida said. "The county ought to board it up. Or better yet—tear the whole thing down." She took another nibble of pie.

"How was your meeting with Mr. Tretheway?" Arlo asked, anxious to change the subject.

"Fine," she said. "Better than I'd hoped, really. We made good progress." She looked at him oddly. "We accomplished so much . . . Well, I was thinking we might go see your grandfather tomorrow . . . if the doctor says it's all right, of course. How would you feel about that?"

Arlo froze with the spoon poised halfway to his mouth. If she'd said they were boarding a rocket ship for Mars at sunrise, he couldn't have been more surprised.

"Really?" he said.

"I think it's time, don't you?"

"Yes." Arlo's mind raced. He conjured images of Poppo in his room. He imagined a trip back to the house to retrieve some of his things—his favorite T-shirts, jeans, video games, and, *yes,* the family album. He could see Sam and find out what they were saying about him in school.

"Is the house . . . livable?" Ida asked. "Because if it is, we could stay there. It's only for one night."

The idea of Ida seeing the way he and Poppo used to live made Arlo squirm.

"It's not as neat as your house," he said. "I mean, Poppo doesn't . . . you know."

Ida smiled. "Are you trying to tell me that Albert's not a housekeeper?"

Arlo blushed. "It's just that you might not be too comfortable."

"I appreciate your concern." Ida placed her spoon sideways on her dessert plate and blotted the sides of her mouth with her napkin. "Maybe it would be best to figure things out after we get there. What do you say?"

"That sounds good," Arlo said. He finished the rest of his pie and ice cream. As they were carrying dishes to the sink, he had another thought. Why had she decided to go now?

Why tomorrow morning, instead of yesterday or two days from now? OK, she said it was because she and Mr. Tretheway had made good progress. But what did that mean? What *kind* of progress had they made? Who had they talked to?

Wait a minute. What if going to Marshboro wasn't really about seeing Poppo at all? What if it was about something entirely different—something like where Arlo was supposed to stay?

"You didn't talk to anyone else, did you?" Arlo asked.

"A few people," Ida said, smiling her tight little smile that sent chills down Arlo's spine.

He should have known something was up. He remembered

that nurse at the hospital talking to Ida the day he first arrived. He remembered the look on Ida's face as she answered the nurse's questions. *I'm not sure about that,* she'd said. *How soon would you need to know?* Her face had gone white first, and then pink, and finally, bright crimson.

She must have had plans all along to turn him over to the authorities. Wasn't it obvious? No wonder she was so happy. One more day and she'd have Arlo off her hands.

"Do you mind if Augusta comes with us?" Ida asked.

Arlo looked at her. His mind was spinning. Would she really abandon him right when he needed her most?

"She offered to help with the driving."

"What? Mrs. Stonestreet? Oh, sure. That's OK with me." What difference did it make who went with them? If you were going to the guillotine, did it matter how many people climbed the steps to the platform with you?

"Fine. First we'll go to the hospital. We'll have a nice visit with Albert and then help him with the move."

"Move?" Arlo asked.   .

"Yes. Didn't I tell you?" Ida said. "They're releasing him to a convalescent facility."

Releasing him? Geez, she made it sound like he was getting out of prison. "I didn't know."

"Yes. Dr. Simon says they've done all they can for him in the hospital. He thinks it would be helpful if we were there to help Albert get settled in a new place."

"But won't he miss Eldon?"

"We talked about that, too," Ida said. "It seems that Eldon is being discharged at the same time. And the residential facility where Albert is going is actually part of the complex where Eldon is moving. They'll be within walking distance of each other."

That was good news. At least Poppo would have a friend, even if things didn't work out so well for Arlo.

"I'm glad for that," Arlo said.

"Yes. It's perfect, really, isn't it?" Ida said. "So, what we'll do is, we'll help him get settled in the new place tomorrow. Then you and I have an appointment at the hospital."

"An appointment?"

"It's at four o'clock."

Arlo's heart dropped even further in his chest. She had had it planned all along, hadn't she? "Who do we have to see at the hospital?"

"Don't worry. It's just a formality," Ida said. "They told me it will only take a few minutes."

To think he'd actually allowed himself to believe she wanted him. To think he could have been so foolish.

He'd allowed his imagination to go crazy, conjuring up all kinds of things—waking up in his father's old room and coming downstairs to find Ida sipping hot tea at the kitchen counter. Fixing hot chocolate for him. Fat chance of that. Arlo should have known better than to believe in fairy-tale endings. Life didn't happen that way. In real life, orphans didn't find a new home with a long-lost grandmother who was dying to take care of him.

He needed to stay calm and think clearly. He needed to stay in control of his life. If getting to Edgewater had been a challenge, imagine how hard escaping foster care would be when the person he had depended on for help turned out to be the person he needed to get away from. A measly mud-and-stick dam wasn't much protection.

It was time for a new plan. He needed the basics. Food and shelter. But he couldn't manage that on his own. He needed help.

And who did he have?

Maywood.

And, maybe, Sam.

Arlo racked his brain all afternoon and into the evening. And then, finally, the answer came to him.

"Arlo?"

"Hi, Sam."

"Where are you?"

"Edgewater."

"You made it?"

"Yeah."

"Are you all right?"

"I'm OK."

"What's going on? Did you find your grandmother? It's been two weeks."

"I know. Sorry. I was going to call sooner, but it's been kind of crazy here. And I don't have a cell phone."

"What's she like?"

"Who? My grandmother? She's uh . . . hard to describe, you know?" *Hint, hint.*

"Oh, yeah. I get it. You think she's listening."

"Exactly." Arlo wasn't sure how much Ida could hear from

the bathroom, but he knew he could hear every word she said on the phone from his father's room.

"Gotcha."

"She said I could call you because we're coming to Marshboro tomorrow."

"Seriously?"

You have no idea how serious I am, Arlo thought. "We have to get together, OK?"

"Yeah. Definitely."

Then Arlo lowered his voice to a whisper. "I need your help," he said.

"What's wrong?"

"Remember that story you told me?"

"Which one?"

"About the rat."

"Yeah?"

"Is it true?"

"Yeah. But what's that got to do with you? You're not going to a foster home, are you?"

"That's right. . . . I mean, I'm not sure. Maybe."

"Oh, geez."

"I know."

"What do you want me to do?"

"Meet me at the hospital."

"When?"

"Four o'clock."

"OK. But where in the hospital? It's a big place."

"The machines in the snack bar in the basement," Arlo whispered. "Do you know where they are?"

"Yeah. I think so. We went there when Aunt Betty's friend was sick."

Arlo whipped around quickly when he thought he heard someone on the stairs, but it turned out to be a shutter creaking in the wind.

"I better go now. See you tomorrow. OK?"

"I'll be there," Sam said.

For a moment after he'd hung up, Arlo sat there, working through each step of his plan. It was all coming together now. He still didn't know how long he could last once he'd escaped, but at least he'd figured out a way to stay out of Miss Hasslebarger's clutches for a while. He went over the plan in his head.

1. Arrive at Marshboro General.
2. Go see Poppo and help him move to convalescent home.
3. Go back to hospital for meeting.
4. Ask to go to snack bar for food on the way to meeting.
5. Meet Sam.
6. Escape.
7. Go with Sam to house.
8. Collect clothes and photographs.
9. Go to Sam's house for food.
10. Hide out in empty apartment over Sam's garage.

The idea of hiding in Aunt Betty's apartment had come to him when he'd been lying in bed, trying to figure out where he could go. *Where was a place that was close enough to Sam, but where nobody would think to look for a missing boy?* He'd started thinking about places where he and Sam had hidden when they'd known they were in trouble. He remembered the time they'd broken the knob off the banister in Sam's great-aunt's house. Sam had taken him to the garage apartment and told him they should stay there until Aunt Betty cooled down.

"She never comes up here," Sam said. "We'll be safe."

It was the perfect hideout.

CHAPTER 35
Bad News/Good News

Poppo wasn't doing so well when they called the hospital before dinner.

"Did I tell you about Eldon?" Poppo asked. "He used to be friends with Frankie."

Arlo's heart skipped. "I think you mentioned him a couple of times."

"I taught Eldon how to do layups. Now he turns up here in the hospital. Right down the hall."

"I think you told me that the last time we talked."

"Did I? Sometimes my memory gets confused."

"That's OK."

"Is somebody there with you?" Poppo asked. "I hear something moving."

"That's just Steamboat trying to jump in my lap."

"Who's Steamboat?"

"Ida's dog."

Poppo chuffed out a sigh. "A dog, huh? Just like you always wanted. I should've gotten you one."

"That's OK." Arlo's heart bumped against his ribs. The last thing he wanted was to make Poppo feel bad.

"Are you still coming to see me?"

"We're leaving first thing in the morning," Arlo said.

"When will you be here?"

"After lunch."

"That's good. I haven't seen you for a long time."

"Two weeks," Arlo said.

"Is that how long it's been?"

Arlo's throat tightened. Poppo would probably have forgotten their conversation before Ida and Arlo finished eating dinner.

Poppo coughed. He was getting tired. Their conversations rarely lasted more than a few minutes these days.

"Maybe you should put that other lady on the phone," he said.

"You mean Ida?"

"Is that her name?"

Arlo swallowed a moan. "I'll get her for you now," he said.

"Thanks, buddy."

"You're welcome. Love you, Poppo."

"I love you, too."

Arlo sat on the prickly sofa and listened to Ida's side of the conversation. All she said was *Yes* and *No* and *I'm not sure.* Finally, she told Poppo she was glad to hear him sounding so good and to be sure to tell his friend Eldon that she and Arlo were looking forward to meeting him.

"Is Steamboat coming with us?" Arlo asked after Ida hung up the phone.

"I wish he could, but we won't have anywhere to leave him while we're visiting with Albert in his room."

"I didn't think about that," Arlo said.

"Neither did I until Augusta pointed it out," Ida said.

Steamboat jumped in Ida's lap and starting licking her cheek.

"Sorry, boy. You know we'd take you if we could," she said.

Arlo reached over and scratched Steamboat behind his ears. "I don't guess we could leave him in the car, could we?"

Ida rolled her eyes. "I'm not trying that again," she said.

"I guess not," Arlo agreed. "So where will he stay?"

"With Maywood. Matthew and Lucius will keep an eye on him while she's in school."

"That won't be so bad." Arlo ruffled Steamboat's ears. "I'll miss you," he said.

Steamboat barked and licked Arlo's cheek.

"He'll miss you, too," Ida said.

A damp chill crept up Arlo's spine. How could she smile when she knew perfectly well Arlo was never going see Steamboat again?

Ida looked at him over Steamboat's head. "I know we should have done this sooner," she said. "I'm sorry, Arlo. All this business about the house has had me in a tizzy."

"That's OK," Arlo said, keeping his eyes on the floor. He couldn't look at her. Two days ago, it would have meant so much to him to hear her apologize for not taking him to see

Poppo sooner. But this trip wasn't really about visiting Poppo, was it?

"We'll leave right after breakfast. How does that sound?"

"Fine," Arlo said. His voice was flat.

"Is something wrong?"

"No. Everything's fine."

She studied his face for a moment until she seemed satisfied that everything was all right. Then she gave a nod.

"Good," she said. "It's settled, then."

The next morning, they had the car loaded and ready to go before seven. Ida packed a bag with Steamboat's dog food and treats, as well as his favorite blanket. They dropped him off at Frog Creek first. Then they swung around the corner and down the street to Augusta's house.

She was waiting for them on her front porch, sitting in her rocking chair with a suitcase and an ancient-looking thermos, which she informed them was filled with hot coffee.

"Right on time," she said as they climbed the porch steps.

Arlo picked up her suitcase and carried it to the trunk of Ida's car.

Ida drove the first two hours. Then Augusta took the wheel and drove until they stopped in Lewisburg for lunch. Arlo's stomach rolled the whole time. What if his plan didn't work? What if Sam wasn't waiting for him at the hospital?

"You're awfully quiet," Ida said over the back of the seat.

"Just tired, I guess." Arlo faked being asleep the rest of the way, hoping they might talk in the front seat and he might overhear some interesting tidbit that would disclose details of her plan for getting rid of him. A single fact might go a long way in helping him fine-tune his escape.

Unfortunately, all they talked about was how much better Matthew's apple cobbler was than the cobbler they served at the Watermen's Café and how somebody ought to make the highway department pave the eastbound lane on the bridge across the river.

The nurse at Marshboro General had Poppo dressed and ready to go when they arrived. His color was better than the last time Arlo had seen him.

"Hi, Arlo," Poppo said, opening his arms. "I've missed you."

"I missed you, too." Arlo's chest was tight. Poppo called him Arlo. He didn't say Frankie. And his hair wasn't sticking up in back. And he didn't have that strange lost glaze in his eyes. When Poppo hugged him, Arlo held on for a long time. Some days it seemed like Poppo was getting better, and other days he didn't seem any better at all.

"It's OK, buddy. I'm not going anywhere," Poppo said. "Other than to my new digs. And you're coming along to help me get settled, right?" Poppo tilted his head so he could see Arlo's face. "You look good," he said. "Ida must be taking great care of you."

Arlo forced his head to move up and down. He didn't want Poppo worrying about him.

"Arlo talks about you every day," Ida said. "He wanted to come sooner, but I had some business I needed to take care of."

Poppo hugged Arlo again. "I'm glad you found this lady," he said, nodding at Ida. "Us fellas were in need of a little assistance, don't you think?"

Arlo nodded again, holding down the tide of feelings that welled up, making it hard to breathe.

"Sorry I let you down." Poppo let his arm slip off Arlo's shoulder.

"You didn't let me down," Arlo said. "You were sick."

"I know, but I should've thought of what might happen." He picked up the plastic cup on his bed tray and took a long sip. "It's just that I never . . ." Poppo's voice trailed off. He exchanged glances with Ida.

"Augusta's waiting for us downstairs," Ida said, using her tight smile again, as if that would smooth over the jagged edges of their conversation. "The nurse told us you'd be leaving in a few minutes, so she decided to wait in the car."

"Is Augusta another relative?" Poppo asked.

"No, Albert. Just a friend. She helped me with the driving."

"Like my friend Eldon," Poppo said, smiling again. "He'll be at the new place. You can meet him."

"I know. That's nice, isn't it?" Ida said. "You'll have a friend as soon as you get there."

Poppo's face brightened. "Eldon says it's a good place."

A nurse appeared at the door with a wheelchair. There was an orderly behind her. Together, they helped Poppo into the chair. Then the orderly handed Poppo his overnight bag, and Ida and Arlo gathered up the bags with Poppo's other things. The orderly pushed the wheelchair down the hall to the elevator.

When the bell dinged and the doors opened, Arlo waited while the orderly wheeled Poppo on board. Then he stepped inside and stood beside his grandfather.

Poppo jabbed Arlo with his elbow. "Here we go," he said.

Arlo smiled back at him. "Here we go," he answered. There was a small jab at his heart as the doors closed and the elevator started moving.

CHAPTER 36
Meeting Eldon

After they'd gotten Poppo settled in his room, after Arlo had carried his Dopp kit to the bathroom and tested out the reclining chair and shared the view out the window with Ida and Augusta and Poppo, the four of them met Eldon in the cafeteria for ice cream.

Eldon was a tall man with a gaunt face and a maze of lines at the corners of his eyes. He looked frightening at first. But then he smiled and all those lines turned into tiny smiles that showed how happy he was to meet Poppo's family.

"So, you're the famous Arlo I've been hearing about," he said.

"He's the one," Poppo said, giving Arlo a wink.

Arlo felt a slight tug as he thought about Eldon filling the spot that Arlo used to occupy. He was glad that Poppo had found a friend. Of course he was. But it was hard sharing the person you loved with a stranger, especially when you weren't sure if you would ever see that person again.

"It's been a long day," Ida said when the orderly came to see if Poppo needed anything. "We should give Albert a chance to rest."

"You leaving already?" Poppo asked.

"We'll be back after dinner," Arlo told him. His stomach churned at the lie. He wasn't coming back after dinner. He was going to the hospital all right, but after he got there, he was going to disappear.

"I'll be waiting," Poppo said.

Water surged against Arlo's dam, ripping away mud and twigs, sweeping over the top, then sliding back and pulling particles of dirt with it. What he was about to say to Poppo—the words forming in his mouth constituted the worst lie Arlo had ever told in his life. Three simple words.

"See you later."

"OK. After dinner," Poppo said. "Right?"

"That's right," Ida said.

Arlo's heart pounded. Did it count as a lie when you pretended something was true even though it wasn't?

Of course it did.

And here was the truth.

At the hospital, Arlo would ask Ida if he could go downstairs to the vending machines, and when he found Sam, the two of them would sneak outside, and that's the last anyone would see of Arlo for a very long time.

"Give me a hug before you go." Poppo held out his arms.

Arlo felt like something was dying inside. He quit trying to hold back the flood. He let it come. He let water pour and spill and ravage and consume.

"What's this?" Poppo asked. "It's all right. You'll be back after a while. And look at me. I'm fine. Doing better than the last time you saw me, in fact. Don't you think so?"

Arlo nodded dumbly. He couldn't speak. Speaking would only confirm the lie. And he couldn't do that, couldn't take it any further. He'd already gone further than he could stand. He hugged Poppo, whispered "I love you," and turned to go.

Walking out of Poppo's room was the hardest thing Arlo had ever done. Two weeks ago, he would have said that running away from Marshboro was the hardest, but this was ten times worse.

Arlo willed his feet to carry him down the hall. He felt like the walls were closing in on him. His heart beat wildly, blurring his vision.

And then, somehow, they were in the car and on the way back to the hospital.

"Is it OK if I get a bottle of water from the machines in the basement?" Arlo asked, struggling to make his voice sound as normal as possible.

"Do you need money?" Ida asked.

"No, thanks," Arlo said. "I have enough."

"Here you go." Ida handed him two dollar bills and a handful of quarters. "I'd like a bottle of water, too, please. If you don't mind. That ought to be enough."

"Thanks," Arlo said.

"We should go on up," Augusta said, pointing to the clock.

"Right," Ida said. "Well, Arlo knows how to find Miss Hasslebarger's office, don't you?"

Arlo nodded.

"Good. Augusta and I will meet you there."

As soon as their backs were turned, Arlo ducked down the stairs to the basement, where the machines were located. He found Sam waiting just as they'd planned.

"Are you OK?" Sam asked.

Arlo nodded.

"You had me worried after that phone call. I was afraid your grandmother was keeping you locked in a closet or something."

"No. She's nice. Well, she was nice. For a while. I mean, she wasn't nice at first, but then she was. And now . . ."

Sam frowned. "You're not making sense."

"Yeah. I know. I don't really understand, either. At first I thought she hated me. But then everybody told me that was just the way she was. Kind of touchy about things, you know? Because she lived alone such a long time—that's what they said. Then after a while, she started acting friendlier. She even told me she wasn't going to move to Richmond after all."

"Whoa, Arlo. You lost me again."

"Sorry."

"What's moving to Richmond got to do with anything?"

"I found out she was going to sell her house and move to Richmond. Everybody in Edgewater told her she shouldn't. Then Mr. Tretheway tried to help her cancel the contract. Things were going real well . . ." Arlo looked down at his feet. "Until she told me we were coming here."

"How do you know she's turning you over to the social worker?"

"Why else would I have to go to this meeting?"

Sam held up his arms in a sign of surrender. "I don't know. Maybe they just need to make sure you're OK. Maybe they want to see the two of you together. You know, just to make sure it's really OK for you to stay with her."

Arlo studied his reflection in the glass on the snack machine. Could the reason for the meeting be as simple as that?

"Did you see your grandpa?" Sam asked.

"Yeah."

"How's he doing?"

"Better."

"Well, that's something, then," Sam said.

"Yeah," Arlo said. "It is."

Footsteps came tapping down the hallway. Someone was headed toward the machines. And they were moving fast.

"We should hurry," Arlo said.

Sam nodded, but before they'd had a chance to move, a shadow fell across the linoleum. Arlo glanced in the glass of the machine again. This time he noticed the profile of someone rounding the corner. A familiar profile. *No.* It couldn't be. She was supposed to be in the meeting.

"Arlo?"

Arlo's stomach dropped. *Busted.*

"Is this a friend of yours?"

"Hi." Sam held up a hand.

"This is Sam," Arlo said.

"Nice to meet you, Sam. I'm Arlo's grandmother."

"Yes, ma'am. You're Mrs. Jones. It's nice to meet you."

"How odd that you ran into each other here." Ida narrowed her eyes at Arlo.

"I was just getting water for us," Arlo said, holding up the quarters she had given him.

"Mmm-hmmm." Ida looked at Sam. "And you," she said. "Were you getting water, too?"

"Well, not exactly. I was just . . ."

"Visiting a relative in the hospital?"

"No, ma'am. I . . ."

Her eyes sharpened. "Meeting Arlo, I suppose."

Sam gave Arlo a panicked look.

"You two didn't just happen to run into each other, did you?"

"Sort of," Arlo started, but then stopped. "No," he said after a pause. He wished he knew how to keep his face from turning red.

Ida looked at him for a long time. Her face was hard at first, but then something changed. She stared at the quarters in Arlo's hand, but he could tell she was thinking about something else. Something far away from the machines and the hospital.

Arlo locked eyes with her. She didn't look as angry anymore.

"You were going to get me a bottle of water, weren't you?"

"Yes," Arlo said.

She nodded at him. "Well, go on. We're here, aren't we?"

Arlo fed a dollar bill and two quarters into the machine. He punched a button for a bottle of water, waited for it to drop, and then handed it to her.

"Now one for you," she said.

Arlo's hand felt shaky as he fed the other bill and quarters into the machine and pushed the same button a second time. What was she planning?

"Sam?" Ida said. "Would you like a bottle of water?"

"No, ma'am," Sam said. "Thank you." He looked like he wished he could push a button and disappear.

If they made a run for it, Ida wouldn't be able to stop them. But somehow that was unthinkable, even if she was about to turn him over. Arlo couldn't run out on her now. Not without a conversation. He eyed the hallway.

"You know," his grandmother said, "Augusta and I would be happy for Sam to join us for dinner. In fact, I should have thought of asking if you'd like to invite one of your friends."

Arlo glanced sideways at Sam, whose eyes were growing rounder by the minute.

"Unless you had something else planned?" She looked from Arlo to Sam and back again.

Arlo's toes itched the same way they had when he was on the bus with Bernice. He rubbed the top of his right foot against his ankle. He didn't want to make up stories anymore. Why was needing a home and someone to take care of him so much to ask?

"We've been getting along so well. And Nathan has things worked out. All we need to do is have this one short meeting."

At the mention of the word *meeting,* Sam looked straight at Arlo. The carving thrummed in Arlo's pocket. Arlo felt

Ida staring at him. She pressed her lips together slowly as she looked from one boy to the other.

"So, that's it," she said. "It's the meeting you're worried about."

Arlo shrugged.

"It's just a formality. We need to go over a few things. Not like when you met with her before. Not like . . ." She stopped again. She started blinking.

Arlo saw the wheels turning in her head.

"You *did* understand this is only to confirm that you're staying with me . . . didn't you? You didn't think . . . Surely you couldn't believe that I would . . ."

Now Arlo was blinking. Salt burned his eyes.

"Oh, Arlo." Her cheeks went from pink to pale white. She moved forward and put her arms around him. "The meeting with Miss Hasslebarger is only a formality. Nathan's arranged everything. You're coming home with me."

Arlo felt his shoulders giving. His pulse throbbed behind his ears.

"It's all right," she said. "I promise. You're coming home with me."

The way Sam looked, you would have thought he was the one being rescued instead of Arlo. Arlo hated crying in front of his friend, but some things couldn't be helped.

"I should have told you sooner," Ida said, "but I needed to be sure everything would work out. I couldn't stand to disappoint you. Not after what you've been through already. It wouldn't be fair."

"It's OK," Arlo said. He hiccupped and brushed the dampness from his cheeks at the same time.

"We may need to make another trip, but you'll want to come see Albert anyway, won't you?"

"Yes."

She hugged him again. "And Sam will have to come visit us."

"I'd like that," Sam said. He looked from Ida to Arlo and back at Ida again. "So everything's OK?" he asked.

Arlo shot him a thumbs-up. "Everything's good," he said.

"Did you mean what you said about coming to dinner?" Sam asked.

"I certainly did," Ida said. "You don't mind sharing a meal with two old ladies, do you?"

"No, ma'am," Sam said.

He rode up with them on the elevator and waited with Augusta in the lounge while Arlo followed his grandmother to Miss Hasslebarger's office.

The meeting lasted twelve minutes.

"Didn't I tell you things would work out?" Miss Hasslebarger said to Arlo as he and Ida were leaving. "You know, you had us worried sick, disappearing the way you did. But now that we know you're safe, I'll admit, it was pretty resourceful what you did. Don't tell anybody I said that. I'm glad you found your grandmother, Arlo. That's what we were all hoping for, isn't it?"

Arlo kept smiling. He didn't open his mouth. When in

doubt, don't stir the soup. That was another one of Poppo's sayings.

"What do you say, Arlo? I think it's time we had some dinner, and then you can take me to see your house." Ida moved toward the door.

Arlo was only too happy to follow. He didn't even care how bad the house looked. Not anymore.

They found Augusta and Sam waiting in the lounge. Augusta had bought Sam a book of crossword puzzles in the gift shop and they were working on them together.

"What's another word for rodent?" Augusta asked.

"Rat," Sam said. He shot a look at Arlo.

Arlo stifled a laugh.

"Ready to go?" Ida asked.

"Anytime," Arlo said.

CHAPTER 37
Home?

They ate dinner at Capellini's. Arlo had spaghetti with mushroom sauce, and Sam ordered lasagna. The garlic toast was Arlo's favorite part of the meal.

Afterward, they went back to visit Poppo.

"Told you I'd see you again soon," Poppo said.

Arlo hugged his grandfather. "You were right, Poppo."

It was hard saying good-bye when they dropped off Sam at his house, but Ida reminded him they would see each other again in a few weeks.

"We'll be back at Thanksgiving," she said. "And Sam's going to visit us too."

When Ida pulled into the driveway, the old house looked smaller than Arlo remembered. The kitchen was just a plain white room with chipped linoleum and fading wallpaper. Nothing more.

Ida and Augusta moved from room to room, keeping poker faces and exchanging whispers.

"Perhaps you'd like to get some things out of your room?" Ida suggested when they reached the top of the stairs.

Arlo was glad Sam wasn't with him. He preferred going through his things on his own. It didn't take long. Arlo knew what he wanted:

four T-shirts (from the 5k and 10k races
    he had run with Sam)
two pairs of jeans
video games
river shoes (in case someone in Edgewater
    wanted to take him out on the river)

Arlo put all those things in the tote bag Augusta had loaned him. Then he added the two Harry Potter books Poppo had given him when Arlo was in fourth grade. Standing in the doorway and surveying the small pile in the bag, Arlo had a sinking feeling that he was letting the house down. First Poppo had left it. And now he was leaving it, too.

He took one last look, letting his eyes sweep the walls, getting it all down in his mind so he could call it up when he needed to remember. There was the poster from the Carnegie Museum and the map of the planets that Arlo used to stare at before he went to sleep. Part of him hated leaving, but another part was more than ready to say good-bye. In a way, the house had already let go of them. It was ready for a fresh start, just the way Arlo was. And the way Poppo was, too.

"Are you ready?" Ida asked.

Arlo nodded.

Augusta was checking windows on the first floor, making sure they were tightly closed so the rain couldn't come in. Arlo heard her whisper to Ida as he carried his bag to the car.

"What will happen to this place?" she asked.

"Not now, Augusta. There are procedures to follow. One step at a time, don't you think?"

"I suppose you're right, dear."

On his way back inside, Arlo detoured into the living room. He slid the family album out of the cabinet and opened to the page with the picture of his parents standing in the orchard in Edgewater. He felt Ida standing behind him.

"I'd forgotten Albert had a copy of that picture," she said.

"It was taken at your house, wasn't it?" Arlo asked.

"In the orchard, I believe. Yes. Do you think Albert would mind if you brought it with you?"

As far as Arlo knew, Poppo never looked at the album. Seeing pictures of Arlo's mother made him too sad.

"I don't think he'd mind." Arlo slipped the photo out of the paper corners that held it to the page.

"Probably shouldn't leave that album in an empty house," Augusta said. She exchanged glances with Ida.

"You're right," Ida said. "I suppose Albert will be collecting more of his things later on. But in the meantime, it would be a shame to let something happen to those photographs."

Arlo closed the album when he sensed Augusta creeping up beside Ida.

"Maybe we could take a few pictures for ourselves and leave the rest for Poppo?" he said.

Ida placed her hand on Arlo's shoulder. "Good idea," she said. "We'll take them to Albert in the morning."

They stayed in adjoining rooms in the motel. Augusta and Ida shared one room. Arlo had the other. For the first time in as many days as Arlo could remember, he was happy to turn out the light and let his head sink into the pillow.

He slept soundly until Ida's knock on the door between their rooms awakened him in the morning.

Poppo and Eldon were watching TV in Poppo's room.

"We brought you this," Arlo said, handing Poppo the album.

Poppo seemed reluctant to take it at first. "It's been a long time since I looked at this," he said, setting the album carefully in his lap.

"I was wondering," Arlo said, running his hand up and down the back of Poppo's chair as Poppo opened to the first page. "Do you think it would be OK if I took a few of the pictures with me? I mean, I don't have to, but . . ."

Poppo reached over and held Arlo's hand. "You're the person I've been saving them for," he said.

He paged through the pictures, lingering over photos of Arlo's mother. A small muscle twitched in Poppo's cheek as he turned each page. Arlo scooted his chair closer so they could look at the pictures together. Poppo paused at the blank spaces where photos had been removed.

"I can put them back if you want," Arlo said.

Poppo shook his head. He tapped the space where the photo of Arlo's parents standing under the apple tree had been. "You've made good choices," he said.

"Are you sure?" Ida asked.

Poppo looked across the room at her. "Positive," he said.

Meanwhile, Augusta was tapping her foot as she stared at the clock. "It's a six-hour drive," she reminded them. "We should be going."

"I'm afraid Augusta's right," Ida said to Poppo.

With a sad nod, Poppo closed the album. He handed it to Eldon, who placed it on the table beside the bed. "You don't want to be out on the highway late at night," Poppo said.

"Give us a call when you get home," Eldon said, standing as they moved toward the door.

Arlo looked back at Poppo. He put down his bag and ran to Poppo's chair.

Poppo returned Arlo's hug. "Don't worry," he said. "You'll be back. And I'm going to be right here."

Arlo's eyes brimmed.

"To tell you the truth," Poppo whispered, "I think I'll get along a lot better with Eldon than I would with those two ladies." He winked at Arlo.

Arlo was quiet in the backseat for the first twenty miles. Augusta drove, and Ida kept her company in the front seat.

They went down the mountain at Sandstone and then crossed the state line just beyond White Sulphur Springs. Somewhere around Staunton, Arlo fell asleep. He slept the rest of the way, dreaming of Mr. Fanucci taking packs of doughnuts out of Poppo's hands. It was a relief to wake up in Ida's driveway.

All these months Arlo had worried day and night about how to keep Poppo from setting the house on fire or getting lost or being arrested for shoplifting food in Fanucci's Market. And now it was over. Arlo had his life back. He hated to admit this, but the truth was, he felt a huge sense of relief. As long as Poppo was happy where he was, then Arlo could feel all right about staying in Edgewater with Ida and Steamboat.

CHAPTER 38
A Setback

The next two days were nearly perfect. Arlo made a list of the people (plus one dog) he was grateful for:

1. Bernice and Tyrone (for bringing him to Edgewater)
2. Eldon (for being a good friend to Poppo)
3. Sam (for always being there when he needed a friend)
4. Steamboat (for making Arlo and Ida laugh)
5. Ida (for taking good care of him)
6. Maywood (for making life interesting)
7. Matthew (for telling stories about his father)
8. Mama Reel (for telling him the truth)

Arlo no longer had to worry about being a runaway. He was where he belonged. *Only a few formalities left to take care of,* Mr. Tretheway had told Ida.

•   •   •

Just when everything seemed perfect, at that moment when Arlo stopped worrying, Mr. Tretheway appeared at Ida's door with news that made the walls of Arlo's dam begin to quiver all over again.

"But I don't understand," Ida kept saying. "You told me there'd be no problem canceling the contract."

"And that's what I thought, too," Mr. Tretheway said, "until I received this letter from the developer's attorney."

Mr. Tretheway extracted a long envelope from his brief-case and set it on the counter. The word CERTIFIED was stamped above the address in bold black letters.

"What does it say?" Ida asked. "And please skip all the legal gobbledygook and just tell me the part that matters."

Mr. Tretheway adjusted his glasses. "The long and short of it is, someone's tipped off the developer that a man from Richmond is interested in your house. In their eyes, you have a potential willing buyer. You agreed to make a good-faith effort to sell. If you don't at least show the house to that person, the developer can say you're not holding up your end of the bargain."

"But how would they know I'm not showing my house?" Ida's eyes blazed.

"People find out things when they want a deal to work," Mr. Tretheway said. "Real estate's a tough business, Ida. People play dirty sometimes."

Ida sank into a chair. "I'll bet it was that Mr. Garringer," she said.

"It's possible." Mr. Tretheway took off his glasses. "The man threw a fit when you refused to show him the house."

"What's the worst that could happen, Nathan?"

Mr. Tretheway pushed his thumbs against each other like poles holding up a tent. "You forfeit your deposit," he said.

Ida gasped. "That's ten thousand dollars," she said.

"Yes, I know."

"Blast!" Ida slammed her fist on the table.

Arlo drew in his breath. He'd never heard his grandmother use a swear word—not that *blast* was exactly a bad word, but still . . .

"Just show Garringer the house," Mr. Tretheway said. "Maybe he won't want to pay the price you're asking."

Ida frowned. "Maybe we could make the house look less appealing," she said.

Mr. Tretheway seemed not to be listening. "You know, it's odd the way the man is so interested in a house he's never seen. I can't help wondering about that. The roof's not even visible from the highway."

"I've thought about that, too," Ida said. "He's never asked to see photographs, either. It's almost as if it's not the house he's really interested in."

"Strange," Mr. Tretheway said.

"If only I'd set the price Augusta suggested. That would have scared him off."

"Your intent was to sell back then," Mr. Tretheway said. "You didn't want to scare buyers off with a hefty price tag."

"If only I'd known." Ida glanced at Arlo and quickly looked away.

Later that afternoon, Arlo sat with Maywood in the tree house.

"Gramma Stonestreet says that Garringer guy is going to look at your grandmother's house this week," Maywood said.

"Mr. Tretheway told her she had to show it to him," Arlo said.

Maywood looked thoughtful as she sipped her lemonade. "We need to make sure he doesn't like it, then," she said.

Arlo gave her a look. "How are we supposed to do that?"

He couldn't imagine anyone *not wanting* to live in Ida's house. Who wouldn't want to wake up in the morning and look out at the river? Who wouldn't want to hear the creaks and moans the walls made at night, as if they were lulling you to sleep? It was so much nicer than the street noises back in Marshboro, where sirens whined on Friday and Saturday nights and trucks ground their gears on the hill, making the walls shake from the vibrations.

"Rats," Maywood said.

"Excuse me?" Arlo stared across the wooden platform toward the spot where Maywood was propped against one of the beanbags. Sometimes she came up with the most outrageous comments. But, seriously, *rats*?

"If I saw a rat in a house, I wouldn't live there for anything," Maywood said.

Arlo thought about Sam. "But if we put a rat in Ida's house, how would we get it out again?"

"I don't know." Maywood shrugged. "We'll put bait outside or something."

"Too dangerous," Arlo said. "Rats bite."

Maywood sighed. "So think of something else," she said.

Arlo thought.

"Too much noise?" he asked.

Maywood waved her hand dismissively. "The only noise at Ida's house is when somebody mows the grass."

"How about water in the basement?" Arlo said. "Our neighbors couldn't sell their house because it got flooded after a bad storm."

"Good idea, except Ida's basement is dry," Maywood said. "I saw it when I helped her stack cans of crab-apple jelly on the shelves down there."

She was silent for a long time. Finally, she sat up. "I have it," she said.

"What?" Arlo asked.

"Squirrels in the attic," Maywood said.

Arlo waved his arm at her. "She already has those," he said. "It's no big deal. The noise scared me at first, but . . ." He stopped speaking midsentence.

"What's wrong?" Maywood asked. "You look like you've seen a ghost."

Arlo smiled. "Exactly," he said.

"Excuse me?" Maywood frowned.

"We'll make Garringer think Ida's house is haunted."

Maywood blinked. "Haunted?" she said. "But how?"

"I don't know," Arlo said. "One of us can hide in the attic and drag chains across the floor or something."

Maywood stared at the table. Slowly, she began to smile. "It might work," she said.

"Of course it'll work," Arlo said. "Remember how we felt at the old Stoneham house?"

Maywood shuddered. "That's different," she said. "That place really is haunted."

Arlo looked at her. "All it takes is making someone *believe* the ghost is there," he said.

Maywood smiled back at him. "OK," she said. "So how do we do that?"

Arlo stood and went to get a piece of paper from the shelf in the clubhouse. Then he came back out and sat down. He started drawing out his idea.

"When Garringer comes to look at the house," he said, "one of us will be in the attic."

"One of us?" Maywood asked.

"Probably you," Arlo said.

"Why not you?"

"Because I'll be the one with Ida, giving Mr. Garringer the tour. We can't let Ida suspect what we're doing. When Ida and I bring Garringer upstairs, I'll give you a signal so you'll know when to make a noise."

"What kind of signal?" Maywood asked.

"I haven't figured that out yet."

She pushed her plate away. "How am I supposed to get up there without someone spotting me?"

"That's easy. I'll sneak you up the back stairs. Ida keeps that door closed all the time. She never uses those stairs. You can go up there ahead of time and hide before Garringer arrives."

"Wouldn't it be easier to sneak into the basement?"

"When people hear noises in basements, they think it's rats," Arlo said. "Attic noises are spookier, especially big attics in old houses. Once we have Mr. Garringer upstairs, you can thump on the floor."

"Thump?" Maywood asked.

"OK. Maybe you could drop something or drag a chain around."

"That sounds better," Maywood said.

They were so intent on their conversation that they failed to notice Matthew standing at the bottom of the ladder, staring up at them.

"What are you two plotting?" he asked.

Maywood peeked over the edge. She pulled up quickly and gave Arlo a zipper-across-the-lips motion.

"Nothing," she said.

"We're reading ghost stories," Arlo said, trying to keep his voice calm while he replayed their conversation in his head. What *exactly* had Matthew heard?

"The sergeant there has a devious look on her face."

"Sergeant?" Arlo asked.

"That's what he calls me sometimes," Maywood explained.

"Only when she's up to no good." Matthew said.

"We're working on a plan to help Ida," Arlo said.

"I'm all for that," Matthew said. "How can I help?"

"We can't tell you anything yet," Maywood said. "It's a secret."

"See what I mean?" Matthew said, shaking a finger at Maywood. "Devious."

Maywood smiled. "Maybe sometimes," she said. "But only when it's absolutely necessary."

Arlo and Maywood spent the next hour reading ghost stories for ideas. Arlo's favorite was the one about the ghost of a Union soldier who had hidden from the Confederates in an attic on a plantation near Edgewater. A hundred years later, the people who bought the plantation found the man's skeleton in their attic. For years afterward, the man's ghost would come to the attic and stand at the window between one and three in the morning.

"You don't really believe in this stuff, do you?" Arlo asked.

Maywood rolled over on her back and stared at the skylight. "People see things they can't explain all the time," she said, "like that crow in the cemetery."

Arlo felt a prickle at the base of his scalp. *Spirits doing their work.* "That was just a bird," he said, though, in truth, that wasn't what he believed.

Arlo called Poppo that evening. Poppo told him he was starting to like his new home.

"They take care of everything for me," he said. "And Eldon comes over to watch TV after dinner every day."

"That's nice," Arlo said.

"Sure is," Poppo said. "How about you? What's new in Edgewater?"

"Did I tell you about the river?" Arlo asked.

"The river? Oh, yeah. I remember it," Poppo said. "It's huge."

Poppo *remembered* the river?

"Like the great grey-green, greasy Limpopo, isn't it?" Poppo laughed. "Are you and Ida getting along all right?"

"We're fine," Arlo said. *Poppo remembered Ida's name, too. He must be having a really good day.*

"How about that other lady? Augusta. How is she?"

"Fine," Arlo said.

"Tell her I said hi. OK?"

"I will."

Arlo heard a voice in the background at Poppo's end of the line.

"Who's that?" Arlo asked.

"Angela," Poppo said. "She's the night nurse. She says Eldon's waiting for me. I guess I'd better go, all right?"

"OK," Arlo said.

"You'll call me again tomorrow, won't you?"

"Sure will," Arlo said.

"Good deal. I'll talk to you then," Poppo said.

"OK."

"Love you," Poppo said.

"I love you, too," Arlo said. Then he hung up the phone. He harbored an unsettling feeling that Poppo was getting along just fine without him.

Shouldn't he be grateful Poppo had a friend?

Of course he should.

Did he feel grateful? Did he feel good?

He did not.

But that was terrible. Arlo knew that. Still, he couldn't help a tiny stab of jealousy. It was hard to let go of the person who'd taken care of him all his life. A tiny part of him longed to go back to the way things used to be . . . over a year ago now. But that wasn't going to happen. It was time to move forward. Arlo wasn't used to doing that, but he was beginning to come around. Moving forward no longer seemed as terrifying as it had the day he escaped on the bus.

CHAPTER 39
More Stories About Wake

Ida was trying to make Edgewater feel like home. Arlo could see that. She'd made space in his father's chest of drawers for his clothes. She'd taken him to the store to select his favorite foods. She'd even started watching his favorite TV programs with him. He appreciated what she was doing. But the day she announced she was taking him to register for school, Arlo thought it was time to slow down. The prospect of being a new kid made his stomach churn. Didn't he have enough to worry about? Contending with creeps like Hafer and Boyle on a daily basis was piling it on.

But Ida insisted. "The sooner you get settled in school, the sooner Edgewater will feel like home," she said.

"It feels like home already," Arlo said.

Ida shook her head sadly. "I know it will be tough at first, but Maywood will help."

Face it. There was only so much a girl could do. Part of letting bullies know how far they could push you was strictly a guy-to-guy thing. Ida couldn't possibly understand.

Despite his protests, Arlo found himself sitting in a classroom with a bunch of strangers a day later. He reassured himself with the knowledge that it could have been worse. The teacher could have stuck him in a seat at the front of the room, the way Mrs. Gretzky did when a new kid joined their class. The teacher at Edgewater Middle School was nice. Her name was Mrs. Previll and she had the good sense to place Arlo in a nondescript seat in the middle of the room. He did his best to melt into the background. It was only at recess and in the halls that he had to worry about Hafer and Boyle. Luckily, neither one of them was in his class.

During one of their study periods in the library, Arlo ran across a faded copy of *The Elephant's Child*. He checked it out and read it that night in his room. Repeating the lines about the "great grey-green, greasy Limpopo River," Arlo heard Poppo's voice in his head. He forgot about being the new kid for a few minutes.

Other people in Edgewater tried to make Arlo feel at home, too. Matthew was great about that. He took Arlo along on deliveries whenever he could. He told Arlo stories about his dad and about the things he and Wake had done when they were kids. And then there was Maywood, who turned out to be a true friend. She asked Arlo to help her get ready for a Halloween party at the bookstore.

"This is the second year we've done it," she said. "We're

having it on the Friday before Halloween. My mom's going to read ghost stories. And Matthew's making caramel apples."

"Sounds good," Arlo said.

"I want to decorate the tree house to look haunted," she said. "Want to help?"

"Sure."

Lucius took them to Val-U-Mart, where Maywood bought strands of fake ivy and moss. They took an old pair of jeans and a flannel shirt and stuffed them with newspapers and then propped them on a chair in the clubhouse with a carved pumpkin for a head. They strung electric lights through the branches and put a light inside the pumpkin head so it glowed through the window.

Everyone loved it, except for four-year-old Melody Walters, who took one look and started screaming. Arlo saved the day by turning on all the lights and showing her that the jack-o'-lantern ghost was nothing but old clothes stuffed with newspapers.

On Saturday Arlo helped Matthew make deliveries to the inns and bed-and-breakfasts up and down the Northern Neck. Matthew regaled him with more stories about things he and Arlo's father had done when they were in school.

"We weren't exactly angels, you know," Matthew said. "Especially in sixth grade."

"That's how old I am now," Arlo said.

"I know," Matthew said. "That's what made me remember."

"What exactly did you do?"

283

Matthew rubbed his hand over his chin. He had an odd expression on his face, as if he were embarrassed to be telling this story, but he kept going anyway. "We used to climb over the fence and break into the city pool," he said.

"Break in? You mean without paying?" Arlo asked.

"No," Matthew said. "That wasn't why we had to break in. It was because we were going to the pool after they'd closed it for the season."

"I don't understand."

Matthew laughed. "Of course you don't. Sounds crazy, doesn't it? Going to a pool after they've drained out all the water."

Arlo nodded.

"Well, here's the thing," Matthew said. "We waited till they'd patched the cracks and put on a fresh coat of white-wash. Then it was perfect."

"Perfect for what?" Arlo asked.

"I don't remember who came up the idea," Matthew said, "but somehow your dad and I started sliding down the walls of the deep end."

"How?" Arlo asked.

"Good question," Matthew said. "You see, the first thing we had to do was, we'd start at the bottom and take a running start and go as far up the side of the pool as we could. It was like going up the side of a mountain — only with fresh whitewash and running shoes, we had some traction, you know? We'd run as far as we could until we started slipping. Then, at the last second, we'd flip over on our backsides and slide down."

"Sounds dangerous," Arlo said.

"Well, the flipping-around part didn't always work so well, I'll admit. A couple of times, we slid facedown."

"Ouch!" Arlo said.

"Yeah." Matthew smiled. "I'll admit there was a little *ouch* from time to time."

Arlo tried to imagine a younger version of Matthew alongside the picture he had of his dad at that age. He pictured them climbing a chain-link fence and dropping down on the other side.

"One day we got caught," Matthew said.

Arlo looked over at him. "Did you get in trouble?"

"Did we ever!" Matthew gave a rueful laugh.

"Who caught you?"

"Well, it's not a person you've met, but you do know his grandson," Matthew said.

Arlo frowned. "I don't know anybody in Edgewater except you and Maywood and Lucius and . . ."

"I'm talking about a person you probably don't think of as a *friend*," Matthew said.

"Oh," Arlo said.

"Yeah." Matthew raised an eyebrow as he stared over the steering wheel.

"Which one?" Arlo asked.

"The one whose father is mayor."

"Uh-huh."

"Back then Hafer's grandfather was the sheriff."

"Oh, geez."

"No kidding." Matthew shook his head. "He made us redo

the paint job on the pool. Said if we did that, he wouldn't press charges."

"At least you survived."

"Better than that," Matthew said.

"What do you mean?"

"Well, you've met the Hafer who hangs around with Boyle, right?"

"Yeah."

"That boy's father was in school with Wake and me. And he thought he could get away with anything because *his* dad was sheriff. So, when he heard about Wake and me sliding down the pool, he figured that sounded like fun. He wanted to do it, too."

"Did he get caught?"

"Oh, boy, did he. Him and another kid. Rodney Wilkins."

"What happened?"

"It was about this time of year. Maybe a little earlier. Hafer's dad was climbing over the fence and got himself stuck up there. He had his pants so tangled up in that wire he couldn't bust loose. Someone saw him and called the police."

"Someone?" Arlo asked.

Matthew's mouth broadened into a smile. "Someone you know," he said. "Let's just leave it at that. Someone who didn't tell the dispatcher at the sheriff's office who the boy *was* hanging off the fence."

Now Arlo was smiling, too.

"So, when the sheriff comes, Hafer-the-future-mayor-of-Edgewater is dangling there by his belt buckle."

"Was he hurt?"

"No. He was even smiling for the picture."

"What picture?" Arlo asked.

"The one the photographer for the *Essex Times* took for the front page after an anonymous caller tipped him off."

"An anonymous caller?"

"That's right." Matthew grinned again.

"What did the sheriff do?"

"Grounded future-mayor-Hafer for the rest of the year," Matthew said. "Told him he had to rake leaves and mow grass and clean out the garage and the basement at his house. Basically made his life miserable for eight months."

"Did you keep sliding down the pool?"

Matthew flipped the blinker to signal a left turn. "That was the end of our pool-sliding days," he said. "After that we moved on to skateboarding in the cemetery."

Arlo looked at Matthew. "You used to skateboard in the cemetery?"

Matthew shrugged. "Way back in the day they used to pave that road leading up the hill. It was a great place to skateboard . . . *as long as you didn't get caught.*"

CHAPTER 40
Swan's Neck Bed-and-Breakfast

"Isn't that the turn at the curve?" Arlo pointed to the sign shaped like a swan.

"You got it." Matthew flipped his blinker and made the turn.

It was their last delivery for the day. Arlo twisted his head all the way around when he spotted the shiny black car in the parking lot.

"Something wrong there, Skywalker?"

"No. It's OK."

Matthew pulled around to the kitchen entrance in the back. A woman waved from the window, then came outside to meet them.

"Morning, Juanita."

"Morning, Matthew. You're just in time. I've got this guest from Richmond who's been sitting in my dining room half an hour now waiting on one of Matthew Healy's famous Morning Glory Muffins."

"Coming right up." In one easy motion, Matthew opened the rear door and slid a long pastry box off the seat.

"What else did you bring?"

"I've got an apple pie, if you want it."

"Thought the apples were all gone."

"These are the last from Tallifarro's Orchards."

"In that case, bring it on."

Matthew nodded at Arlo to take the pie out of the box in the rear of the van. "Say hello to Juanita Stemple," he said. "She's the boss around the Swan's Neck."

"Nice to meet you," the lady said. "But I didn't catch your name."

"Arlo," Arlo said.

The lady stared. "Arlo *Jones*?" she asked.

"Yes, ma'am."

"What a surprise."

"Isn't it?" Matthew said, leading Arlo toward the kitchen.

Arlo guessed that Mrs. Stemple must not be a friend of Augusta Stonestreet's, seeing as how she was the first person he'd met who didn't already know he was in town.

They carried the boxes inside the kitchen. Mrs. Stemple dipped her head in the direction of the dining room. "Better hustle those muffins out to that Garringer fellow. He says he's got some sort of property deal cooking and doesn't have time to waste."

"Did you say Garringer?" Matthew raised an eyebrow.

"A shady customer, if you ask me. I'll tell you one thing"— Mrs. Stemple lowered her voice —"if I were on the other end of that property deal, I'd keep my eyes open."

Arlo's heart sped up. A man named Garringer driving a black sedan, the same black sedan that he and Maywood had spotted in the cemetery.

"There's a man named Garringer trying to buy Ida's house," Arlo said.

"Is that a fact?" Mrs. Stemple exchanged glances with Matthew.

"Tell you what." Matthew opened one of the boxes and started putting muffins on a plate. "How about if I take these muffins out there? I'd like to get a look at this Garringer fellow myself."

"Be my guest." Mrs. Stemple extended her arm, gesturing toward the dining room.

As Arlo and Mrs. Stemple watched, Matthew set the plate of muffins in front of Mr. Garringer.

"Morning, sir," Matthew said.

"Morning." Mr. Garringer offered a gruff acknowledgment without looking up from his newspaper.

Matthew gave Juanita Stemple a conspiratorial nod behind Mr. Garringer's back. Then he started talking in a louder-than-necessary tone of voice.

"Juanita, I don't guess you heard what happened at Ida Jones's house last night, did you?"

Mrs. Stemple looked puzzled for a moment, until Matthew gave her an eye signal to play along.

"Why, no, Matthew, I don't believe I did," she said, winking back at him. "Is Ida all right?"

Now the two of them smiled at each other.

"She's fine," Matthew said. "Just shaken a little."

"What happened?"

"It was yesterday evening. Around dusk." Matthew moved over to the sideboard and lifted the coffeepot off its burner. "Mind if I have a cup?" he asked.

"Help yourself," Mrs. Stemple said.

"Thank you." Matthew poured coffee into a Styrofoam cup. "You know, when I was growing up, I used to hear stories about Civil War spirits haunting the old houses around Edgewater, but I never believed them."

Mrs. Stemple and Matthew exchanged glances again.

"Some very reputable people have reported sightings," Mrs. Stemple said, sliding into a strategic position behind one of the dining room chairs. "Of course, this time of year, people see ghosts all over the place."

"Isn't that the truth," Matthew said. "And I thought it was all hogwash."

Mr. Garringer continued to sip his coffee, staring at his newspaper, though Arlo noticed he hadn't turned a page since Matthew started his story.

"Did something change your mind?" Mrs. Stemple asked as she pushed the small wicker basket of sugar packets and sweeteners in Matthew's direction.

"I've known Ida Jones all my life," Matthew said, "and I've never known her to stretch the truth."

"You're right about that," Mrs. Stemple said.

Matthew lowered his voice. "But you should hear what she told me this morning," he said.

"Go on." Mrs. Stemple leaned closer, and Arlo noticed Mr. Garringer shifting in his seat as well.

"It was while I was waiting for Arlo to get dressed," Matthew said. "Ida told me she'd seen something up in her attic."

Matthew winked at Arlo, and Arlo thought again about the day Matthew had overheard Maywood and him planning to "haunt" Ida's house.

"Ida said she was up in the attic when . . ."

Mrs. Stemple lowered her voice now too. "When what?" she asked.

Matthew's voice was barely a whisper now. Mr. Garringer was leaning so far to his left that his newspaper had dipped into his coffee.

"Ida said she was in the attic searching for old photographs when she felt a chill, like cold air seeping out of the ground."

"Really?" Mrs. Stemple said.

"That's right," Matthew said. He put his hand over his mouth, and Arlo guessed he was covering up a grin. "Now, this is where the story turns strange," he said.

"It's sounding strange already," Mrs. Stemple said.

"That's nothing," Matthew said. "Ida says she turned around and suddenly . . . there he was."

"There *who* was?"

"The soldier."

"What soldier?" Mrs. Stemple asked.

"Ida says he was dressed in Union blue and floating over her great-granddaddy's trunk. She said he had a bloody bandage wrapped around his head. Scared her so bad, she nearly put her hand right through him."

"No."

"That's what she told me."

"When was this?"

"Last night. Around dusk. Like I told you."

Arlo sneaked a fresh look at Mr. Garringer. He had gotten up from the table now and was pouring himself a fresh cup of coffee. His eyes were trained on the hallway where Mrs. Stemple and Matthew were standing. He kept pouring and pouring until the coffee overflowed into his saucer. Meanwhile, Matthew finished telling his story.

"Ida said she'd heard noises before, but she'd always figured they were shutters banging in the wind. Said she'd never given them a second thought. . . . well, not until last night, that is."

Mrs. Stemple handed Matthew a check for the muffins. "I don't guess I ever told you about my great-aunt Thelma, did I?" she asked.

"Don't believe you did," Matthew said. He glanced sideways at Mr. Garringer.

"Well, Aunt Thelma had a ghost who liked to throw towels on her bathroom floor."

"Now, you see," Matthew said, "those are just the kind of stories I never believed."

"Well, I admit I always wondered. Aunt Thelma had a tendency to stretch the truth. Fact is, she drank a little. We never liked to talk about that. But with Ida . . . well, that's a different story."

"Ida's as straight as an arrow," Matthew agreed. "If that lady tells you something, you can take it to the bank."

"She has her feet on the ground, all right."

In the dining room, Mr. Garringer folded up his newspaper. He blotted coffee off his saucer with a napkin, keeping an ear cocked toward the front hallway.

"You'll let me know what you need for Tuesday?" Matthew said.

"I'll give you a call," Mrs. Stemple said.

As they walked out the door, Arlo glanced over his shoulder. Mr. Garringer was peering at them through the front window.

Back in the van, Matthew tapped a victory beat on the dashboard. "We set the bait," he said. "Now it's up to you and Maywood."

Arlo looked at him.

"You and the sergeant ought to be more careful who's listening when you go planning your next caper."

Matthew kept his eyes on the road.

"That was a good ghost story," Arlo said. "How'd you think of it?"

"That story really happened," Matthew said. "Most of it, anyway."

"Not to Ida, though. Right?"

"Of course to Ida. All except the part about the soldier."

"I don't understand," Arlo said.

"Ida really did see a man in the attic. Only, it wasn't a man in uniform. He was wearing a blue sweater."

An uncomfortable chill crossed Arlo's shoulders. "That was a long time ago, wasn't it?"

"About nine years," Matthew said.

Arlo couldn't help thinking about the picture he'd seen in the family album, the photograph of a man wearing a blue sweater, a man who'd died in a car accident nine years ago.

"You all right, Skywalker?"

"I'm fine."

"You don't look so fine."

Arlo leaned his head against his seat and let the music from the radio wash over him. He tapped his pocket till he found the carving. Sure enough, it felt warm to him. Maybe he and Maywood weren't being so creative after all. Maybe putting a ghost in Ida's attic wasn't anything that hadn't already happened before.

As Arlo got out of the car, Matthew reached in the backseat and handed him a bag.

"Fresh doughnuts," he said. "Ida likes the cake kind. I put in a couple of blueberry-filled for you."

"Thank you," Arlo said.

"You available to make deliveries next Saturday, too?"

"Sure," Arlo said. "I'd like that."

Matthew smiled. "I'd like that, too," he said.

As Arlo watched from the gravel path, Matthew followed the curve of Ida's driveway till it straightened out and led him back to the road. Arlo mulled over the story about the man in the blue sweater.

Meanwhile, Ida waved from the kitchen window.

"Arlo? Are you all right?" she said. "You look like you've seen a ghost."

"I'm fine." Arlo bounded up the short staircase and handed her the bag. "Matthew sent you these."

Ida looked up the driveway, where dust swirled in the wake of Matthew's van. "That man," she said. "He's a treasure, isn't he?"

Part III
THE PLAN

CHAPTER 41
How to Haunt a House

The afternoon after Matthew and Arlo made deliveries to the Swan's Neck, Arlo and Maywood worked on their plan for haunting Ida's house. They were in the attic, searching for ideas. Arlo picked up a harness looking thing hanging from a hook on the wall. It had long leather strips studded with ornamental brass buttons.

"What's this?" he asked.

Maywood shook her head. "Looks like some decoration for a horse," she said. "For a parade or something."

"Whatever it is, it's been up here forever." Arlo ran a finger over one of the strips and showed her the dust.

"I'll bet it would make a good noise if you dropped it," Maywood said.

Arlo raised his arm.

"Wait a second," Maywood said. "Where's Ida?"

"In the garden," Arlo said.

He raised his arm higher before letting go. The object hit the floor with a resounding clatter.

"That's perfect," Maywood said.

"Not bad," Arlo agreed.

"We need something else, though." Maywood turned in a circle, examining the contents of the attic. "What's over there?"

She pointed to a dark object in the shadows under the eaves. Arlo walked over to inspect.

"It's an old trunk," he said.

"Try pushing it over the floor," Maywood said.

Arlo gave the trunk a good shove. There was a delicious-sounding scrape of wood against wood.

"*I like it,*" Maywood said.

"So, now all we need are signals for me to let you know when to make the noises," Arlo said.

"And an emergency signal in case something goes wrong," Maywood added.

That evening at dinner, Ida got a call from Mr. Tretheway.

"What's wrong?" Arlo asked when Ida came back to the table.

"Mr. Garringer is coming tomorrow to look at the house," she said.

"On Sunday?"

She rolled her eyes. "At least we'll get it over with," she said. "He's bringing a contractor along. They'll be here at one. He wants to talk about knocking down some walls."

"But he's never even seen the house," Arlo said.

Ida sniffed. "Nathan thinks he's making assumptions based on the age of the place—the fact that it was built in the twenties."

Arlo phoned Maywood right after dinner. He explained what was going on. "Can you be here by twelve thirty tomorrow?" he asked.

"I was supposed to help Dad with inventory, but I'll think of some excuse," she said.

Now there was nothing to do but wait and hope that everything went according to plan.

CHAPTER 42
Not According to Plan

Ida was in her bedroom when Arlo spotted Maywood pumping her bike down the driveway. It was twenty-seven minutes past noon. Maywood steered her bike across the field and through the orchard until she came to a stop behind the garage.

Arlo rushed downstairs to meet her at the kitchen door.

"Is he here yet?" she asked.

"No," Arlo said. "You made it."

"Where's Ida?"

"In the bathroom, changing. Come on. I'll sneak you up the back stairs."

They crept up the dark staircase and rounded the corner to the door to the attic. Ida's bedroom and bath were on the front side of the house, so as long as they stayed quiet, she'd have no idea that Maywood was in the house.

"Did you figure out the signals yet?" Maywood asked.

"When you hear me shut the closet door in my room," Arlo said, "count to ten and then push the trunk across the floor."

"OK," Maywood said. "What else?"

"When I tap on the vent, count to twenty and then drop that harness thing with the leather strips."

"Right," Maywood said. "What about the emergency signal?"

"I'll call for Steamboat," Arlo said.

Maywood looked at him.

"You know, if you hear me say, *Here, Steamboat,* that means, get out of the attic now!"

Steamboat wagged his tail. He jumped up on Arlo's leg.

"Not now, Steamboat," Arlo said.

Maywood shrugged. She leaned down and patted Steamboat on the head. "OK," she said. "If you think that will work."

"It'll work," Arlo said. "Just be sure to go down the back staircase. That way, all you need to do is get from the attic door to the back stairs without being seen."

"That won't even take a second," Maywood said.

"I know."

Steamboat wagged his tail while Arlo held the attic door open long enough for Maywood to slip inside. He let the latch slip back into position at an agonizingly slow pace to avoid making any noise. When it clicked at last, he led Steamboat downstairs and waited for Mr. Garringer and the contractor in the kitchen.

When Ida came downstairs, she pointed toward two

cardboard boxes filled with canceled checks and letters and files that were sitting under the sideboard in the dining room.

"Would you mind helping me carry those to the attic?" she asked. "I don't want strangers snooping through my personal papers."

"The attic?" Arlo said.

"On second thought, maybe there's space under the bottom shelf in the pantry," she said.

"That sounds better." Arlo felt his heart slowing down again.

Ida looked at him.

"That way you won't have to carry them back down two flights of stairs," he explained.

"Right," Ida said. "Let's just get them out of the way before that horrid man arrives."

Mr. Garringer's black Cadillac roared up the driveway at two minutes before one. He gave Arlo a hard stare as he came through the front door with another man. He seemed not to make the connection between Arlo today and the boy he'd seen yesterday at the Swan's Neck B & B.

"We're here to see the house," he announced, stepping into the front parlor as if he already owned the place.

"My grandmother's waiting for you," Arlo said.

He led them through the living room to the staircase in the center hall.

"Nice place," the contractor said, nodding appreciatively at the moldings and the plaster walls. "Looks like solid construction."

"It is," said a voice behind them.

Mr. Garringer whipped around. "You must be Mrs. Jones," he said.

"And you're Mr. Garringer," Ida said without smiling.

Mr. Garringer's mouth twitched. "I've brought Wolfe here to check the construction," he said.

"I'm sure you'll find the house extremely sound," Ida said sharply. She extended a hand toward Mr. Wolfe. "Nice to meet you, sir," she said, indicating by her failure to offer the same pleasantries to Mr. Garringer what she thought about him.

"If I were to buy this place, there would need to be certain modifications for modern living," Mr. Garringer explained.

"Sounds like a good reason not to buy it, then," Ida said.

They stared at each other for a moment. Arlo covered his mouth to keep Mr. Garringer from seeing him laugh. Then Mr. Garringer moved from wall to wall, inspecting Ida's art collection.

"You won't find anything of great value," Ida said, following behind him. "Slocum and I bought those prints when we were in Greece."

"Very nice," Mr. Garringer said, though he'd already moved on to a small engraving hanging beside the bookshelves in the alcove under the staircase.

"Lovely home you have here," Mr. Wolfe said.

"Thank you," Ida said curtly. "I like it."

Mr. Garringer stared at Arlo. "I keep having this feeling we've met before," he said.

Arlo kept his mouth shut.

Mr. Wolfe looked at Ida. "Maybe you could show us around?" he said.

"Of course," Ida said. "That's why you're here, isn't it?" She turned to her left. "As you see, that's the living room you just walked through." Then she pointed to a door on the river side of the living room. "There's a screened porch through there," she said. "And this door in front of us opens onto a path to the river."

Mr. Wolfe tapped on the wall beside the door to the river. Arlo gave Ida a questioning look. She made a slight movement with her shoulders in reply, indicating she had no more idea than he did what the man was up to.

"What's this?" Mr. Wolfe asked when the tapping sound turned hollow. "Is there something behind this wall?"

"A powder room," Ida said. She pulled open a door that had been carefully concealed with wallpaper.

"Must have been added recently," Mr. Garringer said.

"My husband and I put that in fifteen years ago," Ida said.

"What about over here?" Mr. Wolfe tapped on the walls around the bookcase on the opposite side of the center hall.

"There's no bathroom over there, if that's what you're asking," Ida said.

"But there's a funny sound to the plaster here," Mr. Wolfe said.

"Must be something to do with the bookcases," Ida said. "Slocum and I never changed anything over there. And his family was always very careful about preserving things the way they had been."

"Mmmm," said Mr. Wolfe, still tapping. "Do you have any blueprints?"

"I'm afraid they went missing around the time of my husband's uncle's death," Ida said. "He passed away quite suddenly, and there were things that were never found. The plans for the house were among them."

Mr. Garringer and Mr. Wolfe exchanged glances.

"Interesting," Mr. Garringer said. "Isn't it, Wolfe?"

"Very interesting," Mr. Wolfe said.

"Perhaps you'd like to see upstairs?" Ida glared at Mr. Wolfe as he continued to tap on the walls around the bookcase.

"Yes," Mr. Garringer said. "We want to see it all."

They made their way up the staircase, into the master bedroom with the window seat that overlooked the river. Ida ushered them through the adjoining bath, frowning as Mr. Wolfe tapped on every wall and Mr. Garringer inspected each picture.

"That's a birthday card my son made for me when he was a child," she said in a sharp voice. "I had it framed to hang in my dressing room."

"Forgive me," Mr. Garringer said. "You see, I'm a bit of a collector and I can't help noticing art."

Mr. Wolfe tapped the walls in the walk-in linen closet in the hall. "When did you say this house was built?"

"In the twenties," Ida said. "Nineteen twenty-three, I believe it was. It's quite solid construction." She frowned again at his tapping.

"Yes. Yes, I can see that." Mr. Wolfe inspected the crown molding in the open hallway.

Finally, they walked into Arlo's room. Arlo slipped over to his closet and opened the door for them to look inside. When they were finished, he pulled the door closed as loudly as he could without slamming it. Mr. Wolfe gave him an odd look, but then turned and followed Ida into the hall.

"We'll look at the kitchen next," Ida was saying, "and then I'll show you the garage apartment."

"Garage apartment . . . ah, yes. I'd very much like to see that," Mr. Garringer said, trading glances with Mr. Wolfe again.

A dragging sound overhead interrupted them. Mr. Garringer raised his eyes.

"What's up there?" he asked.

"Just the attic," Ida said.

"Is someone living in it?"

"Of course not. Must be a tree branch scraping the wall," Ida said.

Arlo sucked in his cheeks to keep from grinning. Maywood was right on cue.

Nobody noticed Arlo inching over to the vent in the side wall. He gave the metal a swift tap and counted silently in his head until a clatter came from the floor above them. You could see the wheels turning in Mr. Garringer's mind as he played back the story about the Union soldier. He tilted back and stared at the ceiling. Then he looked at Ida.

She looked back at him. *Blink, blink, blink, blink.*

"Who's up there?" he asked.

"Nobody," Ida said. "A squirrel maybe."

"It would have to be an awfully large one," Mr. Wolfe said, "to make a noise like that."

Mr. Garringer took two giant steps to the window, threw

open the sash, and stuck his head outside, twisting his neck to get a look upstairs.

It was at that moment something happened that Arlo hadn't planned on. A cloud passed over what little sun was left. The sky turned black for a few seconds and then there was a boom of thunder.

"Goodness," Ida said, jumping back from the window. She glanced uneasily at the sky. "Better close that," she said. "We're about to have a storm."

"I'm well aware of what's going on outside," Mr. Garringer roared, with his head still sticking out the window. "What I'm trying to figure out is, what's going on in your attic?"

Thunder crashed again, shaking the walls. There was a soft tapping noise coming from above. And then a flash of lightning struck a tree limb in the neighbor's yard.

Mr. Garringer yanked his head back in the house.

"You're lucky you didn't injure yourself," Ida said.

Mr. Garringer glared at her. "Confound it, woman," he said.

Thunder boomed even louder, jarring the house so hard that glass rattled in the windows.

"I don't see what you're so angry about," Ida said. "It's just a storm."

Mr. Garringer screwed up his face. "Someone's in your attic," he said.

Ida stared at the ceiling as though she thought there might be something up there, too. "One of Judge Doerr's cats got up there years ago," she said. "Maybe that's happened again."

Mr. Garringer threw up his arms. "I've had enough of this," he said. "I'm going up for a look."

Ida looked totally perplexed. Arlo was disappointed. The noises were supposed to scare Mr. Garringer, not make him angry. But right now there were more important things to worry about. Maywood. He needed to give her the emergency signal.

"Steamboat?" he yelled.

Ida turned pale. "He's not outside, is he?"

Meanwhile, Maywood commenced a low moaning. At least, that's what it sounded like. Either that, or the wind whistling through a narrow, enclosed space. It started with a soft murmur and then grew. Arlo wondered what was going on. That wasn't part of their plan.

"Steamboat!" Arlo yelled again, louder. He didn't mean to worry Ida, but he had to warn Maywood.

"Good grief, kid, you trying to call clear to the next county?" Mr. Wolfe shot Arlo a dirty look.

Steamboat, naturally, came running from downstairs. He was panting by the time he reached Ida. She sank to her knees and threw her arms around him.

"Thank goodness, you're safe," she said.

The moaning sound came again. It lasted only a moment this time and then stopped abruptly. Mr. Garringer straightened his back and glared at the ceiling.

"I'm getting to the bottom of this," he said. Then he stormed out of the room.

Arlo prayed that Maywood had slipped out of the attic. She must have made the moaning sound on her way down the stairs. He hoped so, anyway.

CHAPTER 43
Ghost of the Tidewater

When they reached the attic, Mr. Garringer went from rafter to rafter, checking every nook and cranny.

"Kitty, kitty, kitty," Ida called.

Mr. Wolfe scowled at her. "There's no cat up here," he said.

"You never know," Ida said. And she went back to calling for the invisible feline.

Out of the corner of his eye, Arlo noticed movement on the far side of the attic, that section that ran over the top of the kitchen on the left side of the tiny garret window. But it wasn't Steamboat. In fact, on second thought, Arlo wasn't even sure it was movement. But there was something. A trick of the light? A cloud passing over the sun? *Something.*

After a few seconds, there was more light—a pale shimmering. Arlo caught Mr. Wolfe staring at it, too. The man removed his glasses, polished the lenses, and then set them back on his nose. Meanwhile, the wood carving thrummed in

Arlo's pocket. He put his hand around it and felt it warming against his palm.

Ida was looking at the same spot, too. Arlo wondered if she was thinking about the apparition in the blue sweater. Was that the spot where she'd seen the ghost of his father?

Arlo moved over to the window. What he saw outside caused the hair on his neck to stiffen. It was Maywood. She was on her bicycle, and she was already halfway down the driveway of the house next door.

But how could she be that far away already?

Arlo's nose prickled at the wet-metal smell that accompanied the rain, which was just beginning to tap the roof.

"There aren't any closets up here, are there?" Mr. Garringer asked.

Ida rolled her eyes. "Why on earth would a person put a closet in an attic this size?"

Mr. Garringer's face was hard. "I don't know what you're trying to pull, lady."

Ida cut him off midsentence. "You're the one who demanded to see the house," she said.

Arlo lost count of her eye blinks. She moved quickly across the attic and shook a finger in his face.

"I resent your tone, sir," she said. "In fact, I resent your very presence in my house. It's time for you to leave."

Arlo stared at his grandmother, marveling at the way she stood up to Mr. Garringer, who was falling in line behind her as she stomped down the staircase. When they reached the kitchen, she turned to Mr. Wolfe.

"And don't you dare tap on that wall," she snapped.

312

Mr. Wolfe froze with his hand raised halfway to do that very thing. He gave her a sheepish look.

"I beg your pardon," he said.

She sniffed. "I'm sorry I ever let either one of you set foot on my property."

Mr. Garringer looked pained. "But we haven't seen the kitchen or the basement."

"Or the garage apartment," Mr. Wolfe added.

"You're standing in the kitchen this very moment," Ida said. "So, you've seen it now, haven't you?"

"Please," Mr. Garringer said. "I'm a student of old houses and I'd hate to miss seeing the rest of this extraordinary property."

"The tour is over," Ida said.

Mr. Garringer's demeanor shifted. "Look, lady," he said. "You signed a contract that says you have to make a good-faith effort to sell, or pay a penalty."

Ida narrowed her eyes. "That contract is none of your business," she said. "In fact, it's privileged information that you have no right to know about."

"Nothing's privileged these days, lady." Mr. Garringer laughed. "All it takes is knowing the right people. I'm a qualified buyer, and you're going to show me your house."

The air grew thick in the room. Mr. Garringer glowered at Ida, and she glowered right back at him.

"Arlo, would you please show these men to the door?" she said firmly.

Arlo's feet felt light as he bounced down the six steps to the kitchen door and held it open.

"Very well," Mr. Garringer said. "We're leaving."

"Finally," Ida said.

"But you haven't heard the last of this." Mr. Garringer shook his fist at her. "Mark my words, woman. You're going to be sorry."

Outside, in the driveway, Mr. Garringer yanked open the door to his Cadillac and jumped inside. Gravel flew as he tore down the driveway.

"Good riddance!" Ida murmured, as she watched the car disappear.

CHAPTER 44
What's Going On?

After he went to bed, Arlo lay awake in the dark, trying to puzzle everything out. The gauzy shape in the attic. Maywood's disappearance. He stared at the shadow cast by a thin strip of paint peeling off one of the shutters at his window.

Later, angry crows worked their way into his dreams. Arlo was standing in line at the bus station. When he stepped forward to buy his ticket, the clerk opened his mouth to speak, but only crow sounds came out. Arlo turned and ran.

He woke up soaked with sweat and found Ida standing at the door to his room.

"I heard you calling out," she said. "Bad dream?"

"Sort of," Arlo said. He felt like he'd barely slept at all. He noticed she was more dressed up than usual. "Are you going somewhere?" he asked.

"Nathan cleared time to see me this morning. I was going to see if you minded going to school a few minutes early."

"Are you going to talk about not selling your house?"

"That and other things," Ida said.

Arlo reached for the T-shirt he'd tossed on the foot of his bed the night before. "I'll be right down," he said.

On their way out the door, the clock on the mantle in the living room began striking the hour. Ida stopped dead in her tracks.

"That clock hasn't chimed in eight years," she said. "Did you wind it?"

Arlo shook his head. "I never touched it," he said.

Ida moved back through the kitchen, straight to the living room. She walked to the mantle and placed her hand on the clock. Then she turned and slowly gazed around the room.

"What's wrong?" Arlo asked.

"Nothing." She ran a finger along the top of the clock. "I haven't cleaned in here for at least ten days, and there's not a speck of dust on this clock. Must have been that Mr. Garringer. The way he went around touching everything in the house. Must have wound the clock. Probably had his eye on buying it, too. Acting as if he owned the place. Honestly. What a horrible man!" She walked toward the kitchen again. "Hurry up, Arlo. We're late."

Was it Arlo's imagination or did something sweep past the window as he glanced toward the attic on his way to the car? He blinked and looked again, but the clouds had uncovered the sun and bright rays glinted off the glass so he couldn't see anything.

When he turned back toward the car, Ida was watching him. She gave him the funniest look.

"I thought I saw something in the attic," Arlo said.

"Light playing tricks on your eyes," Ida said. "Happens all the time." A muscle twitched in her cheek.

Arlo waited for Maywood at her locker.

"What happened to you yesterday?" he asked.

She gave him a quizzical look.

"How did you get out of the attic?" Arlo said.

"Just the way we planned." She turned the dial on her locker and clicked out the numbers of her combination.

"But you couldn't have," Arlo said.

"Why not?"

"Because Mr. Garringer went storming up there as soon as you started moaning."

"As soon as I started what?" She put down her backpack and turned to face him.

"You know. That *was* you moaning, right? When the storm hit."

Maywood frowned. "I have no idea what you're talking about," she said. "I left as soon as you started calling for Steamboat. Just the way we planned."

A clammy feeling settled on the back of Arlo's neck. "If it wasn't you . . ." he started, leaving the sentence unfinished.

"I never did any moaning," Maywood said.

"But there couldn't have been anybody else."

"Must have been the wind," Maywood said. "That was a terrible storm. I was soaked by the time I got home."

"I don't think so," Arlo said.

Maywood unzipped her backpack and lifted her history

317

book into her locker. "As long as we fooled Mr. Garringer," she said. "As long as we made him think the house was haunted."

Arlo sighed. "He doesn't think it's haunted. He thinks we were playing a trick on him."

"Well, he's right about that," Maywood said.

"I know, but not the way he believes."

"I don't understand."

"That's because you weren't up there when it happened," Arlo said.

"When *what* happened?"

Arlo sighed. He wasn't sure how to explain what he'd seen. "Did you notice anything *unusual?*" he asked.

Maywood frowned. "Unusual how?" she said.

Arlo tried to demonstrate the shimmering with his hands, but it was basically hopeless. "I don't know," he said finally. "Just something you didn't expect."

Maywood watched him closely, as if Arlo were suddenly speaking a foreign language and she was trying to decipher his words.

"I saw the same stuff you and I saw when we were up there before. Boxes, trunks, ice skates, Christmas wreaths, suitcases . . ."

"Besides that."

She shook her head. "Not really," she said.

Arlo stared at the pile of papers in his locker. He was going to have to explain. She was looking at him like he was crazy. Maybe he was. Who knows? The whole thing was strange.

"Arlo?"

318

"Yes?"

"What are you trying to tell me?"

"There was something up there," he said. "It wasn't just me. Ida saw it, too. And so did Mr. Wolfe."

"Saw what?"

"This . . . thing." He repeated the same shimmering motion. "I'm trying to explain it to you." He waited while she put the rest of her books in the locker except for math and science. "You're the one who's always talking about ghosts," he said.

Maywood nodded as she twisted the dial on her locker. "Wait a minute," she said, turning to look at him. "Are you telling me you saw a ghost?"

"It was this shimmery light thing."

"You saw a ghost and you didn't tell me?"

"I'm telling you now," Arlo said.

"I can't believe this. I wait all my life to see something like that and you're in Edgewater for barely any time at all, and practically right off you see a ghost. It's not fair."

"I'm not sure what it was. It's just that strange things are happening. Like the clock on Ida's mantle. It's not supposed to chime, but it did."

"Now you really aren't making sense." She zipped up her backpack and hoisted it onto her shoulder.

"It's just another weird thing that happened. That's all. Ida thinks Mr. Garringer wound it. Maybe he did. I don't know."

Maywood started toward the classroom. "I can't believe I was up there and never saw anything," she said.

Arlo followed her. "Don't get mad at me," he said.

They turned into Mr. Raffo's class.

"I'm not mad," Maywood said, "except I can't believe we went through all that and we didn't even scare him."

"I know," Arlo said. He sighed as he slumped into his seat.

What Maywood said was true. That was the worst part.

CHAPTER 45
Matthew Tells a Story

The next week passed slowly. Arlo still hated being a new kid, but he was beginning to adjust. At least his teachers were nice. They didn't make demands on him. And Maywood helped him feel less isolated. But he missed Sam. He missed knowing what to expect. One thing he didn't miss was Mrs. Gretzky's math tests.

On Saturday he helped Maywood shelve new books. Later, he helped Matthew make a delivery to the Swan's Neck. As they carried boxes to the kitchen, Mrs. Stemple told them Mr. Garringer had appeared very agitated when he came back to the inn the evening after looking at Ida's house.

"He was angry about something," she said. "There was another man with him. Mr. Wolfe is his name. They stayed upstairs a long time. I think they were planning something."

"Why do you say that?" Matthew asked.

"It was when that Mr. Wolfe left," Mrs. Stemple said. "Mr.

Garringer called down the stairs after him. 'A few more days and we'll be set for life.'"

"Set for life? That's what he said?"

"Yes."

"What does that mean?" Arlo asked.

"No idea," Matthew said. "Sounds like they're planning something all right."

"There's something evil about that man," Mrs. Stemple said. "I don't trust him."

"Me, either," Matthew said. "How long is he staying?"

Mrs. Stemple gave Matthew a meaningful look. "That's just it," she said. "He checked out this morning."

"So he's gone?" Arlo said.

"Not a minute too soon, as far as I'm concerned." Mrs. Stemple shook her head.

Matthew raised an eyebrow. "Well, now. Isn't that interesting? Did he say he was coming back?"

"Not a whisper of that," Mrs. Stemple said. "I'm happy to report."

"Do you think he's coming back?" Arlo asked when he and Matthew were in the car on the way home.

"Probably," Matthew said.

"I think it has something to do with the way Mr. Wolfe was tapping on all the walls." Arlo closed his eyes and replayed the memory. "It was like he was looking for something."

Matthew didn't say anything. After a few minutes, he flipped the blinker and made a left turn off the highway.

He followed a two-lane dirt road to a sign marked WILDLIFE REFUGE.

"Are we making another delivery?" Arlo asked.

"No. There's something I want to show you." Matthew followed the path to a sandy parking lot on their left.

"Does this have something to do with Mr. Garringer?" Arlo asked as they were getting out of the car.

"No," Matthew said. "This is about your father."

Cliffs rose on the opposite side of the river. An osprey's nest sat atop a wooden pole.

"That's an empty osprey nest, isn't it?" Arlo said.

Matthew looked impressed. "You know birds, do you?"

Arlo shrugged. "Not really," he said. "Ida and I saw an osprey on the way home a few weeks ago. And then Maywood and I saw an empty nest, and she told me about them leaving for the winter and coming back to the same nest every spring."

Matthew nodded. "Those birds were about gone when your daddy and I used to come here," he said.

"When was that?" Arlo asked.

"Junior high and high school. Right over there's the spot where we pitched a tent one night." Matthew pointed to the spot where the dunes rose to a point above the river. "It was that summer I was telling you about, after your dad came home from camp."

As they walked closer to the water, Arlo noticed a sign.

NO CAMPING OR FISHING.

He cocked an eye at Matthew.

"Didn't used to be that way," Matthew said. "Camping was still legal back then. The government didn't restrict this area till fifteen years ago. The whole place was getting too crowded. They wanted to protect the eagles. Closing the campground helped."

"Must have been nice back in those days," Arlo said.

"Just about perfect," Matthew said. His mouth flattened into a line as he stared at the river.

Arlo looked at the river, too. He tried to imagine his dad and a younger version of Matthew camping here. If he stared at the water long enough and concentrated really hard, he could almost see them. As the image grew clearer in his mind he felt the carving growing warmer in his pocket. When he put his hand over it, it felt like it was moving again.

"You still with me, Skywalker?"

"I'm here," Arlo said.

"Thought I lost you there for a minute."

Arlo shrugged. "I wish I could talk to him sometimes," he said. "I know that sounds crazy."

"Doesn't sound crazy at all," Matthew said.

"It doesn't?"

"No."

They stood silently watching the water for a minute.

Matthew picked up a stick and broke it in half. He handed one piece to Arlo and kept the other piece for himself. As Arlo watched, Matthew heaved the stick as far as he could into the water. "Your turn," he said.

Arlo raised his arm and aimed for the spot where Matthew's stick had gone.

"Nice job," Matthew said.

"Thanks."

Matthew turned to look at him. "You know, this might sound a little strange, but there's nothing that says you couldn't go ahead and talk to your dad sometimes."

Arlo kept on looking at the spot where his stick had disappeared.

"I don't mean you have to do it out loud or anything, but shoot, for all we know, he could be out there listening. . . . I mean, from wherever it is people go."

Arlo nodded.

They lingered a few moments, watching the sun turn pink as it sank lower in the sky.

"Better get going," Matthew said finally. "Ida will be wondering where we are."

CHAPTER 46
Ida's Turn

When Arlo walked in the house, he found Ida sitting on the floor in the dining room, going through photos in a green cardboard box. He remembered seeing that box up in the attic. It had been on the middle of a set of built-in shelves in the space above Ida's bedroom. Ida had three photographs spread out in front of her. Arlo pointed to the one in the middle, a picture of his father wearing the blue sweater — the same picture he'd seen in the album back home.

"I'd forgotten I still had this," Ida said, handing it to him. "It was taken right after you were born."

Arlo stared at the picture.

"There's a resemblance, you know," she said. "That spot in your left eyebrow."

Arlo touched the thin spot on his forehead. "Can I ask you something?" he said.

"Go ahead," Ida whispered. Her eyes were misty.

"How come you never came to see us?"

She blinked, then leaned down and gathered up the photographs, tucking them into the pocket of her sweater.

"I tried," she said without turning around. "After Slocum died, I tried to see you a number of times."

"How come I don't remember that?" Arlo asked. He knew he was being hard on her, but he deserved answers, didn't he?

When Ida turned around to face him, her cheeks were pink. Water pooled in her eyes. "Albert wouldn't allow me to see you," she said.

Arlo couldn't help noticing little prickles of anger creeping up his spine. It happened every time she criticized his grandfather.

"Poppo wouldn't do that."

Ida sighed. "I understand why you feel that way. But, the fact is, he *did* do that. Augusta and I drove all the way to Marshboro once. When we got there, Albert refused to let me see you."

Arlo stared at her. "But where was I?" he said.

"At school," she said, her voice cracking on the word *school*.

"Why would Poppo do that?"

Ida pulled the tissue from her pocket and blotted her eyes. "You have to understand," she said. "Albert was hurt. And angry. And he needed someone to blame."

"Blame for what?" Arlo asked.

Tears spilled onto her cheeks. "For losing your mother." She walked over to the window and stood there a long time without saying anything.

"But it was an accident," Arlo said.

"Yes," Ida said. "It was." When she sighed, her whole body shivered. "In your grandfather's eyes, everything that happened was my fault. Or Slocum's fault. Or it was both of our faults."

Arlo felt water pounding against his dam. The walls shook, threatening to let loose everything he'd held inside.

Ida ran a thumb over the swollen knuckles of her hand. "I said terrible things to your mother, Arlo. Heaven knows I regret that now. But when your father won that scholarship, I had such hopes. . . . He was on his way out from under Slocum's thumb. He could be his own man."

When she turned around, Arlo spotted a tear making a slow track down her left cheek.

"But then he found your mother. And he was crazy about her. I didn't think he was old enough to know what he was doing. I was afraid he was throwing his life away, giving up everything just to get away from Slocum."

She took a tissue out of her other pocket and blotted away the dampness.

"And when he told us Amy was expecting and he had asked her to marry him . . ." Her voice cracked. "Sorry. I didn't mean to say that."

Arlo watched his grandmother's face. The picture was becoming clear.

"You didn't want them to have me?" he said.

She had difficulty swallowing. "I didn't mean it that way, Arlo. You know I didn't." Her face had a bruised look, as if tiny blood vessels had burst beneath her skin.

Arlo's heart pumped harder. He didn't know what to think or who to believe.

"Did you really try to see me?" he asked.

Ida nodded. "After Albert refused to let me see you, I made Augusta drive to the school yard. We parked across the street and waited until the bell rang. I saw you walk out with another boy."

"Sam," Arlo said automatically.

"The boy I met at the hospital?"

"Yes."

"That's probably who it was. I don't know. Augusta and I waited until you were all the way down the street. I needed to make sure you were all right. And I could tell you were. You were laughing and talking with your friend. And I knew that Albert was devoted to you. I understood he was trying to protect you — even though *it broke my heart.* . . ."

"He wouldn't let me talk to you?"

"No."

Arlo studied the photograph of his father. If only he could feel something, some connection to that face, to the look in his father's eyes. But the truth was, Wakeford Jones was just a face staring back at him. It could have been any face, except for the fact that they both shared that same narrowed spot in the left eyebrow. Arlo wanted what other kids had — a place in his memory where his father was always alive.

"Could you . . . ?" Arlo started.

"What?" Ida leaned toward him.

Now it was Arlo's voice that cracked on the words. "Tell me about him?"

She studied the photograph.

"Because Matthew's told me some things," Arlo continued. "But I need to know more."

She tucked the tissue back in her pocket. "Maybe you could help me get started," she said.

"OK." Arlo tried not to look at her. Maybe that would keep her from feeling uncomfortable. "What should I do?" he asked.

She thought for a moment. "Ask me questions," she said. Then she nodded to herself. "Yes, I think that would help. If you could ask me something specific about him, that would give me a place to start."

Arlo stared through the window. He had no idea what to ask.

"Take your time," Ida said. "Ask anything."

Arlo searched the room for clues. The first thing he noticed was the high-school graduation photo on the mantle in the living room. That was as good a place as any, wasn't it?

"Was he smart?"

Ida smiled. "Smart as a whip, though his grades didn't show it at first. Not until high school, anyway. That's when he got serious. Before ninth grade, Wake had other things on his mind."

"Things like what?"

"Canoes. Paddling on the river. He liked to be outside."

"I like that, too," Arlo said.

"Yes," Ida said. "I believe you two are a lot alike."

She smiled then. And Arlo sat quietly for a moment.

"What else?" he asked finally.

Ida spread her hands over her knees. "So many things," she whispered.

"Tell me one."

"All right." She stared into the fireplace. "Here's something I'll always remember about Wake, how he hated wearing shoes."

"Why?"

She laughed then. "Who knows? Maybe I let him wander outside barefoot too often when he was a toddler. I've no idea, really. When he started first grade, his teacher called and told me I needed to speak to him. *I can't have a student going barefoot in class,* she said. *It sets a bad example and then every other boy wants to do the same thing.*"

Arlo laughed. "Did he stop?"

"He did *eventually*," Ida said. "But it took a long time."

"What else?" Arlo asked.

Ida put the lid back on the box of photographs. "Wake hated unhappy endings. He refused to finish a book if it turned sad. Switched off the TV in the middle of movies sometimes. That used to drive your grandfather crazy."

"Tell me one more thing."

Ida reached for Arlo's hand. "He loved every minute of being your father," she said. "If he could see you now, it would make him very proud."

Arlo choked, though it came out as more of a hiccup. "I wish I remembered him," he said.

"I wish you did, too. But it's no one's fault. It's just something that happened. And now we have to make the best of it."

Arlo nodded.

The sun shifted, throwing light across the table. The flood inside had subsided now and somehow, *miraculously,* Arlo's dam was still intact, a little pockmarked maybe, but still standing.

"You did the right thing coming here," Ida said.

"I did?"

Their eyes met over Steamboat's head.

"You kept me from selling my house." She squeezed his hand tightly. "You kept me from losing the chance to know my grandson."

Arlo's heart pushed against the back of his throat.

"Do you think . . . ?" his grandmother started. Then she stopped and cleared her throat. "What I mean is, do you think you could be happy . . . living here with me?"

Arlo felt as if the earth had taken a momentary pause from spinning on its axis. "What about Poppo?" he whispered.

Ida looked pained. "I know," she said. "What *can* we do about your grandfather?"

"I think he'd like to stay near Eldon," Arlo said. He watched for Ida's reaction.

She lifted an eyebrow. "Do you think he could be happy in one of those apartments?"

Arlo thought about his recent conversations with Poppo. He thought back to their visit to Marshboro and the way Poppo and Eldon had laughed as they shared old stories. He thought about how relieved Poppo had seemed when he found out how well Arlo was doing in Edgewater.

"I think so," Arlo said.

Ida tilted her head. "And what about you?" she asked.

"I'm OK," Arlo said. *"Now."*

She smiled. "Good." She reached over and hugged him.

Steamboat barked and wagged his tail.

"Don't worry, boy. Arlo's not going anywhere." Ida patted Steamboat on the head. "He staying right here with us."

Sometime after midnight, Arlo woke with a start. Something drew him downstairs. He walked to the alcove and stood looking at the shelves. *What is it?* he thought. *What am I looking for?*

Finally, he went into the kitchen and drank a glass of milk. On his way back upstairs, he had the same nagging feeling, as if there were something in the alcove he needed to see. He paused on the landing, waiting for . . . whatever it was, but nothing came to him, so finally he climbed the stairs and went back to sleep.

CHAPTER 47
Strange Sounds

By Monday morning, Arlo had forgotten about the funny feeling he'd had in front of the alcove. He had overslept and was rushing to get ready for school.

"I have a meeting with Nathan at four forty-five," Ida said. "That's the only time he could squeeze me in. We need to get some papers in the mail to Miss Hasslebarger. Why don't you go home with Maywood after school?"

"OK. Sure," Arlo said, happy for an excuse to delay doing homework.

That afternoon, he and Maywood went bike riding. Arlo borrowed Lucius's bike since he didn't have one of his own in Edgewater. They rode over the sidewalks at Saint Ann's and down to the public beach and the creek below Augusta Stonestreet's house. Then they took the path to the park and followed it all the way to the marina and beyond. They rode and rode until they were at the turn to Ida's house. By that time, they were hot and thirsty and tired and they were ready to take a break.

"I have a house key," Arlo said. "And there's lemonade in the refrigerator."

"Good," Maywood said. "I need to stop and rest. Ida won't mind if we help ourselves, will she?"

"No," Arlo said. "Why would she mind?"

They made the turn onto the driveway and rode past the orchard to the circle. As they neared the house, Arlo spotted a familiar-looking black sedan parked in front.

Maywood drew in her breath. "What's *he* doing here?" she asked.

"No idea," Arlo said.

They pushed their bikes through the yard to the side of the garage. Maywood jabbed Arlo with her elbow. "I thought Ida left Steamboat in the house when she wasn't home," she whispered.

"She does," Arlo said. "Unless she takes him with her."

"Then how come he's over there?" Maywood raised an arm and pointed through the gap in the hedge to the yard next door. Steamboat was standing in the neighbor's driveway, having a staring contest with a cat. As they watched, the cat flicked her tail and Steamboat barked and backed away.

"Ida never leaves him outside if she's not home," Arlo said.

"Well, he had to get out somehow," Maywood said. "Come on. We should see what's going on."

"I don't know," Arlo said, "but we need to catch Steamboat before he gets in trouble."

They parked their bikes behind the garage and crept toward the driveway next door.

"Steamboat first," Arlo said.

"OK," Maywood said. "But hurry. We need to find out what's going on."

CHAPTER 48
Intruders

Steamboat was happy to follow Arlo back to the house. Arlo stroked Steamboat's head to keep him quiet while they slipped through the kitchen door. A strange toolbox blocked the entryway. Muddy footprints left a track from the door to the basement steps.

"Now what?" Maywood said

Arlo put a finger over his mouth. "Listen," he said.

Voices drifted up from the basement.

Arlo sent Maywood a message with his eyebrows. "Up there," he whispered, pointing toward the kitchen. He lifted Steamboat into his arms, then led Maywood up the steps. Ever so slowly, Arlo pulled the door to the pantry open just enough for the three of them to slip inside. Arlo sat on the lid of the steel garbage pail. He signaled to Maywood to sit on the cardboard box that was filled with empty canning jars. Steamboat nestled between them. Then Arlo pulled the door shut and the three of them huddled together in the dark.

"What are we doing?" Maywood whispered.

Arlo pointed at a vent in the floorboards. In a few seconds, voices floated up from the basement. Arlo leaned toward them, straining to make out the words.

"You sure this house belonged to the same guy that was in those letters?" a male voice asked.

"I am now," the other voice said.

Arlo recognized them both immediately. Mr. Garringer and Mr. Wolfe. He kept his head tilted at just the right angle so he could understand what they were saying.

"It was sweet the way those two delinquents led us straight to the statue, wasn't it?" Mr. Wolfe said. "You had it figured out all along. That Malachy guy was buried in Edgewater. He lived in this house."

"You can gloat later," Mr. Garringer said. "Right now we need to find that painting."

Maywood's eyes bulged. Arlo shrugged. He nodded toward the vent and then pointed at his ear. Maywood understood. She leaned closer to listen, too.

"There's nothing down here," Mr. Wolfe was saying.

"So where do you suggest we look?" Mr. Garringer asked.

"I'm telling you, there's something behind those bookcases," Mr. Wolfe said. "If you ask me, that's where Malachy stashed the Brokenberry."

There was a long pause, following which Mr. Garringer said, "All right. Let's have another look."

Steamboat squirmed in Arlo's lap. When footsteps pounded up from the basement and across the kitchen floor, Arlo squeezed Steamboat tighter. The dog let out a tiny yelp.

On the other side of the door, the footsteps stopped. Arlo's heart nearly stopped as well.

"Did you hear something?" Mr. Wolfe asked.

"Nah," Mr. Garringer said. "You're too nervous. Old houses make funny noises. Come on. Let's find that painting."

Arlo started breathing again.

The footsteps moved toward the center hall.

Arlo patted Steamboat on the head. "Good boy," he whispered.

Soon they heard tapping on the wall of the alcove.

"Now what?" Maywood whispered.

"Now we wait," Arlo said.

"For what?" Maywood asked.

"I'm not sure," Arlo said.

There were more knocks and the sound of books being tossed on the floor. Soon a loud scraping sound set Arlo's teeth on edge. It was as if someone was moving furniture, only it must have been something a lot bigger than a sofa or a table because it sounded like a piece of the house was being moved.

After a while, the sound turned softer, as if they had finished one stage of whatever they were doing and moved on to something else. Then there were squeaks like footsteps over creaky floorboards.

"Now?" Maywood whispered.

Arlo nodded. "Now," he said.

They made their way quietly out of the pantry. Arlo held on to Steamboat's collar to keep him from running ahead of them. They crept through the dining room, taking care to stay on the thickest and softest part of the worn carpet. When they reached the main hallway, they saw what had made the noise.

The bookcase on the wall beneath the stairs had been moved. It was standing open, like a giant door leading into a small room underneath the stairway and part of the wall. At the back of the room was a doorway and what appeared to be steps.

Arlo picked up Steamboat again and carried him, with Maywood following behind, through the room and partway down the steps.

At the bottom of the steps was another room, much larger than the space under the stairway. It had wood floors and plaster walls and a low ceiling. And it appeared to extend the entire length of the living room above it, though there was not enough light to be certain of that. Mr. Garringer and Mr. Wolfe were both down there. They were standing under a bare lightbulb, which hung on a wire from the ceiling. Along the walls on either side of them were wooden racks with what appeared to be bottles stacked on their sides.

Arlo felt Steamboat's breath on his hand. He prayed the dog would stay silent long enough to see what the men were up to before he and Maywood crept out of the room.

It wasn't until Mr. Wolfe stepped to one side that Arlo spotted the painting. It was on an easel between the two men and beside it, on the floor, was a dusty bedsheet that must have been covering the painting. Arlo wasn't close enough to have a clear view, but still he could see the bottom portion of the canvas, that place where the artist had painted what appeared to be twigs of berries resting on a silver platter. Solomon Brokenberry's hallmark. *On a painting in a secret room inside his grandmother's house!*

Arlo turned to Maywood and gave her an eye signal indicating they should leave. They backed up the steps and tiptoed through the secret room and into the house.

Arlo put Steamboat down and began pushing on the bookcase immediately.

"Help me," he said. If the bookcase made the same noise going back into place as it had made when the two men opened it up, they needed to work quickly.

Maywood pushed, too. The wall began to move — ever so slowly at first, but then faster as they came closer to latching it tight. They heard footsteps coming up from below.

"Hurry," Maywood whispered.

Arlo heaved as hard as he could. Maywood threw her body against the wall as well. There was a loud click as the bookcase snapped into place. The secret doorway was closed. Hands pounded on the other side. Mr. Garringer and Mr. Wolfe shouted in angry voices.

"Let us out of here!"

"Where's Steamboat?" Arlo asked, his heart hammering at the thought that Steamboat might be trapped inside with the two men.

"Over there," Maywood said. She pointed toward the living room.

Arlo let out his breath. "Call the police," he said.

Maywood picked up the receiver and punched 911.

Then they waited.

CHAPTER 49
The Painting

Sirens whined. Gravel ricocheted under the tires of three sheriffs' cars as they careened down Ida's driveway. A minute later, the sheriff and three of his deputies burst through the kitchen door.

"In there!" Arlo yelled, pointing toward the center hallway. He led them to the bookcase under the stairs.

Steamboat stood and barked as everyone crowded around.

"In there?" the sheriff asked.

Arlo nodded. "They were after a painting," he said.

"A painting?" The sheriff screwed up his face. "What kind of painting?"

"It's in a secret room," Maywood added.

One of the deputies elbowed another one. He rolled his eyes.

"There's a room behind that bookcase," Arlo said. "It leads to a stairway that goes to a room under the living room."

"This better not be a false alarm," the cranky deputy said.

"Calm down, Pete," the sheriff said. "You saw that black Caddy in the driveway, didn't you? There's something fishy going on here. That's for sure. And I don't think it's these kids."

Another deputy was running his finger around the edges of the bookcase. Then he ran his hand along the bottom side of each of the shelves.

Meanwhile, the sheriff started firing questions.

"How many of them did you say there were?"

"Two," Arlo said.

"And do you know who they are?"

"Sure," Maywood said. "It's Mr. Garringer and Mr. Wolfe."

"Who are they?" the sheriff asked.

Arlo told him.

"You're sure you saw them down there?" the sheriff asked.

Arlo nodded. "They were looking at a painting."

"Do they have weapons?" the sheriff asked.

"I don't know," Arlo said.

"Nice job," the deputy who was checking out the bookcase said. He gave Arlo a nod.

Steamboat wagged his tail as if the deputy were praising him.

"He wasn't talking to you," Maywood said.

Steamboat looked crestfallen until Arlo patted him on the head and Steamboat perked up again.

"Bingo," the deputy who was searching the bookcase said. He showed the sheriff a button on the bottom side of the third shelf.

"OK," the sheriff told his deputies. "Form a line. You kids go outside and wait. And take the dog with you."

As Arlo carried Steamboat through the dining room, he heard the sheriff's voice behind him.

"This is the county sheriff. I've got three deputies with me. And we're armed. So what we're going to do is . . . I'm going to open this bookcase real slow. And when I do, I want to see the two of you with your hands up."

"Come on," Maywood said. She tugged on Arlo's arm.

Part of Arlo wanted to stay and watch, but he was also afraid Steamboat might break loose and get hurt. Nothing was worth risking that. So he followed Maywood outside to the driveway.

"How long do you think we'll have to stay out here?" she asked.

"No idea," Arlo said. "But I guess they'll let us know when it's OK to go back in."

Arlo threw a ball for Steamboat and waited while Steamboat retrieved it and brought it back to drop at Arlo's feet.

A few minutes later, the sheriff and three deputies led Mr. Garringer and Mr. Wolfe outside. The two men were hand-cuffed. The deputies put Mr. Garringer in one car and Mr. Wolfe in another.

Then the sheriff came over and asked Arlo and Maywood to follow him inside.

The bookcase was still standing open. The sheriff led them back down to the secret room. There was the painting on the easel. Arlo leaned in close to examine it.

It was a picture of two boys standing in front of a large wooden table in what appeared to be the grand hallway of an old house. One of the boys was seated, and the other stood beside him. On the table a small silver platter held two clusters of red berries.

Maywood whispered one word. "Brokenberry."

Arlo gave her a nod. "Exactly," he said.

"You kids know who painted this picture?" the sheriff asked. He gave Arlo a funny look.

Maywood explained about Solomon Brokenberry and the upcoming exhibit at the museum in Richmond. The more she talked, the more amazed the sheriff looked. He kept shaking his head.

"I should put you kids on the payroll," he said.

"It's because of Mama Reel," Arlo said. "She told us all about him."

Mama Reel and Lucius arrived a few minutes later. They found their way to the secret space under the living room.

"How did you ever discover this?" Lucius asked.

"The robbers led us here," Maywood said.

Lucius's eyebrows popped up.

Meanwhile, Mama Reel stared at the painting. "It can't be," she whispered.

"Is it really by that Brokenberry guy?" Maywood asked.

Mama Reel bent down and examined the painting closely. She stared at the berries on the platter and lingered over the artist's signature at the bottom of the canvas.

"Mind you, I'm no expert," she said. "But this looks like

345

the famous lost painting." She glanced at the sheriff and looked back at the picture. "But that can't be. Can it? How on earth would it end up here?"

The sheriff raised an eyebrow. "Lost painting?" he said.

Mama Reel kept talking. "All this time," she whispered.

"All what time?" the sheriff asked.

"Since 1907," Mama Reel said. "Well, it didn't disappear until 1930 or so. After the Crash."

"You lost me," the sheriff said. "Who lost the painting?"

"Sorry," Mama Reel said. "I'm rambling, aren't I?" She straightened her glasses. "Here's the story, Sheriff. Solomon Brokenberry was an artist from a family that had ties to this area. In 1907, he exhibited a painting that looked exactly like this one at the Salon d'Automne in Paris. It created quite a stir."

"You keep calling it the *lost painting*," the sheriff said. "What does that mean?"

"After the exhibition, Brokenberry's dealer sold the painting to an American collector from Baltimore. That man's name was Weiderman. He had the painting shipped home. There was an article about it in the Baltimore newspaper in 1912, with a photograph of the painting in Mr. Weiderman's living room."

"Then what happened?" asked the sheriff.

"When the stock market crashed in 1929, Weiderman lost everything. He died of a heart attack in 1930. When his estate was settled, a European collector tried to buy the painting, but no one could find it. The Brokenberry canvas had disappeared."

"The famous *lost painting*," the sheriff said.

"Exactly," Mama Reel said.

"How valuable is it?" the sheriff asked.

"It's a museum piece," Mama Reel said. "I don't know what kind of price you would put on it, but it would be a high one. I can guarantee that."

The sheriff stared at the painting. Then he looked all around the room. He walked over and inspected the bottles on the racks along the walls. "You ever hear any talk about Slocum's Uncle Malachy being a bootlegger?" he asked.

Mama Reel stared at the bottles. Then she glanced up at the sheriff. A look of understanding passed between them. "That would explain things, wouldn't it?"

The sheriff stroked his chin. "I suppose a bootlegger wouldn't mind taking a valuable painting in payment for his whiskey," the sheriff said. "Especially after the Crash." He whipped out his cell phone and punched in some numbers. "Karen," he said, "this is Sheriff McMillan. I'm here at Ida's house and there's something I need to speak to her about right away. Is she there with Nathan?"

Ida arrived ten minutes later. Her hands shook as she leaned forward to inspect the painting.

"Slocum never breathed a word about a secret room," she said. "Or bootlegging or a painting or anything like that."

"I doubt he ever knew," the sheriff said. "It was Mr. Garringer and Mr. Wolfe who led Arlo and Maywood here."

Ida's knees wobbled.

"Maybe we'd better help you upstairs," the sheriff said.

Ida nodded. She held on to his arm as the sheriff guided her to the staircase.

"What's a bootlegger?" Maywood asked her father an hour later when they were all gathered in the living room.

"That's someone who sold illegal liquor back during Prohibition," Lucius said.

"What's Prohibition?" Arlo asked.

Lucius shook his head. "Don't they teach you American history in school?"

"We're only up to the Boston Tea Party," Maywood said.

Lucius sighed. "In 1919, there was an amendment to the Constitution that made it illegal to manufacture, sell, or transport liquor in the United States. It lasted until 1933, when the Constitution was amended again. During that time, a lot of people smuggled wine and beer and whiskey into the U.S. from other countries."

"That's what those bottles in the basement are?" Arlo asked.

"Sure looks like it," Lucius said.

"So my great-great-uncle was a bootlegger?"

Lucius rolled his shoulders in an apologetic gesture. "I'm afraid it looks that way."

"What will happen to Mr. Garringer now?" Maywood asked.

"For starters, they've got him for breaking and entering. And then there's the fact that he was clearly trying to steal that painting."

"Does that mean he won't buy Ida's house?"

Lucius smiled. "I think that's a safe bet," he said.

"Not that he had any intention of buying it in the first place," Ida said.

Everyone turned to watch her coming down the stairs.

"Well, it's obvious, isn't it?" she said. "All he wanted was the opportunity to get inside and look for the painting. He never had any interest in the house."

"That explains a lot, doesn't it?" Lucius said.

Arlo looked around the room. In three days, he would turn twelve. He'd never expected to spend his birthday with his grandmother Jones. It was hard to believe how much had happened since he'd sneaked into that bus station in Marshboro. He checked his pocket for the wood carving, and when he held it in his hand, he was sure he felt something coming back at him.

CHAPTER 50
Great-Uncle Malachy

It wasn't until Mr. Garringer, on the advice of his lawyer, agreed to plead guilty to a lesser charge that the whole story came out. That was all anyone could talk about when Ida invited Lucius and Delia and Maywood and Mama Reel and Matthew and Augusta and Nathan Tretheway and even the sheriff to dinner at her house on Thursday.

"It's the famous lost painting, all right," Mama Reel said. "Delia talked to the lady from the Smithsonian. They're verifying a few details, but she said she's ninety percent certain it's the real thing."

"Hard to believe, isn't it?" Ida said. "All these years no one ever guessed Uncle Malachy was a bootlegger."

"And Mr. Weiderman was one of his best customers," the sheriff said.

"That's how he got the painting," Delia added.

"And that's why he hid it under the house," Lucius said.

"No way to explain buying something like that in the middle of the Depression."

"But why didn't he tell somebody before he died?" Maywood asked.

"Most likely, he meant to," Mr. Tretheway said. "It's not uncommon for people to carry secrets to the grave."

"Uncle Malachy died in 1936," Ida said. "Prohibition had just ended a few years before. He probably felt like it was too soon to tell anyone about what he had hidden."

"So how did Mr. Garringer know to look for the painting in Ida's house?" Maywood asked.

"He didn't exactly *know* it was here," Mama Reel said. "He came looking for it. Isn't that right, Sheriff?"

"That's a fact, Aurelia. It turns out Garringer's a dealer himself. Recently he bought up all the inventory and the records that belonged to Brokenberry's old dealer. Among the papers was a letter saying that if someone wanted to find the lost painting, they ought to 'ask Mr. Weiderman's bootlegger about it.'"

"Did the letter say who that bootlegger was?"

"According to Mr. Garringer, the letter said there was a man named Malachy Jones who lived in the Tidewater area and who might know something about the painting. It was all very sketchy."

"So that's why he was snooping around the cemetery," Maywood said.

"Somehow he discovered there was a Malachy Jones who had died in Edgewater. He came looking for his grave so he could verify if that man had been alive during Prohibition.

He needed to be sure that the Malachy Jones he'd found could have been the bootlegger in question. Once he confirmed that, he needed to find out where he had lived."

"So that's where Hafer and Boyle came in," Maywood said.

"Exactly," the sheriff said. "Garringer didn't want to call too much attention to himself by snooping around the cemetery, so he told Hafer and Boyle what he was looking for. They led him straight to the grave."

"So what was in the envelopes he gave them?" Arlo asked.

Maywood rolled her eyes. "Money, of course," she said.

Arlo blushed.

"Garringer paid them for information," the sheriff went on. "They told him where Malachy Jones's house was."

Ida moved forward in her chair. "So all that tapping on the walls was those two men searching for a secret hiding place?" she said.

"That's right," the sheriff said.

"So what happens next?" Matthew asked.

"Well, we won't be worrying about Mr. Garringer moving to Edgewater. That's for sure," the sheriff said.

"And that painting will bring a tidy sum," Mama Reel said. "Ought to put Arlo through college."

Ida closed her eyes. "I never would have believed life could turn around so quickly," she said.

"Pass the potato salad, would you, Sheriff?" Nathan Tretheway asked.

"Sure thing." The sheriff passed the bowl to Delia, who passed it to Mama Reel, who passed it to Lucius, who handed it to Ida, who dolloped a scoop of potato salad onto Mr. Tretheway's plate.

"What about the painting?" Arlo asked.

"Ida plans to loan it to the museum in Richmond for the exhibit," Mr. Tretheway said. "We hope they'll buy it."

"That's enough talk about business," Delia said. "This is a party." She sent a look in Lucius's direction.

Lucius got up from the table and went over to turn out the lights. At the same moment, Ida gave Matthew a nod. Matthew and Maywood went to the kitchen. Someone struck a match, and a sharp sulfur odor burned Arlo's nostrils. Next thing he knew, Maywood was carrying a cake with twelve candles toward his place at the table. Everyone started singing. Steamboat tilted his head and howled.

Ida carried a stack of cake plates to the table and set them alongside Arlo's place.

"You knew it was my birthday?"

Ida put her hand on Arlo's shoulder. "I've always known when your birthday was," she said. She handed Arlo an envelope with a card in it. "And Albert remembered, too."

"You need to make a wish," Maywood said.

Arlo took a deep breath. He concentrated on the wish as he blew out every single candle. Then he looked around the table. Could it really have been only a month since he'd arrived in Edgewater? Already the people sitting around the table felt like family.

CHAPTER 51
Home

That evening, Arlo and Ida sat on the back porch drinking lemonade and watching boats on the river. Shadows climbed the trunks of the pine trees as the sun sank lower in the sky. It was around seven when the phone rang. Ida rose to answer it and then called Arlo inside.

"It's Albert," she said.

Arlo gave her a worried look.

"It's all right," she said. "He sounds perfectly . . . clear-headed."

Arlo took the phone. After Poppo had asked him how he was, and after Arlo had asked Poppo how *he* was, Poppo said he had an important question to ask.

"The truth is, I don't know exactly how to say this," Poppo said.

Arlo's heart pumped faster.

"But Eldon thinks you'll understand."

"Thinks I'll understand what?"

Poppo sighed. "Ida tells me the two of you are getting along pretty good," he said.

"That's true," Arlo said.

"She says you've made a friend there. That girl you told me about."

"Maywood," Arlo said.

"That's right." Poppo cleared his throat. "She says you ride bikes and do a lot of exploring and read books."

"Yeah?" Arlo waited.

Poppo cleared his throat. "You know," he said, "I'm doing a whole lot better than I was when you left, but the fact is . . ." Poppo coughed. "The thing is, the doctors tell me, I'm always going to have a little trouble with my memory. In fact, they say it's going to get worse."

Arlo's heart dropped lower in his chest.

"But you already knew that, didn't you?" Poppo said.

"Yes," Arlo said, in a quiet voice.

"So you know we can't really go back to living in the house together the way we were doing before. Don't you?"

Arlo took a long time to answer. "I guess so," he said.

Poppo's voice cracked. "Not that I wouldn't love to do that, you understand."

"I know," Arlo said. The knot that had formed in his throat made it hard to speak.

Poppo blew his nose at the other end. "We've had some good times, haven't we?"

"Really good," Arlo said.

"And we'll have some more," Poppo said. His voice was growing strong again. "They'll just be . . . different."

"I know," Arlo said.

"If you and I were out on the road somewhere and I had one of those memory spells . . ."

"It's OK," Arlo said.

Poppo took a deep breath. "You remember me telling you there might be an apartment in the complex where Eldon lives?"

"Yes?"

"Turns out it's going to be available in a couple of weeks. And my doctor thinks it would be a perfect place for me. The only problem is, it's just for old folks. You know what I mean?"

Arlo knew exactly what Poppo meant.

"'Course, we can have guests. There's plenty of room for someone to come and spend the night every now and then."

There was a long pause.

"The other thing is, I've been talking to that lady Miss Hasslebarger. You remember her?"

"Sure," Arlo said. "The social worker from the hospital."

"That's the one. She's worried about you. She says she thinks you're doing well there in Edgewater. In fact, she told me she thinks it might be a good idea for you to stay there for a while. 'Course, I told her that was out of the question unless you were happy with the idea. It would only be for a trial period, you understand. You wouldn't have to stay if you didn't want to."

Arlo imagined more days of sitting around the table in Ida's kitchen and listening to her stories. He imagined Sunday drives in the country and doing homework in the tree house with Maywood. He went through the items on his list of reasons to stay in Edgewater versus reasons to stay in Marshboro. He thought about Sam and his other friends at school. And he thought about Poppo. What would happen if he said he didn't want to stay with Ida? He thought about Poppo giving up the opportunity to live near Eldon. That would be a mistake. Poppo needed to take that apartment. And Arlo needed to stay where he was. In Edgewater. With Ida. It felt like the right choice. It felt like what he was supposed to do.

"I think that sounds OK," Arlo said. "I think we should try it. You know. For a while, at least."

Arlo could hear the relief in Poppo's voice. "You don't mind if I tell Miss Hasslebarger, do you?"

"No," Arlo said. "I don't mind."

Ida came out of the kitchen with a fresh cup of tea. She was nodding her head up and down, so Arlo understood she had been listening on the other line.

"Ida says we'll come visit real soon," Arlo said.

When he looked to Ida for approval, she gave him another nod.

"Good." Poppo sounded like someone had lifted about a thousand pounds off his shoulders. "That reminds me," he said. "Eldon told me there's a fishing pond near these apartments. We'll need to check that out when you're here."

"I'd like that," Arlo said.

"Me, too," Poppo said.

They talked on for another ten minutes, until finally, Poppo said the nurse had to give him some medicine.

"I'm glad we got this worked out," Poppo said.

"Me, too," Arlo said.

"I'll see you soon, right?"

"You bet," Arlo said. "Maybe next weekend."

"Well, all right, then," Poppo said.

"Love you," Arlo said.

"I love you, too," Poppo said.

The wood carving thrummed in Arlo's pocket. He tapped it three times for luck. He looked at the staircase and the living room and the door that led to the path to the river. He thought about Poppo and Eldon and about the future here with Ida and Steamboat and Maywood. He thought about being at home in a new place that was really an old place. A place where he was probably meant to be all along. He drew in a long, slow breath and let it out again. Then he stood and headed for the stairs.

Author's Note

The references in this book to the artist who painted the "famous lost painting" were inspired in part by the life of Henry Ossawa Tanner, who was born in Pittsburgh in 1859 and grew up to become the first African-American painter to be celebrated in both America and Europe.

Tanner's middle name, Ossawa, was a tribute to abolitionist John Brown and the town of Osawatomie, Kansas, where Brown led a raid against pro-slavery forces in 1856. Tanner's mother was born a slave in Virginia and escaped on the Underground Railroad. His father was born a free man in Pittsburgh and became a minister and later, a bishop in the African Methodist Episcopal Church.

Tanner decided he wanted to become an artist at the age of thirteen, when he went on a walk with his father in Fairmount Park in Philadelphia and observed a painter at work. He enrolled at the Pennsylvania Academy of the Fine Arts when he was twenty-one and fell under the tutelage of renowned American artist Thomas Eakins.

After two years, Tanner left the Academy and struggled to achieve success as an artist. In 1888, he moved to Atlanta, where he hoped to establish a livelihood by running a photography studio and teaching at Clark College. He was unsuccessful, but he did manage to capture the attention of a prominent Methodist Episcopal bishop named Joseph Crane Hartzell who, along with his wife, arranged an exhibit of Tanner's work in Cincinnati. When none of the work sold, the Hartzells purchased all of Tanner's paintings themselves. Tanner used the money to fund a trip to Europe.

It was when Tanner arrived in Paris in 1891 that he found a home among fellow expatriates. He thrived in the absence of the racism he had experienced in America. He joined the American Art Students' Club of Paris and took classes at the Académie Julian. During the summers of 1892 and 1893, Tanner fell ill and was forced to return to America. It was during this time that he painted what was to become one of his most famous works, *The Banjo Lesson*. That canvas was accepted into the Paris Salon of 1894. Another painting, *Daniel in the Lions' Den*, won an honorable mention in the Paris Salon of 1896 and a silver medal at the Universal Exposition in Paris in 1900.

Tanner spent the remainder of his life in France, dividing his time between Paris and a farm near Étaples, in Normandy. In 1899, he married Jessie McCauley Olssen, a Swedish opera student. They had one son, named Jesse. Though Tanner said he maintained great respect for America, he did not feel he could be a successful artist if he had to spend a lot of time fighting racism.

In 1923, Tanner received France's highest honor when he was made an honorary Chevalier of the Order of the Legion of Honor. In 1927, he became the first African American to be named a full academician of the National Academy of Design.

Tanner's painting *Sand Dunes at Sunset, Atlantic City* was acquired during the Clinton Administration by the White House Foundation and is the first painting by an African-American artist to enter the White House's permanent collection. It hangs in the Green Room.

Tanner's work was the subject of an exhibition *Henry Ossawa Tanner: Modern Spirit*, which was organized by the Pennsylvania Academy of the

Fine Arts in Philadelphia, and presented in 2012. The exhibit also appeared at the Cincinnati Art Museum and the Museum of Fine Arts in Houston. While Solomon Brokenberry in *All That's Missing* is a figure of my imagination, I relied upon many of the facts of Tanner's life in order to construct a plausible story.

SOURCES AND SUGGESTIONS FOR FURTHER READING

Hartigan, Lynda Roscoe. *Sharing Traditions: Five Black Artists in Nineteenth-Century America.* Washington, DC: Smithsonian Institution Press, 1985.

Marley, Anna O., ed. *Henry Ossawa Tanner: Modern Spirit.* Berkeley: University of California Press, 2011.

Mathews, Marcia M. *Henry Ossawa Tanner, American Artist.* Chicago: University of Chicago Press, 1969.

Ringgold, Faith. *Henry Ossawa Tanner: His Boyhood Dream Comes True.* Pierpont, NH: Bunker Hill, 2011.

Acknowledgments

Writing a novel is a daunting proposition, but no less daunting is the thought of thanking all those people who helped along the way. Unfortunately, there is not space to name them all.

Offering moral support were the good people at the Kanawha County Public Library, the West Virginia Library Commission, Read Aloud West Virginia, the West Virginia Commission on the Arts, and the *Sunday Gazette-Mail*. Thanks also to Colleen Anderson, Ancilla Bickley, Denise Giardina, Kate Long, Ann Pancake, Arla Ralston, Mary Kay Bond, Susan Turnbull, Carol Campbell, Jeri Matheney, and Cindy Miller.

Thanks to all my Vermont College mentors and friends — especially Jane Resh Thomas, Liza Ketchum, Kathi Appelt, Leda Schubert and Bethany Hegedus, all of whom read early drafts of this novel. Thanks also to Ellen Levine (now sadly missed) and Carolyn Coman, workshop leaders who asked just the right questions, and to advisors Phyllis Root and Louise Hawes. Thanks to my writing group — Jane Buchanan, Debby Edwardson, Nancy Thalia Reynolds, and Maura Stokes for sage advice. Thanks to fellow Wild Things (Vermont College Class of Winter 2005) for team spirit. And, special shout-outs go to Tami Lewis Brown, Nicole Griffin, Helen Hemphill, and Deborah Wiles for positive energy and encouragement.

Thanks to Straton Beamer—local natural-history expert and gardener extraordinaire—and to the knowledgeable staff at the Rappahannock River Valley National Wildlife Refuge for answering questions about ospreys and eagles. Also thanks to the people at Charleston Area Medical Center for answering questions about social workers.

This novel would never have been completed without the quiet space generously offered by Bailey & Glasser, LLP.

I owe a *huge* debt of gratitude to patient and long-suffering editor Hilary Breed Van Dusen, who saw possibilities in the manuscript I first submitted in the spring of 2011, who urged me on with insightful editorial letters, and who never complained about my obsessive revising (though she did once threaten to come to my house and grab the manuscript out of my hands if I failed to hit the SEND button by Thursday). Thank you, Hilary! Thanks also to Miriam Newman for valuable editorial insight and comments.

Thanks to everyone at Candlewick for making the world of children's books the most glorious space on earth and, unbelievably, for allowing me to be a part of it.

Finally, thanks to Marshall, Jenn, Jennifer, Mike, and Chana for understanding all those times when I was revising and unwilling to carry my laptop across the river in a canoe. And to my husband, Rick, there are not words to express my gratitude. Twenty years ago, I told you I wanted to write a novel and you never stopped believing I would.